D1240555

P R A I S E   F O

D A N C I N G   N A K E D   I N   D I X I E

"Get ready for a great time as you travel along with Julia
as she yearns to fall in love with life, family, and syrupy
Southern sweet tea..."

DATE DUE

AUG 1 2 2013

AUG 1 9 2013

AUG 2 9 2013

OCT 0 4 2013

OCT 2 3 2013
NOV 0 8 2013

NOV 2 6 2013

"I

AUG 1 9 2015
OCT 2 3 2015

"I

JUL 1 0 2017

"A s

DISCARDED

Praise for Lauren Clark & *Stay Tuned*

"Riveting and much recommended…"
MIDWEST BOOK REVIEW

"A great read!"
REBECCA BERTO,
NOVEL GIRL

"Realistic and refreshing!"
MICHELLE ADAMS,
BOOK BRIEFS

"Clark's first attempt at story-telling - fiction story-telling -
is a prize for any reader to have on his or her shelf."
BECKY HOLLAND, *MACON EXAMINER*

"Stay Tuned is a great read with vivid characters and an
entertaining plot. "
JENNIE COUGHLIN
AUTHOR, *WELCOME TO EXETER*

"Kudos to Ms. Clark on a wonderful debut…I look forward
to reading more of her books."
KATHLEEN ANDERSON
JERSEY GIRL BOOK REVIEWS

"*Stay Tuned* is as fast-paced as a real-life newsroom."
DEVON WALSH
WKRG-TV ANCHOR

"*Stay Tuned* is a great read! Lauren Clark writes so well
you can feel what the characters feel."
LAUREN DAVIS
WVLT-TV ANCHOR

"Loved it and you will too. The book will draw you in and
leave you wanting more."
ANNE RICHTER
WWNY TV ANCHOR

STARDUST SUMMER

ALSO BY LAUREN CLARK

Dancing Naked in Dixie

Stay Tuned

STARDUST SUMMER

LAUREN CLARK

CAMELLIA PRESS

For information contact:

CAMELLIA PRESS

Camellia Press LLC
2029B Airport Blvd. #274
Mobile, AL 36606

FOR PATRICK

Chapter 1

IN THE RUSH to escape the scorching rays of the swollen Mississippi sun, the plain brown package could have been missed all together.

As she fumbled with her keys, Grace wished for the faintest hint of a breeze. It was ninety-five in the shade, she noted, as a bead of sweat tickled the back of her neck. Nearby, her son kicked a loose stone on the concrete, his face flushed the color of his canvas backpack.

Grace jiggled the lock one more time, and the door finally swung open, releasing a welcome blast of chilled air. Evan slipped by, and she heard the bump of his bag as he dropped it on the wooden floor; the thud-thud as he kicked off his tennis shoes.

It was then she noticed the small package, tucked in the corner of their white wooden porch swing. Adrenaline pumped through her veins as Grace knelt down and reached for the delivery.

"Mom? Did you hear me?" Evan called out.

Startled, Grace looked up. "No. I'm sorry, honey. What is it?"

Her son stuck his head out the door, brow furrowed. "Can I go over to Adam's?"

Attempting a wide smile, Grace nodded. "Sure, sweetie. But, before you go, I think Papa sent you a surprise." She tossed the box to her son.

With a whoop of joy, Evan caught the package in both hands and ran back inside. Grace followed close behind, holding her breath. After peeling off rows of tape, Evan pulled out a small card with several bills tucked inside. Below that, beneath layers of tissue paper, his grandfather had also included a pair of swimming goggles.

Evan unfolded the note and scanned the lines. "Papa wants us to come to the lake," he said, grinning and examining his new treasure. "Can we, Mom, this time, *please?* School's almost over."

Grace stiffened. She would call her father with regrets tomorrow between classes. Grace earned a tiny salary—barely enough for the two of them to live on—but working as a teacher's aide allowed her to stay close to her son.

"We'll see," she said, trying for a casual response.

Undeterred, Evan hummed to himself and stuffed the cash into his pocket. After setting the goggles on the table, he headed for the door. "There's something else in the box for you. Later, Mom."

The door closed tight with a bang.

Grace stared after her eight-year-old son and blinked. *Later, Mom?* When had Evan become such a little man? So grown up?

So much like her own father.

Evan possessed Henry Mason's easy smile, his throaty laugh, and smart sense of humor. Her son had the same head of thick, dark hair, identical bright, inquisitive eyes, and an even jawline that matched her father's.

For two people separated by fifty years in age, a dozen states, and one time zone, the similarities were remarkable.

They barely knew each other, though her father called every week and mailed gifts once a month without fail. Henry had moved from Mississippi shortly after Hurricane Katrina; he'd taken a new job on a Wednesday in August and moved the following Friday, assuming the role of Vice President of Keuka College easily. To Henry Mason, the change was no more complicated than shrugging on a new sport coat and tie.

Grace squeezed her eyes shut. He'd invited them to visit a dozen times. It didn't matter. Henry Mason could send round-trip, first-class plane tickets, a million dollars, and Santa Claus with his sleigh and reindeer. She still wasn't coming. And Evan wasn't either.

Which was why Grace rid the house of reminders, *anything* extra her father mailed. In fact, she'd do it right now. With a shaking hand, she reached for the cardboard package and tissue paper.

As Grace tilted the box to one side, an embossed invitation, a letter, and photograph spilled out. She stared, willpower evaporating, and unfolded the loose, white page. At the mention of Kathleen's name, her spine stiffened.

Grace, I officially retired yesterday—for good this time— can you believe it? I'll be staying busy with my boat and the house, and, of course, driving Kathleen crazy.

Hope you'll make it to the Mason Library dedication...it's your name on the building, too.

I found this photo the other day. Doesn't this beautiful girl look happy? Give Evan a hug.

Love, Dad

Gingerly, Grace picked up the picture. It was faded, the edges yellowed. In the image, she was about as old as Evan, with dark pigtails, hair curling up at the ends, and a huge smile that showed gaps in her teeth.

Thick rows of Mississippi sugarcane, jointed and dense,

filled the background. Grace caught her breath. She could almost smell the sweet, earthy fragrance, and she imagined the green fronds waving in the breeze, like an army of soldiers marching home.

Grace pressed the photograph to her chest, hoping Evan wouldn't burst through the door. He didn't need to see his mother sobbing over a silly memory.

What was her father doing? Trying to convince her that they were still a family? That she should come to New York for a big reunion?

Grace wiped her cheeks. Henry Mason charmed everyone, even total strangers. He was always the life of the party—and would be at the Mason Library Dedication—with his jokes and fantastical stories. By the end of the night, he'd sing a line or two from 'Stardust.'

Just like when she was little. He'd convince her that everything would be fine.

This time, not a chance.

Henry Mason made his choice. She'd made hers.

Mississippi was home. Nothing would change that.

Chapter 2

T HE SCREAM OF an ambulance siren pierced the air. Grabbing his white coat and keys, Dr. Ryan Gordon bolted out the door, past his office manager, and waved at his first few patients of the day. "Be right back," he promised.

Ryan cranked his pickup, turned the wheel, and called the ER. The nurse on duty had sketchy details: Henry Mason had collapsed in the kitchen after his regular morning run. A neighbor, looking to borrow garden tools, found him sprawled on the floor, and called 9-1-1.

Kathleen, Henry's wife, was attending a ladies' breakfast at church. She'd been notified, and was already at the hospital.

At the next intersection, Ryan gripped the wheel, tapping it with his fingers, waiting for the light to change. He needed to be there. Henry was his patient. More than that, Henry was his friend.

Inside the ICU, the attending cardiologist couldn't offer much reassurance. Despite valiant efforts from the local rescue squad, chest compressions, and two rounds of defibrillation, Henry had suffered a stroke. Moments ago, he'd slipped into a coma.

Through the glass, Ryan saw Kathleen. She rushed to meet two doctors, friends of his, at the door of Henry's room. They took turns, talking in low tones as Kathleen raked her eyes across her husband's motionless body. One physician patted her on the back stiffly. The other squeezed her hand. Ryan watched as they paused, nodded, and exited the small space.

Kathleen, now alone, sank into the seat next to Henry, clasping his arm. Monitors flashed and broke the silence with an occasional beep. The ventilator sighed and hissed.

Ryan waited for Kathleen to turn, look up, and see him, but she sat perfectly still, as if carved from stone.

The sight of Henry's wife, almost trance-like, unnerved Ryan. He'd rather a spouse cried or got angry, even yelled for answers or demanded endless explanations. Then again, no rules defined this sort of situation.

Perhaps Kathleen was praying. Or deep in thought.

There was no reason to interrupt, Ryan told himself. He wasn't family. And, at least for now, Henry's condition seemed stable.

THAT SAME AFTERNOON, back in his office, Ryan pressed a button on his cell phone to silence the noise. He scanned the message, his fifth in the last hour.

The answering service connected him with a distressed and tearful mother, at home with her sick infant. She described the baby's symptoms; he had a history of nasty ear infections. Ryan listened closely, took a few notes on a pad on the counter, and asked if she could bring the boy to his office in the next fifteen minutes.

He glanced at the clock. Sure, it was Monday evening and he was leaving soon, but he had time, Ryan explained. He always had another few minutes. Everyone in the community knew that.

Long hours were part of being a doctor. Ryan still had a

practice to build, a reputation to maintain, and patients who needed him. Every day, he left the house at dawn for hospital rounds and walked back in the door after dark. He didn't hesitate to answer questions in the grocery store, at the bait and tackle shop, or on the sidewalk downtown.

Ryan's dedication wasn't in question, but he'd forgotten one important lesson in the time since medical school graduation. A promise he'd sworn to abide by every day of his life.

Primum non nocere. First, do no harm.

One tenet of the Hippocratic Oath.

True, Ryan did serve, heal, and save lives, but he'd neglected to nurture his own marriage.

Almost two years after his wife left him, Ryan never quite accepted that Lori wasn't coming back. Additional responsibilities at the hospital, weekend office hours, and taking call for other physicians all allowed Ryan to bury himself deeper in his cocoon of work.

During any downtime, usually on Sundays, he sailed in the mornings with Henry Mason. Later, he'd swim or bike until it was too dark or too cold. Just keep moving, he told himself. Don't give yourself time to think.

But today was different.

He thought about Lori. And Henry. Especially his good friend.

His phone rang again. The display showed a familiar number and Ryan answered. A colleague of his, a neurosurgeon, confirmed that Henry had suffered another stroke. His friend had only a few days left. Seventy-two hours, maybe less. A pinprick of time.

In the privacy of his office, Ryan let down his guard to grieve. He detested this part of his job. End of life was never easy, but the senseless, untimely deaths were hardest to take. During his residency, everyone warned against getting attached to patients. They also said he'd get used to the loss of life, but he never did. They were failures. His failures.

It haunted him those first years, especially the children who died in his arms fighting cancer or incurable disease. They were the hardest to take. Now, years later, the feeling was down to a dull ache, but nothing he could fully ignore.

Ryan pulled open his laptop and clicked through several pages, stopping when he reached Henry's information. There, his friend's life was displayed in dizzying quantities of numbers and letters. He scrolled through, looking for the smallest hint of an answer.

Henry's chart revealed years of check-ups recorded, medicines added as he got older, remarks about a winter cold or an occasional bout with the flu. He showed up for appointments on time, took his medicine, exercised, and ate right. He was only fifty-seven. They'd joked about Viagra, but he'd never needed it. Everything was under control.

What had he missed?

Thirty minutes later, he shut the laptop and closed his eyes. They felt grainy and dry from lack of sleep and stress. He had been working too hard, his nurses told him. *Go home.* Every day, around seven o'clock, it was the same mantra.

Take a break, schedule a vacation, do something other than come to work. His staff chorused like a hundred-person choir, singing from the same sheet music at the top of their lungs.

Ryan rubbed his head and grabbed his stethoscope, slinging it around his neck. Maybe they were right, but there was no time for rest today. The little boy with the ear infection was coming soon.

And he'd promised himself another stop by the hospital. He had to see Henry one last time.

O N HIS WAY to the ICU, Ryan took the stairs two at a time. He hoped, by some miracle, that Henry might be awake. It was possible that he would open his eyes long enough for

Ryan to reach over and squeeze his hand, just to let him know he was there.

Kathleen might even need a short break by now. He would send her to the cafeteria for coffee, get her to stretch her legs.

Ryan pushed the metal door open, nearly blinded by the florescent lights beaming above the nurses' station.

As he blinked and stepped onto the floor, a few doors away, a monitor flat-lined. A rush of pounding footsteps filled Ryan's ears. Hospital employees in scrubs shouted urgent questions.

Everyone had converged in the corner. Room 214. His eyes moved right, to the last name and initial on the white board behind the nurses' station.

It couldn't be true.

Ryan forced his feet forward. Looking. Searching. And finally, seeing.

Henry. Ryan's limbs congealed, his muscles atrophied. Time stopped, faces blurred, voices bellowed into an angry chorus.

In the chaos, Kathleen Mason was pressed to the corner, white-faced, wide-eyed, away from the fray.

Her lips moved apart, forming one word.

Ryan understood.

Kathleen had said goodbye.

Chapter 3

I MIGHT AS WELL *be in a casket, the way I look.* Kathleen grimly surveyed her slim figure, clad in a dark sheath and sensible heels. In the full-length mirror, smoothing the long sleeves, she thought of childhood Sunday dresses; how she would wriggle and fight the scratchy lace.

Fifty years later, the face looking back at her was pale, with more than a few wrinkles. Her skin was highlighted with pink blush and soft lipstick, the hues complementing the strand of pearls around her neck. She smoothed a piece of short-cropped silver hair away from her forehead.

In the shadows of her bedroom, her blue eyes were flat and cloudy. The lines around her mouth were deeper, more pronounced.

It was an effort to think, a momentous task to move—as if a giant weight had pushed her body underwater and held it there, the pressure building around her brain.

If Henry were here ... She couldn't finish the sentence. He would have made her laugh, made her angry, and tease her until she was ready to strangle him.

If Henry were here ... He would be up early and go for his morning sail with Ryan, then a run along the road that followed the lake's edge, logging five or more miles.

He would be the first one to dive off the dock when the sun peeked out from behind the trees. He would swim for an hour, doing laps from their property to the lake point a half-mile away. He was in better shape than most men half his age with twice the energy. Or so they thought.

The past eighteen hours had been hell. The final five minutes, devastating. Another stroke had damaged Henry's brain beyond repair. Afterward, following the attack, his face looked peaceful again, his body normal. But the man Kathleen knew and loved was never coming back.

She'd numbly signed a stack of white papers with a nearly-dry ink pen, allowing the doctors to remove all of the tubing and machines.

Finally, it was only Henry and Kathleen. The two of them, alone one last time.

A FTERWARD, KATHLEEN HAD refused to accept a ride and made herself drive back to her empty house. She'd been standing in front of the mirror for God knows how long. Finally, legs beginning to tremble, she moved away, unable to look any longer.

Slowly, as if she were wading through knee-deep mud, she made her way to the kitchen and sank into the nearest wooden chair. She was so very tired.

The next thing she knew, Kathleen woke with her head pressed to the tablecloth. She jerked awake at a loud noise outside.

It was the sound of a boat engine churning on the lake, a quarter-mile away. She listened for the cast and pull of a fishing line, the rhythmic whirr of a reel. All familiar sounds, all part of her world. The noises were usually soothing.

This morning, only a dull ache existed. She felt as if a hammer had been buried in her brain.

Kathleen's eyes pricked with tears. She fumbled to find her watch and look at the time. Already eight-fifteen in the morning. She needed to call Keuka College and let everyone know. She had to cancel the library dedication.

And there was Grace. Kathleen had to deliver the news about her father, and make sure she was coming to the funeral.

Henry's daughter, whom she'd spoken to hours before. The same woman she'd reassured that her father was okay. *Resting comfortably. Stable. The doctors are doing all they can.*

Kathleen's hands shook. She fumbled through papers to find her stepdaughter's contact information. Anyone else would have it memorized, a little voice played in her head.

But finally, beneath a tumble of scratch pads and pens, stuck to a yellow post-it note, was a small white card with Henry's writing.

Her breath caught in her throat when she saw it. *Grace at school*, the paper said, with ten numbers scrawled beneath it. Her hands shook as she punched the keys, one by one, and listened to the ringing, waiting for someone to answer.

An operator's voice came through clearly with a hint of Southern drawl in the greeting. Kathleen hesitated, gathering her thoughts, and the woman patiently repeated her greeting, this time, with more of a question in her voice.

Following a deep breath, Kathleen let the words spill out. She needed to speak to her stepdaughter, it was an emergency, and could she please find her. Immediately, music blared. Kathleen held the phone out at arm's length and shut her eyes at the noise, waiting. She couldn't think of what to say, or how to say it.

When the music stopped and Kathleen heard Grace answer, it stopped her cold. Hers was such a grown up, confident voice, and a person she didn't know very well.

Grace paused expectantly for Kathleen to talk. The sound of children, chattering and giggling, echoed in the background.

"I'm calling about your father. He seemed to be doing better. He was stable, and then, last night, he had another stroke." Kathleen inhaled and made herself say the next sentence. "The doctors...I'm so sorry, Grace," her voice broke, "he didn't make it."

Kathleen closed her eyes tightly, trying to shut out the pain in Grace's voice. The syllables she heard were cutting and sharp, bending at the end into tears.

After the sobs and exclamations of disbelief, there were questions. Patiently, Kathleen tried her best to answer each one. Grief washed over Kathleen again, listening to her stepdaughter mourn.

She had never felt so helpless.

In the end, though, it was done. And Grace, who'd sworn she would never visit her father again, was finally coming home for Henry.

Chapter 4

E VAN CHATTERED AWAY on the short drive to the airport, peppering Grace with questions about their trip.

Shifting in her seat, trying not to cry, Grace concentrated on her son's voice, thinking carefully before answering. It was difficult enough for adults to comprehend death; trying to explain it to an eight-year old was like dissecting the theory of relativity using crayons and construction paper.

"So, where did Papa go?" Evan repeated, wrinkling his forehead.

"To heaven," Grace finally replied, smiling through her grief. It was the logical choice, the response that made sense. She wasn't particularly religious, but she did believe in God, and was comforted by the promise that a beautiful afterlife existed—in whatever form it took.

"So," Evan said thoughtfully, shifting his dark brown eyes out the window. "Is he with the angels, then?"

The idea made Grace happy, and she immediately pictured Henry ambling along the clouds, surrounded by dozens of white-cloaked, feather-winged beings. He would be in his glory, she thought, telling stories, listening to music, and making new friends.

"Yes," Grace said, glancing over at Evan with a smile, "if anyone is, Papa is certainly with the angels."

Evan digested this, becoming quiet as they passed the large sign marking the entrance to the Gulfport-Biloxi International Airport. Through the car window, he gazed out at the long, sleek terminal building and the planes nearby, waiting to be filled with passengers.

Grace's heart beat faster at the sight of the gleaming, mirrored windows and a jet landing on the runway. *She and Evan were leaving Mississippi. They were really going to New York.* Grace took a deep breath to quiet her nerves.

After maneuvering through the maze of the parking lot, finding an empty space, and dragging their bags to the terminal, she squeezed Evan around the shoulders.

As the ticket line inched forward, Evan slipped his hand into hers; the fit was warm and exactly right. For a few moments, Grace let herself believe they were on their way to a much-needed vacation—the Bahamas, Bermuda, St. Lucia—it didn't matter as long as they were together.

The squawk of the overhead page interrupted her daydreams. She edged her bag closer to the counter, pushing the canvas edge with the toe of her shoe. The man behind her slid his briefcase into her ankle a second time. She winced at the pain, letting out a small cry.

"Sorry," the man said as she glanced back. His face was frowning, sincere.

"It happens." Grace flashed him a wry smile. "Don't worry about it."

The small airport was unusually busy, with groups of people crowding the lobby. The terminal was newly renovated and beautiful. But even with its high ceilings, sky lights, and hallways that seemed to stretch for a mile, the noise level matched that of a sold-out football stadium.

Evan nudged Grace. It was their turn.

"May I help you?" The agent flashed a practiced smile. Grace couldn't help but notice the woman's long, pink fingernails, the tips covered in rhinestones.

Grace slid her driver's license across the counter, the small photo of herself looking up at the ceiling. The agent picked it up, checking her vital statistics—long, dark brown hair, hazel eyes, a little taller than most women, with a lean, athletic build.

"Going to Rochester, New York?" The woman behind the counter didn't wait for an answer, her rhinestone-studded fingers flying over a hidden keyboard. "Coming back Wednesday?"

Grace nodded, confirming the words. "On Wednesday."

For her father's sake, surely she could survive that long with her stepmother. Nine days wasn't too much. When she made the reservation, looking at the calendar, seven seemed too few, fourteen too many. She was second-guessing herself again, a trait she had relentlessly perfected for much of her 36 years.

The travel agent interrupted. "Business or pleasure?" Tap. Tap. Tap.

Since when did ticket agents need to know? The man with the ankle-breaking briefcase shifted impatiently behind her.

Grace couldn't think of an answer. It didn't matter. Her reply was not one of the choices. "My father passed away," she offered, looking straight at the woman's tooth.

The agent's pink lips formed a small "o," her fingers frozen above the keyboard. She avoided Grace's eyes for a moment.

"Sorry," she said. "Is that home for you?"

Grace shook her head. "Mississippi."

Tap. Tap. Tap.

"All righty," the agent chirped. "You're all set. Here are your boarding passes. Gate B-4. Have a good trip."

Evan's chatter about the airport, the plane, and the passengers had kept her mind off the inevitable. Evan took the seat by the window as Grace settled their carry-on bags.

She watched as her son's brown eyes darted back and forth, following the burly baggage men loading the suitcases, one by one on the black conveyer belt. After a while, Evan's chin drooped just slightly and his eyelids closed as the flight attendant smiled broadly and began to demonstrate the safety features of the CRJ-200.

The jet engines gunned to life just about the time Evan dropped off to sleep. Grace held back from sweeping the piece of dark hair sliding near his eye. She'd surely wake him up if she did.

Grace gripped her armrest tightly and checked for the second time that her seatbelt was securely buckled. She pushed herself against the seat back, trying to find a comfortable position as the jet taxied down the runway.

She thought about her father as they pushed through the clouds, white and gray surrounding them. If heaven existed, they were certainly closer at thirty thousand feet above the earth. *Was her father there? Was he watching over her and Evan?*

The idea of it made Grace wonder about her own mother—her biological mother. A drunk driver in downtown Gulfport had killed her instantly in a head-on collision. She'd never met her own grandson.

Grace's eyes filled with tears. Her throat tightened. Never had she felt so desperately off-kilter. Her world was upside down. Her father was gone forever and Grace hadn't been able to say goodbye. *If there only had been more time, another day, more warning...*

Pressing her head against the seat, she closed her eyes and hoped that her father hadn't suffered. Grace wiped her cheeks, hoping no one had seen her cry.

Henry wouldn't want her to be sad. If her father was sitting there, on the plane, he would be the first person to remind Grace that she hadn't lost everything and everyone.

She and Evan had each other.

That, Henry would say, was a gift.

Chapter 5

KATHLEEN HAD CHOSEN Garrett Memorial Chapel to honor Henry. Stone-carved and rustic, the granite structure seemed to grow out of the rugged rock foundation of Bluff Point on Keuka Lake.

She and Henry loved the story behind the chapel, built almost eight decades earlier by Paul and Evelyn Garrett. Their son, Charles, had contracted tuberculosis and tragically passed away at age twenty-six. His parents erected the chapel in his honor and as a memorial to life, faith, and family.

Just six months earlier, Kathleen and Henry had talked about their own final wishes. They'd spent a long afternoon at their attorney's office, making final changes to their estate plan.

Over glasses of wine a few hours later, they had actually joked about eschewing the traditional funeral arrangements— holding a celebration of life instead on the lakeshore, with friends, food, and family around them.

Henry had made Kathleen promise that there would be no gaudy flower arrangements wrapped in satin ribbon, no body laid out to view, and no hideous, cake-like makeup. He swore that he would come back and haunt her if she allowed awful organ music and a long, boring service.

Kathleen remembered laughing until her sides hurt at Henry's description. They clinked their glasses together, poured more wine, and watched the sky explode in reds, purples, and pinks as day faded into night.

They had years to live, after all. She had believed that.

Now, it was almost time to say her final farewell.

The chime of the grandfather clock sounded and Kathleen forced herself to her feet. Thirty minutes until it was time to leave.

Kathleen began to pace.

For once, she wanted to find Henry's grassy footprints in the house or a pile of dirty clothes at the end of the neatly-made bed. Kathleen searched the house, half-expecting to find another blob of toothpaste to wipe up or a cereal bowl, with milk and floating pieces of cereal, in the sink. But, the counters shone and the windows gleamed in the sunlight, untouched, free of fingerprints and specks of dust.

She knew at least a couple of newspapers were sitting at the foot of the steps outside. Would someone bring them to the door? Part of her, now, didn't care about rising gas prices, global warming, and more problems with the local school board. None of it seemed to matter anymore.

Kathleen stared at her calendar, filled with once-important notes in black ink about this meeting or that dinner. Her life with Henry was ordered, predictable.

A stack of invitations sat next to it. She picked up the first and examined it. In flowery scroll, it invited them to the wedding. The next was for a dinner party. An anniversary was being celebrated in June. An engagement party for a friend's granddaughter was set for July.

The words on the last piece of ecru cardstock seemed to blur together. For so long, her life had been connected to those little pieces of paper. She couldn't read another one. In one swift motion, she gathered them all. On impulse, she held them over the wastebasket and let go. The papers fluttered a goodbye as they landed, one by one.

Now, Kathleen needed a map, directions, maybe a compass. She needed someone or something to tell her how to get through the day and the next day and the rest of her life, without Henry.

TREE BRANCHES, THICK with foliage, hung like a shelter of dark green over the road. The open window let in a cool breeze as Kathleen pressed the accelerator gently. The simple stone chapel came into view. The carved stone youth holding the globe above the entrance greeted her like an old friend. It was small, only space enough to seat thirty people.

The sun, streaming through the trees, warmed the granite, in twisted colors of gray-green and black. It awed Kathleen, yet made her feel safe. The chapel was strong, something that would stand up to the wind and the rain and snow, like love itself. It was a quiet symbol of the feelings even death couldn't take away.

Kathleen parked in the furthest space from the chapel and rolled up the windows. She leaned over and touched the box cradled in the seat beside her. Gingerly, as if she might damage it, Kathleen picked up the container of Henry's ashes. It was made of mahogany and heavier than she imagined. Kathleen hugged it close, like a china doll that might break if she dropped it. The back of her neck tingled and Kathleen tensed, feeling like someone was watching her. Nerves, she decided.

She was early, so the parking lot was empty, save for one small van that must have belonged to the minister. Kathleen stepped onto the gravel and closed the car door behind her.

Inhaling the smell of pine and fresh air, she made her

way carefully toward the giant wooden doors. The hinges were big and metal, curling out toward the center—what she imagined graced the doors of castles in the Middle Ages. Kathleen always thought they gave off the impression that everything in the world would stand still when she stepped through them.

Inside, the cool air felt good on her skin. Her footsteps echoed on the slate floor. Her legs felt heavy, like she was walking in water. Up the stairs a deep, friendly voice called out, followed by a familiar, round smiling face, and cloaked figure at the top of the stairs.

"Kathleen?"

Chapter 6

GRACE GLANCED AT her watch again. Evan was awake now and playing his Nintendo 3DS intently, missing out on the scenery floating by at sixty-five miles an hour.

Listening to the voice on the GPS, Grace turned a few miles out of her way to travel along the edge of Seneca Lake. It wasn't *Henry's* lake, but it was beautiful in its own right. Its water sparkled in the sunlight and she watched three sailboats seem to dance on the waves.

In long, rambling letters to Grace, her father had explained the history of the Finger Lake Region. It had been glaciers, giant and powerful, that had carved out the eleven lakes in the area, side by side. Grace envisioned fearful images of icy masses grinding and cutting through what was now pristine water and lush rolling hills, dotted by thriving wineries and dairy farms.

Grace pointed the car south and east, toward Penn Yan. The village sat at the northeastern tip of the lake. From there, it stretched 18 miles to Hammondsport and back up to Branchport, making the outline of a Y—instead of long and narrow body of water.

Next stop, the college, Grace thought. She gripped the wheel in anticipation and sat up a little straighter, wondering if Evan had noticed the change in posture. He didn't.

The school's main building housed a bell tower that stretched high above the other brick structures on campus and looked out on the water. The chapel sat beyond, near the shoreline. Residence halls nestled into a hillside, among trees.

As Vice President of Keuka College, Henry had loved the atmosphere and soaked up the vibrant life on campus. Grace could tell from the way that he talked about his job, the faculty, and the students. It was small and safe. It would have been the perfect place for Grace to attend college and later teach, he'd said on more than one occasion.

Grace had opted for the sprawling University of Georgia in Athens. She'd floated through three years at the school when she met and fell headlong into Steven, the biggest mistake of her life.

Steven Sanders was a history professor with a delicious accent and European airs. American born, the professor traveled the world, knew good wine, and could speak several languages fluently. He openly admitted he preferred international cities over the nightlife of New York and Atlanta, and talked at length about his home on Lake Como and flat in Munich. After a month of whirlwind courtship, Grace was infatuated, dazzled with the idea of becoming his wife.

After all, it was Grace's senior year; many of her friends were planning weddings and talking nonstop about buying houses, joining country clubs, and having babies. Smitten with Steven, Grace let her grades slide, stopped attending class, and planned every minute of every day around his schedule.

As was his pattern, five months later, Steven grew tired of his relationship with Grace. By the time she realized anything was wrong, Professor Sanders had moved on—with a much younger woman.

Grace discovered her mistake the day she confessed to him she was pregnant with Evan. Heart full to bursting with love for Steven, she nearly fainted when a towel-clad nineteen-year-old answered the door of his two-story brick house.

With a cry, Grace dropped the grocery bag with her pregnancy test on the front steps and ran away, crying as if her heart would break.

Days later, he confessed he would never marry her. Steven offered to pay for an abortion. Grace refused.

Professor Sanders quietly explained that he had accepted a job with a university in Munich. He was leaving at the end of the semester for one year. The young girl Grace had met at the door was his new assistant. She would be accompanying him to Germany.

There was silence then. Neither Steven nor Grace said a word.

Struggling to breathe, Grace nodded and clutched at the tiny swell of her belly. If Steven didn't want their child, she did. Nothing would change that.

She would raise him, alone, and love him unconditionally.

Without another word, Grace rose out of her seat and walked toward the door. Steven wouldn't look in her direction, though he attempted to grab her arm before she left the house.

Grace turned and shook off his grasp, lips pressed tight.

With a groan, a weak, semi-apologetic noise, Steven held out cash—hundreds of dollars. A peace offering? A payoff?

Grace paused and considered the gesture through narrowed eyes. She lifted her hand, the slightest movement, but he still wouldn't meet her gaze.

Heart splintering like broken glass, Grace hesitated, then slapped Steven across the face. As his cash fluttered to the floor, she walked out of the room, head held high. The door closed with a quiet click behind her.

GRACE TUCKED THE memory away and slowed down to allow a young couple to cross the street. They waved like they knew her well, and she managed to wave back and smile. Summer session at Keuka College was starting soon, and a few students trickled by with their backpacks on. A group of kids played Frisbee on the campus square with a lively German shepherd.

She pointed them out to Evan, who glanced up from his Nintendo 3DS long enough to see the dog catch the Frisbee in his mouth. Evan laughed out loud, music to Grace's ears, as they made the final turn off the main road.

Grace sighed and shifted in her seat. Evan moved and glanced up at the noise. She smiled and patted his leg. Evan went back to battling monsters, his thumbs and fingers pressing wildly back and forth across the buttons.

Grace paused as the lake came into view. For a moment, she held her breath, slowing down the car, drinking in the scenery. It was striking, long and lean, cutting a blue, shimmering streak in between the hills of brown and green.

A longing welled up inside her. All of it was so lovely— the sounds of nature, the pristine lake, and the neat, pretty cottages dotting the shoreline.

Then, in a flash of blinding sun through the windshield, she saw an image of her father. It was from a photograph, one he'd sent recently. He was smiling, holding the mast of his sailboat, surrounded by crystal clear water for miles.

Grace tried to squeeze back tears. Her eyelids burned with saltiness.

She swallowed, trying to push her fear and sadness back, deep inside her, to the place those feelings had been hidden for so long.

Chapter 7

THE CHAPEL WAS almost full. Every face was familiar—
Ryan recognized patients and neighbors, community
leaders, and family friends—all gathered to honor Henry Mason.

Ryan had arrived with minutes to spare, and chose to sit
in the very last pew, wanting to be alone with his thoughts.
There would be plenty of time for conversation at Kathleen's
house after the service.

As he gazed at the light streaming through the stained
glass windows, waiting for the service to begin, Ryan heard the
heavy wooden door creak open. Hushed words were spoken
and a young woman and a boy hurried past, making their way
toward the front of the chapel.

Ryan sat up straighter and watched as they slid into the
pew with Kathleen. He'd seen dozens of photographs. Grace
was even more lovely in person. Her son, Evan, was a carbon
copy of Henry. The same bright eyes, the same chin and shock
of dark hair—though Henry's had been peppered with silver.

Though he didn't know the details, Ryan was aware there
had been problems between Henry and his only daughter. According to Kathleen, the two rarely spoke, and Grace didn't

visit, though numerous invitations had been extended.

If it had taken a heavy toll on his heart, Henry had covered the pain well. His neighbor was happy, always jovial, with a ready smile, and a helping hand. Henry had a lovely home, a job he enjoyed, and active life, and an adoring wife.

Ryan frowned. Perhaps he had been too wrapped up in his own work and relationship issues to really take notice.

LAST WEEK, HENRY had come down the hill toward the dock with a steaming cup of coffee for his wife. It was early morning and Kathleen was tending her vegetable garden, gathering a basket of ripe peppers and tomatoes.

Ryan, docking his sailboat, watched Henry greet Kathleen as if they hadn't seen each other in years. He smiled down at his wife, caressed her cheek, and kissed her lips tenderly.

Not wanting to interrupt, Ryan began making his way back to his cottage. Before he reached the steps of his house, Henry was already calling him back.

"Hey, good morning," Ryan waved and ambled over, throwing his towel around his shoulders.

"Isn't it, though?" Henry answered, shaking hands with his neighbor. "Every day is a blessing—especially with my lovely Kathleen." He winked in his wife's direction, making her cheeks blush berry-pink.

Ryan felt his own face redden. He stared at the ground and shuffled his feet until Kathleen broke the silence.

"Henry, I've been thinking," Kathleen said, beaming up at her husband. "Isn't it time for Ryan to get out there again?" She smiled up at her husband. "He needs to find someone special... and maybe, we can help."

Henry considered this and grinned. "Absolutely."

R YAN DIDN'T NEED matchmakers, though the idea had amused him to no end. Henry and Kathleen were great neighbors and knew he must be lonely. Ryan would push on. He deserved to be alone; he had already found and lost his someone special.

Fresh out of residency, married just a few months, he and his wife, Lori, fell in love with the community. After being recruited by Soldiers and Sailors Hospital in Penn Yan, they picked out a lovely house on Keuka Lake, attempted some minor renovations, and moved in.

With a loan that would have made his parents life-long income seem small, Ryan purchased a retiring physician's practice, a new computer system, and opened for business.

Lori had been his anchor. She encouraged him, cheered him on, and tried to wait up on nights Ryan made rounds. By the time he crept in the door, it was dark, Lori was often asleep on the sofa, and dinner was cold.

They had talked of starting a family, soon after the practice was running smoothly. That idea, along with a boat for the lake, landscaping the yard, or scheduling a vacation, all went by the wayside. There simply wasn't time, Ryan explained.

After another year, Lori stopped asking. Ryan barely noticed. He took call every day of the year, made rounds early in the morning, and went to the office to see patients on weekends. When he was home, Ryan buried himself in medical journals or spent time on the Internet, keeping up on the latest health trends and pharmaceutical breakthroughs.

Lori decided to leave just as his practice started booming. He had forgotten their wedding anniversary, circled in red on the calendar.

He remembered her face the day she left. Her cheeks were swollen from crying, her hair tied back in a messy ponytail, still beautiful.

"You're a wonderful physician, Ryan," Lori said in the doorway, her hand resting on the frame. "Your patients love you. But you don't have time for me." She winced. "Can't you see that? Does it matter?"

Ryan didn't answer, his pride fighting the urge to beg her to stay. He clenched his jaw, trembling inside beneath a stony exterior.

Lori waited a beat, then picked up her suitcase, her voice barely above a whisper. "All right then, I'll pick up the rest of my things next week while you're at work."

Lori turned and walked up the path to the car. Ryan watched her, her golden hair falling softly on her shoulders, reflecting the sunshine.

You'll be back, he thought to himself. *You'll miss me. You'll need me.* But a week went by and Lori never appeared. A month passed, and then two more, and still no word.

Then, one day, a crisp white envelope appeared in his mailbox. Lori was in Atlanta, working at an art gallery. She wanted a divorce.

Wracked with denial, Ryan ignored the delivery. It couldn't be true. Lori would change her mind. Surely she would realize the mistake she had made.

It didn't happen. Lori stood her ground. She wasn't coming back.

Three months later, after a harsh phone call from his wife's attorney, Ryan signed the papers and put them in the mail.

He was divorced in time for Christmas. Ryan spent it alone, by the fireplace, with a bottle of wine and his cell phone. For once, even the answering service didn't call.

Ryan pushed the thoughts from his mind. It wasn't time to think about his life. What was missing. What he could have fixed or done differently. Today was about Kathleen and Henry.

The minister took his place at the front of the chapel, Bible in hand.

"We are here to celebrate the life of Henry Mason…"

Chapter 8

IN THE CHAPEL, pressed against the hard back of the wooden pew, Kathleen heard the words and music, but couldn't digest them. She stole a glance at her stepdaughter and grandson instead, focusing on what was real and right in front of her. Something, anything that didn't hurt as much as Henry's absence.

Grace's long dark hair was pulled back at the nape of her neck. She looked thinner, Kathleen thought, and her face was pale. Evan, on the other hand, had grown about a foot taller since his last school photo. He would turn out to be a fine young man, and his grandfather would be so proud.

Grace, avoiding Kathleen's gaze, had looked anxious when she slid into the seat, her eyes red-rimmed. She sat an arm's width away, with Evan on the other side. Kathleen was aware that the space was necessary—Grace needed to guard herself—but the inches felt like the expanse of the universe.

Kathleen forced herself to look up at the pulpit, biting her bottom lip to keep from running from the tiny sanctuary. She linked her fingers, pressing the knuckles together so that she wouldn't begin to sob. So far, it had worked.

Reverend Spencer, of course, was still talking about Henry. He spoke at length about his virtues and personality, his helping nature and giving spirit.

It was true, every word. Everyone loved Henry. People couldn't help it. Complete strangers became his best friends in a matter of minutes. He'd strike up lively conversations with grocery store clerks, talk with couples in line at the movie theatre, or recommend novels to people shopping at Long's Cards and Books on Main Street.

Kathleen glanced at her hands. The diamond in her ring glinted back at her. It reminded her of the way Henry used to wink when they shared a secret or a joke. She missed that. She missed Henry. It had only been two days.

His face was there, smiling, on paper, surrounded with a gold frame. The minister had suggested the photo. It was something for people to look at, a reminder since there was no casket and there would be no burial. The photograph sat to the side of the mahogany container.

Then, Reverend Spencer announced it was time for Kathleen to release Henry's ashes. Kathleen stood up mechanically and followed the minister outside to the small white gazebo that overlooked the water. Row by row, friends and acquaintances filed out and formed a small semi-circle, quietly waiting. Kathleen held onto Henry's ashes tightly as Reverend Spencer began another prayer.

As Kathleen grasped at the lid, a strong breeze suddenly pushed through the small gathering. The edges of the minister's robe lifted. Grace swayed at the force and grabbed at Evan to hold her balance. Kathleen braced herself on one of the posts and tucked a loose strand of her hair back behind her ear.

"Excuse me." Kathleen heard herself say. It didn't even sound like her voice.

Reverend Spencer stopped mid-sentence.

"Yes, Kathleen?" His voice was quizzical and kind.

"I'd like to say something." She cleared her throat.

"Of course." Reverend Spencer stepped aside gracefully, with a sweep of his arm, like it was the most normal thing in the world for someone to interrupt a funeral eulogy.

Kathleen turned and faced the rows of guests. Grace was wide-eyed. Even Evan had lifted his head, curious as to what was going to happen next.

For a moment, time stood still. Kathleen waited, gathering her thoughts. It seemed everyone, including her, was holding his or her breath. When she finally spoke, her voice came out, louder than she expected.

"I can't let him go right now. What I mean is…" Kathleen looked at the box, her hand on the lid. "Instead, I'm going to share something with all of you. Henry's favorite song."

And her voice lifted, loud and clear. Kathleen sang, off-key, but strong.

"And now the purple dusk of twilight time steals across the meadows of my heart. High up in the sky the little stars climb, always reminding me that we're apart."

She didn't look at anyone for fear she would think too much about it and stop. She had to do it for Henry and for herself.

In those moments, Kathleen willed herself to live at least one more day. Somehow, she would manage. As much as she feared it, she wouldn't let her spirit die with Henry.

"Though I dream in vain, in my heart it will remain…my stardust melody. The memory of love's refrain."

Chapter 9

G RANDMA DOESN'T REALLY know how to sing, does she?" Evan looked up at Grace with his eyebrows raised. He wasn't old enough to be thoroughly embarrassed, though as a teenager, her son might have claimed the performance would have scarred him for life.

"Well, she tried. But no, I guess not." Grace smiled a little at the remark. She was still trying to make sense of the afternoon, glad for the temporary protection that the rental car offered. She had been wishing an earthquake might swallow them up during her stepmother's tribute to Henry, though the odds of a natural disaster were not particularly in her favor.

"So why did she do it?" Evan questioned again. He was in a persistent mood and Grace knew he'd keep asking until he was satisfied he had been given the most brutally honest reply.

"I think she felt like she needed to," Grace heard herself say. "It was her way of showing that she loved your grandfather."

Evan scrunched his nose. "Oh. People do weird things when they're in love, then." He sunk back against the gray plush of the seat.

Grace laughed out loud at the comment. She was glad to have something to think about other than the funeral. "You're right, sweetie."

The windows were open, as there was rarely a need for air conditioning in Upstate New York, even in the dead of summer. Grace felt the breeze caress her face as she navigated through the one-lane road, barely paved, around potholes and over tree roots.

Evan fiddled with the radio, turning the dial to find music that he liked. It was mostly static, with an occasional blare of music coming through, and then fading. Eventually, he gave up and searched for his Nintendo 3DS.

Grace bit her lip and brushed a piece of hair off her face. "You know, Grandma doesn't like those things."

Evan glanced up from the screen. He pressed the pause button with one finger, raising an eyebrow.

"She's kind of old-fashioned, remember?"

Grace could see Evan was trying hard to think. "Yeah, I guess so."

"Anyway, we'll probably just stow it until we leave. You can keep it in the car. Nothing will happen to it."

"Do you really mean it?" Her son frowned.

"And there's no TV." Grace said quickly. "Unless it's to watch the news or check the weather."

Evan's eyes grew wide in disbelief. "What?" He scratched his head. "Why not?"

Grace thought for a minute. She gathered up what she had been told as a little girl, hoping it made sense and sounded believable. "Papa used to say that water has magic all around it. Oceans, rivers, lakes, it doesn't matter."

"Okay," Evan said from the corner of his mouth. He pressed his head against the window, staring out at the landscape.

"And Papa always thought that TV and electronics got in

the way of people finding it," Grace added.

Evan thought about this. He wasn't happy, but understood that he had to follow the rules. "Fine."

Grace pursed her lips. It was exactly what she would have said thirty years ago. She reached out a hand and squeezed his knee. "Thanks, honey."

She eased the car to the side of the road and double-checked the numbers on the mailboxes. Satisfied she was at the right place, Grace parked and cut the engine.

Outside, Grace stretched and peered up at the massive trees overhead. The foliage was so dense it made the road dark and cool, tricking you into thinking it was late afternoon or early evening, until splinters of bright light flashed through breaks in the branches and leaves.

Her father had found the house of his dreams five years ago, paid a good price for it, and spent every weekend fixing it up. Grace had seen photos in various stages of the repair process and had to admit that the finished product was more than impressive.

The two-story cottage was painted a deep khaki color, trimmed in white, with a wrap-around porch. The grass, lush and green, was interrupted only by a gravel path running out to the edge of the lake. Grace knew that the landscaping was her stepmother's project, and the yard looked like a page out of *Better Homes and Gardens* magazine.

Now, the house was Kathleen's alone. Grace wondered who was going to mow the lawn, get the mail from town, and make the repairs? All the things her father had just taken care of every day. Grace frowned and ran a hand through her hair.

What was she thinking? Her stepmother, being the consummate organizer and ultimate perfectionist, probably hadn't missed a beat. There was no doubt, she had it all worked out already.

Grace didn't need to worry. It wasn't her problem. She was leaving in eight days.

Chapter 10

THE BOWL IN Ryan's hand wobbled precariously. He stopped and set it down, adjusting the plastic wrap over the top to keep the contents from spilling out.

He had worked hard on the fruit salad, carefully slicing and cutting the pieces of pineapple, strawberry, melon and orange – nearly slicing his finger off in the meantime. It was all tossed in a gooey, sugary mixture of powdered sugar and juices. Lori's recipe. She had made it look easy. It took him hours. He grunted in frustration, glad it was finished.

Ryan thought more than once about tossing the whole thing and running to the grocery store to have a tray made, but kept on out of principal. He wanted it to be special for Kathleen and Henry. Something he had made himself.

People had already started arriving from the church service. He heard cars pulling up and parking, the sound of voices, loud and soft, floating through the air. A few children shouted and ran down the path, only to be shushed by their parents. Doors opened and shut.

Ryan took a deep breath and picked up the bowl again,

looking down at the colors, deep red, cheerful yellow, and bright orange staring back at him. Stepping out into the sunshine, he walked the few yards to the house next door on the path Henry had built of brick pavers. Carefully laid out, it snaked though the green grass, straight to their door. A small sign proclaiming "Bless this House" hung over the doorway.

Inside was crowded and noisy, with a long table loaded down with food. People he knew or recognized were sipping out of glasses or sampling the sandwiches, neatly lined up on a tray. As Ryan set down the bowl in an empty place on the table and unwrapped it, he felt a cool, soft touch on his shoulder.

He turned to see Kathleen.

"How sweet of you." She reached out and squeezed his hand. It was cold as ice and shaking slightly. Her eyes, usually bright and sparkling, looked tired. She smiled at the fruit.

"Made it myself."

"I'm impressed. Henry would be too."

"Took me forever, I'm not exactly experienced in the kitchen," Ryan said, putting a hand in the center of his chest and heaving a mock sigh. "But for you, anything!"

"Well, thank you." Kathleen managed a wink. When you get a chance, I'd love for you to meet Grace and Evan. They're around here somewhere." Kathleen searched the room, her eyes darting over and in between the crowd.

"I'd love too." Ryan's voice trailed off.

But his neighbor wasn't listening; she had taken his elbow and was trying to lead him over to the porch to a group of chattering women.

"Over here!" One of them called out.

Kathleen smiled and signaled for Ryan to wait just a minute. He paused as she turned to chat with her friends, all of whom took turns hugging her.

Then, Ryan eased away, giving his neighbor her space. He saw her every day—many of her friends had driven from hours away—some from out of state.

There was a table set up in the corner, people were signing a book and looking at photos of Henry and the family. He stepped closer. The mahogany box was there, in the center.

Ryan thought about Kathleen not being able to let go of Henry's ashes. He didn't blame her, and there was no designated timeframe. When there was nothing left but memories, it was easy to cling to something tangible. *It was why he hadn't moved Lori's things*, a voice inside him said.

Ryan shook his head, trying to rid the nagging thoughts, and focused instead on the pictures.

The photos on the table were arranged in no particular order; some were in black and white, some color. There were small photos of Henry as a boy in suspenders, one of him as a teenager, football in hand, with another boy.

Kathleen had taken some of Henry on his Sailfish, blue and white stripes floating behind him. There were a few of Henry swimming in the lake. The last photo was of Henry at the kitchen table in this very room, birthday cake in front of him with dozens of candles glowing beneath him, Kathleen at his side. It was almost as if he could see the happiness surrounding them. Ryan had taken the picture only months before.

An older couple made their way to the table and smiled at the photos. The man pointed at one. "He was a good man."

"A good man, he certainly was," Ryan echoed.

"Henry and I worked together at Keuka College." The man stuck out his hand in greeting. "And you are?"

"Ryan Gordon, Henry's doctor." The man looked at him carefully, searching his eyes. He dropped his hand quickly. "And neighbor," he added.

"Nice to meet you..." the man said. His voice trailed off as his wife or companion interrupted, murmuring something into his ear and they abruptly turned away.

Ryan watched as they disappeared through the crowd. *Odd.* Coincidence or not? He wondered if people thought he was to blame for Henry's death. The thought gave him chills. He had done everything he could, ruling out the most minute details.

His head swam with guilt and negative thoughts. Did Kathleen think he had failed? All of a sudden, Ryan needed air. He needed to get away from the crowd, as quickly as possible.

Ryan turned, running straight into Kathleen's stepdaughter.

Grace gasped as her chilled drink splashed over the front of her dress. She was so startled that the glass slipped from between her fingers. In seemingly slow motion, the goblet turned end over end, finally landing on the wooden floor. With a loud crash, the crystal wine glass smashed into a million pieces.

"Don't move," Ryan cautioned, grasping one of Grace's arms to steady her. She was shaking, and so pale; her skin had taken on a luminous, ghost-like pallor. All around her feet, jagged shards of glass poked through a large pool of red liquid.

"I'm so sorry," he exclaimed. As a doctor, he was used to fixing people, not knocking them over. "Would someone toss me a mop or broom, please?"

Ryan kept his eyes on Grace, realizing that she might be in shock. She'd travelled a long distance, then sat through her father's funeral service, only to be doused with fruit punch by a complete stranger.

To someone who hadn't witnessed the collision, Kathleen's room floor looked like a fresh crime scene.

An elderly woman from church disappeared to find supplies. The room was quiet for a minute; a few faces looked curiously in their direction, and then buzzed with gentle conversation again. The crowd around them thinned, making room for the clean-up. Kathleen, who had heard the noise, was rushing over to survey the damage.

Ryan released Grace from his grasp as the color returned to her cheeks. She blinked, looking as if she'd just woken from a nine-hour nap.

"Are you all right?" Ryan asked.

"Don't worry about it," Grace said in a quiet voice and backed away, stepping over the spilled drink like she was walking a tightrope. "It's fine."

"But…" Ryan persisted.

Grace shook her head emphatically. She murmured an apology, and disappeared through her stepmother's front door.

Chapter 11

KATHLEEN WAS EXHAUSTED after floating through the afternoon in a semi-conscious state. Though the crowd had thinned, the room still seemed to whirl with the dull roar of voices, ebbing and flowing around her.

If it hadn't been for Henry dying, it would have felt like one of their regular summer parties. She did better, felt better, when she imagined Henry still at work, busy at the college, set to walk in the door at any moment. He'd throw down his briefcase and call out to her that he was home.

Hanging on to that thought, Kathleen was able to go through the motions. "We'll see" became her pat response after the tenth time someone inquired about upkeep on the cottage or whether she was going to sell Henry's boat. Deep down, she knew they were asking because they cared, but at the moment, she couldn't make a single decision.

She might as well have been Scarlett O'Hara, telling herself she'd "think about it tomorrow." Henry would have made a fine Rhett Butler, although his leaving had nothing to do with an argument on the steps of a mansion in Georgia.

Kathleen managed to smile at the thought as the last guests said their goodbyes. After closing the door behind them, she picked up a few wine glasses and carried them to the sink. Grace was there, washing dishes and setting them out on thick towels to dry.

Evan sat near her, at the end of the kitchen table, alternating between bites of a sandwich and drinks of milk. He had endured endless gushing over his looks, how he favored Henry. Kathleen smiled at a lipstick mark, bright pink, on the edge of his forehead.

S HE NEEDED TO try and relax for a few moments, allow the tension escape her neck and shoulders, but Kathleen was worried about Grace. Her stepdaughter wasn't speaking to anyone. Not to her, not to Evan.

Kathleen began cleaning up the table. She covered casseroles and plates of cookies. She took a deep breath and turned toward Grace, gesturing at Ryan's fruit salad. "Can't you eat some of this?"

"No, thanks, Kathleen, I've had enough." Grace looked over her shoulder and wiped her hands. She set the towel down in a heap next to the tower of clean dishes and folded her arms. "Actually, I don't feel very well."

"I'm sorry, what can I do to help?" Kathleen asked.

Grace pursed her lips, chin tilted toward the ceiling, her eyes filling with tears. "There isn't anything you can do, Kathleen."

Evan looked up from his sandwich, surprised at his mother's reaction.

"Sweetie, Mommy's just sad about Papa," Grace explained, wiping her eyes. "Why don't you run and wash your hands while Grandma Kathleen and I talk for a minute."

Sliding out from his seat, still looking at his mother, Evan walked to the guest bathroom. A few moments later, the water began to run.

Grace cleared her throat. "You didn't say anything about having my father cremated. You didn't even *ask*." Her voice broke as she emphasized the last word.

Kathleen swallowed hard. "I thought that you knew. He was very clear about it. I wouldn't have kept that from you—"

"What's cremated?" Evan was listening from the open door.

Grace closed her eyes.

Kathleen's mind raced. Maybe she should have asked Grace. Or not. Everything was so confused. It had been Henry's wish, after all.

She looked over at Evan and hesitated, trying to think of the simplest explanation.

"It's when they take a person's body after they die and turn it into ashes, instead of burying it in the ground." The words came out fast, like if she said them quickly enough, he wouldn't hear or understand them.

"That's what they did to Grandpa?" Evan made a face, his eyes wide. "Gross. Yuck. Why?"

"It's what he wanted." Kathleen tried to make her voice firm.

"Evan, we can discuss this later, just the *two* of us," Grace interrupted and shot her stepmother a curious look.

"Oh, okay," said Evan. He shrugged and picked up his sandwich again.

Kathleen pressed her lips together and went back to cleaning up stray glasses and silverware. Clearly, she wasn't wanted or needed—not by Grace, anyway. But she could still have a relationship with her grandchild.

After stacking a set of dishes and carrying them to the sink, Kathleen made a suggestion. "Why don't you go down to the dock, Evan? There are some great rocks you can skip on the water. Do you know how to do that?"

Her grandson downed the last of his milk with triumph.

He wiped away the white foam on his top lip with his tongue. "Sure I do." Evan jumped down from the chair with flourish. "Can I go swimming too?"

"Absolutely, honey. Good idea," Grace answered. She bent down and ruffled Evan's hair. "I'll find your bathing suit, sweetie." Grabbing her suitcase that had set in the far corner of the room, she pulled it toward the bedroom, running the wheels along the wood floor.

"You'll have to have your mom or me there when you go in the water, okay?" Kathleen said. "It's pretty deep."

"I'm a good swimmer," Evan said. "Mom had me take lessons. I can even go off the high dive now."

"That sounds scary," Kathleen said. She clapped a hand over her mouth and made her eyes wide in mock horror.

Evan chuckled to himself as Grace reappeared, wrapped in a beach towel and holding her son's swim trunks.

"Found them. Here you go."

Evan snatched up the bathing suit, ran into the bedroom, and returned in a flash, changed and ready to go. Without waiting for further instruction, he kicked off his shoes and ran outside, making a beeline for the gravel walkway down to the lake.

Grace paused by the door, struggling to meet her stepmother's gaze. "I have to go watch him."

"Of course." Kathleen said lightly. She wasn't going to bring up the memorial service, her husband's cremation, or anything else remotely upsetting. "Go and enjoy yourself. Try to relax."

"Thank you," Grace said in a small voice, clearly struggling to keep her emotions in check. "Please understand that I don't know how to feel about any of this." She took a sharp breath. "And I'm sorry for snapping at you."

"Don't give it a thought," Kathleen said. "It's been hard on all of us."

Grace nodded and looked away. She slipped through

the door, following Evan down the path. He was almost to the water's edge.

Kathleen watched Grace catch up with her grandson. Her stepdaughter shrugged off her towel and walked to the end of the dock, holding Evan's hand.

From the open window, Kathleen could hear peals of laughter. Evan began to count, swinging his mother's arm.

"Ready?" he yelled. "Okay. Three. Two. One."

Grace and Evan jumped together, shrieking as their bodies disappeared into a splash of water.

And Kathleen grinned, wide and strong, for the first time since Henry died.

Chapter 12

Back on the dock, Grace exhaled some of her stress, toweling off as Evan continued to swim and play in the lake.

She sat cross-legged on the edge of the wooden planks, legs dangling, and let the fading light bathe and warm her. She took some deep breaths, filling her lungs deeply and exhaling, wishing she knew tai chi or yoga.

Evan ran around on the beach, examining stones, pausing to toss some. The sight brought Grace back to her own childhood. Her family had always vacationed by the water, renting a house on the ocean every Memorial Day weekend.

It wasn't the clear, fresh water of Keuka Lake in Upstate New York, but Orange Beach, Alabama had its own irresistible charm. Grace had always loved the white sand beaches and salty sea water.

C'MON, CHICKEN," HER *father called out. It was their an-nual ritual—the game of who could jump into the water first. It had been a cool Spring, and for the last weekend in May, the ocean was still breathtakingly chilled.*

Her mother had turned to go back inside, flatly refusing to participate in the antics. She shook her head and walked away, back to the house and her list of chores. The edge of her dress swayed like a bell in the breeze, back and forth.

"If you get sick…" she had warned both of them sternly, patting the edge of her hair. But she was beaten and she knew it. Her words fell on her father like spring rain, evaporating almost instantly.

Birds called to each other and swooped over the water in the distance, searching for dinner.

"Let her go, who cares?" Her father whispered once she was safely out of sight. His eyes twinkled at Grace irresistibly.

Grace couldn't help but giggle, feeling a rush of devilish pleasure run through her body. She threw her towel down and stretched her arms to the sky, feeling the anticipation.

"All right!" Her father clapped his hands together.

"It's too cold," Grace protested. She said it every year, out of principle. She was almost twelve, after all.

"Okay, if I have to go by myself, I will." He set his face in a mock frown and started marching toward the dock, his long legs striding purposefully toward his mission. After he turned away, there was a smile on his lips. Grace could tell, even from the back of his head.

Grace's heart lurched with the thought of being left be-hind. She balled up her fists and pushed against the soft ground with the toes of her flip flops. "Wait!" She called out to him.

He turned and smiled, holding out his hand.

Grace grabbed for his palm, her fingers getting swal-lowed up in his firm grip. She stood with him after kicking off her shoes behind him. She was breathing hard, feeling the beating of her heart in her chest.

"Ready?" Her father turned and looked straight across the lake. "One, two, three…"

Grace and her father jumped together, at once feeling weightless, crashing down with the shock of the water taking both their breath away.

Grace came up, sputtering and laughing. They were still holding hands.

"That's my girl!" Grace heard her father exclaim proudly.

And she knew that she was.

A N HOUR LATER, Evan emerged from the water, hungry and tired. After drying off and getting him into pajamas, Grace fixed him a grilled cheese sandwich and hot cocoa.

Belly full, Evan brushed his teeth, and rolled into bed. Grace perched on the edge of the mattress and began to read from one of his favorite books, *Tom Sawyer*. Kathleen had left it, along with a stack of other classics, on the nightstand.

Her son didn't make it through the first chapter. Breathing heavily and sleeping peacefully, Grace tucked the covers around Evan's shoulders, kissed him goodnight, and slipped out of the room.

The main rooms in the house were empty as she tiptoed through the kitchen. Relieved that she didn't have to make small talk with Kathleen or apologize again for her behavior, Grace eased into her bedroom.

She looked out the window. The sky was streaked in gorgeous shades of purple and red, setting the hillsides on fire. The lake below was still; not a ripple broke the surface. As she watched the scenery fade to black, the moon, rising in the sky glowed silver-bright in the distance. All around, where the light grazed the treetops and cottage roofs, it *did* look like stardust

Grace understood then why her father loved it here so

much, and didn't want to leave. It was peaceful and perfect. And yes, almost magical.

The suitcase unzipped easily, making a whirring sound as she pulled it open. The clothes she had packed were thrown in hastily, most not ironed.

Grace lifted the shirts and pants out one by one, laying them of the bed and smoothing them with her hands before folding them and placing them into an open drawer.

She set the invitation her father had sent on the corner of the dresser.

Yes, despite everything, Grace was Henry's girl, and always would be.

Chapter 13

In the morning light, Ryan watched Kathleen struggle with the Sailfish. He'd held back for the last half-hour, not wanting to intervene.

The boats, by design, were light and sleek in the water and relatively simple to maneuver. It was about twelve feet long, painted white, with small wooden railings, and enough space for two adults to sit comfortably.

Ryan rubbed his head, trying to remember a time Kathleen had piloted the boat by herself. Henry always held the rope and the rudder while his wife enjoyed the sun and the breeze, dangling her toes into the water.

His neighbor struggled a few minutes more, wiggling the center mast and attempting to drag the boat from its perch. Unable to stand by, Ryan finally strode down the yard connecting the two properties.

"My, you're up early." Kathleen said and gave him a wry look. Her sunglasses were perched on top of her head jauntily, and she was wearing the brightest orange life vest Ryan had ever seen, well-worn on the edges. It must have been Henry's from his college days.

Ryan grinned under his baseball cap and waved in the direction of the Sailfish. "Saw a damsel in distress."

"I'm not in *distress*," Kathleen said, pursing her lips in frustration. "This boat is just stuck."

Ryan nodded and surveyed the situation while his neighbor stood back. With a heave, he slid the boat off its stand and into the waiting water. Before Kathleen could argue, Ryan plunged his feet into the lake, his running shoes filling with water.

Grinning up at Kathleen, he held the Sailfish in place. "C'mon, you climb on."

Kathleen maneuvered onto the smooth wooden surface and scooted to the rear. She grabbed the rudder and held it still while Ryan loosened his grip on the ropes holding the sail in place.

The breeze was soft and caught at the fabric, making it flap once or twice. Kathleen let the sail out to catch more of the wind. It arced into a wide C shape.

"You'll have to take her out sometime," she said, tilting her head toward the center of the lake. "Henry would like that."

Ryan, keeping one hand on the Sailfish, grinned. "I'd like that, too."

Kathleen fluttered her eyelashes. "If you tried getting home from work at a decent hour, maybe you'd have time to do something fun."

Ryan rolled his eyes and, for show, let out an exasperated sigh. "I hear that all the time—from my staff. Now I have to hear it from you, too?"

His neighbor nodded in agreement. "Those ladies are right."

The water sloshed around Ryan's waist as he stepped further from shore, holding the sailboat. He'd be over his head if he went much further. "Okay, okay! I'll try to get home earlier one night next week," he gulped. "Sound good? Ready to cast off?"

"Yes. Thank you." Kathleen, safe and mostly dry, nudged the centerboard into place. Ryan gave the Sailfish a push toward the center of the lake.He watched her for a while, standing near the dock, as the breeze helped the boat move further away from him. After a few minutes, Kathleen and her life-jacket became just a speck of orange in the distance.

His neighbor's words echoed in his ear.

Ryan couldn't remember the last time he'd left work early—or had fun.

Maybe, just maybe, Kathleen was right.

Chapter 14

GRACE WOKE TO the sound of the lake lapping against the pebbly shore, as comfortable and familiar as a pair of old shoes. Morning light streamed in through the edges of the blinds covering the windows.

She noticed the dark tufts of Evan's hair peeking out of the covers and smiled. He was breathing deeply, one arm slung over his head. Despite being eight and more grown-up, he still took every opportunity to climb into bed with her.

Carefully, she lifted her side of the sheets and pulled them back slowly. It was a new day and Grace was glad. It had been a long and weird afternoon yesterday, topped off with her stepmother's performance at the funeral.

Grace sighed long and deep. She slipped on her robe and shut the bedroom door behind her carefully, so as not to wake Evan. If she had to guess, her stepmother was probably awake an hour ago. She peeked around the corner into the living room, expecting her to be standing there.

It was empty, and the door to Kathleen's bedroom was open just a crack.

"Hello?" Grace said in a loud whisper.

No answer.

Grace let her shoulders relax. Kathleen was probably outside walking or gardening, maybe talking to one of the neighbors. Her father always said that her stepmother could never stand still.

Grateful for the reprieve, Grace decided to make coffee. As expected, everything inside the kitchen cabinets was stacked neatly and labeled. Grace inhaled the nutty aroma as she measured out a few scoops of dark brown granules, added the water, and flicked the switch.

As the coffee pot began to gurgle, Grace inspected the living room. It looked completely different without a crowd of people. The space was clean and white, with a sofa and loveseat in the corner, both set an equal distance apart from the coffee table. The floor, wide-planked and wooden, was aged to mellow golden color.

Framed pictures hung on the walls. There were lovely panoramic shots of Keuka Lake, two of her father and his Sailfish, and several snapshots of Evan.

The majority of photographs, however, were of Henry and Kathleen. Grace moved closer, studying the details, and found herself mesmerized by the similarities. In each one—location aside—her father and stepmother were smiling. In Italy, in China, and France. On the campus of the college where her father worked, on the shore of the lake, and inside the house where Grace was standing.

Every time the shutter clicked open, Henry and Kathleen had their heads bent together and arms entwined. They glowed with happiness and love.

Grace stepped back and turned away, feeling her throat choke with emotion.

It hurt to look too long at her father's face.

GRACE SLID OPEN the heavy glass doors to the outside porch and stepped out onto the sturdy wooden planks, wishing the coffee would finish.

She shivered when the cool breeze hit her face and tugged the robe around her tighter. A tiny ant ran across the top of the wood, clinging for dear life in the breeze.

The chairs on the porch were empty. She looked further, down along the shoreline, for signs of life. The deck and pebbly beach were empty too.

Out of the corner of her eye, familiar blue and white stripes came into view across the aquamarine of the water. It looked hauntingly like her father's sailboat. The trees near the deck bent in their branches, leaves rustling noisily.

The Sailfish was her father's prized possession, the boat he'd bought in college for only three hundred dollars. Henry had lovingly taken care of it over the years, sanded carefully and painted the brightest white at least a dozen times.

Grace kept her eyes focused on the tall mast, bobbing slightly as it made its way across the water. She could make out a single figure in an orange life vest. One person on board. It could be Kathleen, but she wasn't sure.

Then, the wind slowed, gusted once again, and sputtered. As the sun rose about the hilltops, the air became absolutely still.

Grace waited for the breeze to pick up, anticipating the brush of air against her bare skin. Her heart began to beat faster. She glanced around for other boats in the area—a fishing boat, a rowboat, anything.

The lake was empty. The sail hadn't moved.

Shading her eyes, Grace held the boat in view, starting to walk toward the dock.

Another agonizing minute passed.

The boat's mast teetered, causing the sail to shake from side to side. Grace blinked to make sure what she was seeing was real.

It was Kathleen.

Chapter 15

KATHLEEN HADN'T COUNTED on the Sailfish being this difficult to manage. She had been on it a thousand times with Henry and chided herself for worrying.

Her husband had patiently shown her how to trim the huge sail and make the boat go faster. She remembered that letting out the rope allowed the Sailfish to slow down. Kathleen knew how to move the rudder, and when to pull up the centerboard.

But she never had asked—or didn't remember hearing—exactly what steps to take when stuck in the middle of the lake. By herself.

Kathleen, in her hurry to enjoy the morning solitude, hadn't thought to bring her cell phone. She didn't leave Grace a note. And, of course, by now, Dr. Ryan Gordon was long gone, driving into work, his mind squarely focused on the dozens of patients waiting for him at the office.

If Henry could see her, Kathleen thought, he was probably having a chuckle. She looked up at the few white puffs floating by against the blue and leaned her head against the steel mast.

Kathleen scanned the horizon. It was daybreak. Lights were just starting to come on in houses dotting the shoreline. A few birds swooped down, nearby, in search of breakfast. They paid her no attention, darting and calling out to each other. Otherwise, the lake was empty. Even the Sheriff's boat would have been a welcome sight at this point.

She considered her options. Kathleen could try to paddle back to her dock using the centerboard, which was awkward and unwieldy. She could try to swim back, as she had the life vest on, but she'd have to leave the boat. She could wait. Or, if it wasn't so early, she might try to yell or scream and attract some attention.

The latter, however, was out, she decided. She'd rather not completely lose her dignity. The talk in Penn Yan would be nothing but stories about the crazy woman who lost her husband, and a day later, tried to drown herself in the middle of Keuka Lake.

Paddle it was, Kathleen decided.

At least she was facing the right direction. Letting the rope go slack, she tugged at the slippery centerboard. It wouldn't budge. Kathleen set her jaw and tried again, readjusting her grip. With a small grunt, she yanked hard, finally freeing the centerboard.

The effort threw Kathleen off balance, and out of the corner of her eye, she watched the rope unfurl and slip into the water. A second too late, she grabbed for the thick, white strand, but felt the braided edges brush past her fingers.

Trying not to panic, Kathleen tucked the centerboard behind her, eased toward the edge of the Sailfish, and slid one leg into the water, trying to catch the rope with her toes.

No such luck. Kathleen slapped at the lake in disgust, causing droplets to spray her nose and mouth. With the back of one hand, she wiped at her face, trying not to cry.

How had she ever gotten herself in such a predicament?

Kathleen rubbed at the back of her neck and blinked away tears. She glanced around, hoping to see another sailboat or a swimmer. She saw no one, but noticed with increasing concern that the sky had grown dark. Thick clouds were rolling in from the South, covering what had been a perfectly blue horizon.

A few droplets of rain fell against her leg and spattered the boat.

Kathleen let out a tiny moan.

Gusts of wind now pushed persistently at the sail, rocking the Sailfish from side to side. Kathleen clung to the rails, unable to think. She shifted back, inching closer to the mast. When her tailbone hit something hard and cold, she jumped.

The splash, directly behind the boat, stopped her cold. With horror, Kathleen realized she had lost her only other means of saving herself. Holding her breath, she turned her head.

The centerboard was in the water, floating away. *Damn!*

Wind, causing the lake to whitecap, whipped at Kathleen's hair. The strands played on her cheeks and eyelashes, making it difficult to see. Before she could tuck them out of the way, a bigger gust took the sail and spun it.

There was an awful scraping sound, metal on metal.

All at once, the long, silver boom swung around, gathering speed, and hit the back of Kathleen's neck. She winced in pain and grabbed at nothing, too late. The Sailfish tilted up, unsteadily, then back. Water washed over her legs and feet, pulling and dragging her away.

Kathleen plunged into the dark, cool lake. The last thing she remembered was watching the sail crash to the water next to her head.

Chapter 16

AFTER REALIZING THAT he'd left his briefcase on the kitchen counter, Ryan returned to the house, parked his pickup, and ambled down the gravel driveway. One step away from his front door, a woman's scream sliced the morning air.

Ryan took a detour to the lakeshore, quickened his pace to a jog, and caught a glimpse of Grace running for the dock full speed. Peering out into the distance, he saw what had given Kathleen's stepdaughter such a scare.

Henry's Sailfish was capsized, with no one making any effort to right it. He thought he saw a small corner of Kathleen's bright orange life vest bobbing in and out of the small waves, but couldn't be sure. What was worse, the sky, turning black and spitting rain, rumbled with huge thunderclouds.

Ryan slid on the nearest lifejacket he could find, grabbed the keys to his wave runner, jumped on, and cranked the engine. It sputtered to life, sending a stream of water arcing from the tail.

Grace, desperately trying to lower Henry's power boat, wasn't having much success working the lift. She was so consumed with her task that she didn't notice that Ryan had driven over and was trying to get her attention.

"Hey! Jump on." There was no time for formality. Ryan waved his arm and called out a second time, making his voice bellow. "Grace! Come on. You're wasting time!"

This time, Kathleen's stepdaughter whirled around, one hand clinging to the lift mechanism. Her eyes darted out to the water. "But the boat. My stepmother..."

"I know," Ryan yelled, circling the wave runner to stay close. He slowed and puttered toward the end of the dock. Holding out a hand, he grabbed for the metal ladder and hung on.

"Get on!"

Grace blinked back at him, and finally seemed to understand what he was trying to tell her. She snatched up a bright blue life vest from the boat, took hold of Ryan's shirt, and jumped on the back of the wave runner.

Ryan gunned the motor and coaxed it as fast as he could without causing another accident. Glancing side to side, he was grateful it was so early. Had it been a weekend afternoon, he might have to dodge speedboats or watch for the occasional crazy driver who'd had a few too many beers.

The spray in his face, Ryan crouched close to the handles, navigating through the swells of the water. He could see Kathleen, looking dazed, her head above the water, thankfully. Henry's crazy orange life jacket had saved her.

As they drew close, even in the darkness, Ryan noticed the blood immediately. Grace muffled a gasp as slowed the wave runner.

"She's going to be fine, Grace," Ryan said, making his voice calm and firm. "I'm going to dive off and get her. You stay on here and steer."

"Okay." Grace sounded unsure. Her hands felt shaky on his back, but Ryan wasn't about to hesitate now. She could manage it, even if he had to coach her from the water. "Ever drive one of these things?" he called behind him.

"No." Grace replied though tight lips.

It didn't matter.

"Just lean to the left and I'll get off." With the words just out of his mouth, Ryan plunged into the lake, hoping Grace had listened.

Pulling the water toward him in strong strokes, Ryan was at Kathleen's side in a matter of seconds. Her eyes were open, but glazed. She was blinking slowly and treading water, one arm outstretched.

"Ryan." Kathleen was surprisingly calm. She gazed at him with an amused look on her face. "Whatever are you doing out here?"

Chapter 17

I'M AMAZED HE'S still asleep," Kathleen said, smoothing a damp hair away from her face. She leaned back against her lawn chair as Grace sat down in the seat beside her.

"I know," her stepdaughter agreed, shooting a wary glace at the sky. "I'm amazed all of the wind and rain didn't wake him up." Grace then squinted out at the dock and tugged at the towel around her shoulders. "Is Ryan finished?"

"I hope so." Kathleen watched her neighbor carefully as he unlashed the rope connecting the wave runner and sailboat. *He was clever. And brave. Not just anyone would have thrown all safety aside to save her life.*

Ryan had thought out the rescue carefully, pulling Kathleen onto the wave runner while Grace tied a spare rope to the Sailfish. Her stepdaughter had clung to the back of Henry's boat, and in minutes, Ryan was maneuvering both vessels and carrying the two women back shore.

It had been awkward and slow-going, but better than leaving someone, exposed and vulnerable to lightning, waiting in the middle of the lake.

Kathleen and Grace, safe and sound, watched from the relative comfort of his covered back porch as Ryan finished dragging the Sailfish onto the beach.

Grace broke the silence. "You're still bleeding."

With a jolt of realization, Kathleen touched the back of her head gingerly. Her head still hurt, but she'd decided it was just the impact from being struck by the boom. When she examined her fingers, they were stained blush-red at the tips.

"It's nothing," Kathleen scoffed a little, shifting in her chair. She'd wait until Ryan came up to the cottage and let him take a look.

Grace frowned and leaned forward for emphasis. "Kathleen, listen. I really think—"

"Ahoy, mates." Ryan called out, shaking the water from his hair. "Kathleen, stay right there so I can take a look at your war wound."

"Stay here?" Grace muttered to herself.

Kathleen waggled her fingers and smiled brightly at her neighbor. "Yes, of course."

With a scrape of chair legs against wooden planks, Grace pushed back, nearly knocking her seat end-over-end. She stood up, shook her head in frustration, and met Ryan on the back steps, blocking his path.

Before Kathleen realized what was going on, before she could interject or explain, her stepdaughter raised her voice and looked directly at Ryan.

"Excuse me, but my stepmother needs a doctor," Grace said sharply. "We'll be going to the nearest emergency room."

"Not necessary," Kathleen chimed in.

Grace swiveled her head back at her stepmother. "You are going to the ER and that is final. Your neighbor doesn't know a thing about what's wrong with your head."

Both Ryan and Kathleen burst into laughter simultaneously. The look on Grace's face didn't help matters. The poor thing was so confused that it just added to the amusement.

Finally, Ryan coughed and wiped tears from his eyes.

Grace folded both arms across her chest and waited patiently for an explanation. "What ever is so funny?" she demanded.

"Ryan *is* my doctor." Kathleen giggled.

Grace blinked.

"This," she swept a hand toward her neighbor, as if making formal introductions, "is Dr. Gordon."

Chapter 18

KATHLEEN SAT AS still as she could next to Ryan's kitchen table. She had been there before, many times, for dinner parties and social gatherings. Open and inviting, it was decorated simply, with a huge window overlooking the lake, tree branches framing the view of water and sky. A fireplace sat in the far corner of the room, hand-built from slate and stone. The aroma of coffee filled the air.

Ryan worked quickly and gently, cleaning the wound and inspecting for other scrapes or cuts.

Trying not to think about her aching head, Kathleen concentrated on the scenery outside. An occasional seagull swooped by the window, looking for breakfast. The wind was picking up and gray storm clouds were gathering in the distance.

Grace had left in a huff, and was no doubt walking off some of her frustration and embarrassment. Kathleen wished she could soothe whatever bothered her stepdaughter so much, but she doubted that Grace would ever let her close enough to try.

Ryan patted her shoulder. He was finished, or so it seemed. He came around the table and gazed down at Kathleen as he packed up his medical supplies.

"Looks like you lucked out this time," he grinned ruefully.

"Ten stitches?" Kathleen said, trying to make a joke, but bracing herself for the worst.

"Nah, it's a little cut. It's not gaping, so there's really no need to stitch or staple it up. Head cuts just tend to bleed more. Makes it look worse than it really is."

Kathleen grimaced. She had to be a bit more careful, especially since she was by herself.

"Can I get you some coffee? I even made a fresh pot this morning."

"Thank you, yes. That would be wonderful. And thank you again for this morning. I hate that I interrupted your work day. All of those patients."

Ryan shook his head and glanced away, trying to look lighthearted. "The office staff handled it. They diverted any real emergencies to the urgent care center or the ER. Anyone else was rescheduled. No worries."

"Well, that's good," Kathleen exhaled deeply. "And that must mean that I have you all to myself for the rest of the morning, right?"

She was teasing, but saw a sad, dark look cross Ryan face. The expression lasted for just for a moment, then it was gone again. Her eyes followed his to a small photo in a silver frame.

"Absolutely. Especially since we're both by ourselves now." Ryan said, then paused. "It's hard, isn't it? Losing someone?"

"I miss Henry every minute."

Ryan nodded thoughtfully. "It's been a long time since Lori left."

Kathleen knew it was hard for him to say the words, admitting it was real. Everyone had seen it coming but Ryan.

Oblivious to the end.

More than once, Kathleen had tried to make Henry "talk some sense into the two of them," but Henry insisted it was between Ryan and Lori. He had been correct, as always.

Ryan took a few steps away from Kathleen across the hardwood floor. Straightening his shoulders, he shivered slightly and ran a hand through his hair.

"We'll just have to look out for each other." Ryan tried to smile, but Kathleen could see he was struggling. Ryan cleared his throat. "How about that coffee I promised you?"

A knock on the door startled both of them. Evan's head was visible through the screen door. He was squinting and trying to see through the mesh.

"Grandma?"

"C'mon in!" Ryan called out, pasting a cheerful smile on his face.

"Where's mom? Can I go swimming? It stopped raining." Evan's voice was a mixture of urgency and confusion.

Kathleen stood and waved a hand at Ryan. "I'll get the door and help myself to the coffee. You go change. Get some dry clothes on."

"It's a deal. Be back in a few minutes."

Kathleen opened the door and let Evan in. "Good morning!" He was in a rumpled t-shirt and sweatpants, his hair standing on end from being pressed against a pillow. She hugged her grandson to her chest, rocking him back and forth.

Not a moment later, Ryan reappeared, changed into clean, dry clothes.

"Evan!" Ryan exclaimed. "You've grown three feet since the last time I saw you!"

Evan blushed with pleasure and stood a little taller. "Wait a minute," he said, and looked at Ryan thoughtfully. "That was yesterday!"

Kathleen let out a giggle. "You're a smart boy."

With a chuckle, Ryan rubbed Evan's head and laughed. As he sat down at the table next to Kathleen, Grace's son looked around suspiciously at the wet towels and clothing draped over the furniture. "Wait. Did you go swimming without me?" Evan asked accusingly.

"Not exactly," Kathleen answered. "Grandma had a little accident with the sailboat, but everything's okay. Your mom and Ryan helped me."

"So, where *is* my mom?"

"I think she took a walk. She'll be back soon."

Ryan changed the subject quickly. "Evan, help yourself to any of the books and magazines there. Grace will be back in a few minutes, I'm sure. He winked at Kathleen over Evan's head. She nodded back, detecting the sincerity in his voice. It was a rare quality in a person these days, to worry about a child's feelings.

A crack of thunder echoed in the distance.

Her neighbor smiled, stood up, and promised to be right back. Kathleen nodded, focusing her gaze on Evan, as he disappeared into his bedroom.

Meanwhile, her thoughts raced, skipping from Grace to Evan, then bouncing back and landing on Ryan. She rubbed at her temples, thinking about the strange morning, but mostly about the conversation she and Ryan had just shared.

Her neighbor, always open, friendly, and jovial, had been absolutely relieved that their talk had been interrupted.

Chapter 19

A FTER ABOUT A mile, Grace had walked off most of her
frustration. Going to the house and cleaning up had
been her first thought, but she had changed her mind at the
doorway. The road behind the house was narrow and quiet
and offered the perfect place for biking and walking. A few
cars passed by, slowing to a crawl as they went by her on the
narrow road.

Behind rows of trees, Grace could see portions of the
lake. It stretched nearly a mile across to the green, tree-lined
hills on the other side. She inhaled deeply and listened to the
sound of crickets and frogs croaking. Homes, large and small,
looked out on the water, their docks stretching out into the
water.

It had been warm when she started walking, but the air
felt sticky and heavy now. She thought about walking to the
university campus, but it was much too far.

Grace stopped and stretched her calves, leaning against a
wooden fence post. The muscles in her legs were protesting and
her hair was sticking to the back of her neck. Her clothes were

a bit drier and her tennis shoes had finally stopped squeaking and leaking water. They were probably ruined.

She kicked a stone and watched it skip down the black-top. It must be getting late. Out of habit, Grace glanced down at her wrist. Her watch was missing. She hadn't had time to put it on this morning.

She wondered if Evan was up. Grace turned around toward her stepmother's house and quickened her pace.

She'd just have to control her temper a little better and be more patient. Her stepmother was just under a lot of stress. Acting strangely was to be expected, wasn't it? It was enough that she had lost her father and Kathleen had lost her husband. They were both on edge.

With everything that had happened, she didn't want to argue, especially in front of a stranger. An almost-stranger whom she had just insulted, she reminded herself. *It's not like we're staying that long*, Grace rationalized. She would simply have to avoid him.

Grace started to jog slowly, then picked up her pace. Around the corner, the house came into view. Something wasn't quite right. The side door was open slightly and creaking back and forth in the wind. Grace frowned. Surely Kathleen hadn't left it like that. Her feet pounded the steps. It was certainly loud enough to wake Evan up.

"Evan? Kathleen?"

The clock ticked loudly. No answer. Grace stood expectantly in the doorway, waiting for Evan to stroll out of the bedroom. She glanced around the living room nervously. Hands on her hips, she decided everything was in exactly the same place she had left it. That was hard to believe, especially if Evan was around. He could tear up a room in thirty seconds flat.

Grace strode over to the window and looked down at the dock. It was empty.

"Evan? Come out right now. This isn't funny!"

Grace looked behind doors and under the kitchen table.

Evan was obviously playing with her or he was missing.

Grace's breath caught in her throat. She felt dizzy and held the table with her hand. Television news reports with photos of kidnapped children flashed before her eyes.

Grace ran out the door again, this time, yelling Evan's name as loud as she could. It started to rain in earnest, first a light shower, then faster. Grace felt herself getting drenched all over again as she strained her voice to yell louder.

Suddenly, she spied her stepmother's life vest and towel outside the neighbor's door. Almost sliding across the still-damp grass, Grace ran to the porch, up the stairs, chest heaving from screaming Evan's name. Heart pounding, she didn't think to knock. Flinging open the door, Grace panted for breath.

Kathleen sat at the table with Ryan, calmly talking and sipping coffee. Both had looks of surprise when Grace burst in, unannounced.

"Evan… he's not in the house."

Ryan raised his eyebrows in amusement. Grace ignored him, waving her hands around wildly. "I've looked everywhere!"

"Grace, calm down." Kathleen set her coffee cup down hard on the table. Brown liquid sloshed out one side.

"I'm serious. He isn't…"

Kathleen cut her off. "Evan's right here." She moved to one side, cocking her head and taking in Grace's disheveled appearance.

Grace leaned in to look around her stepmother's legs.

Evan sat cross-legged on the floor behind the table, a book in his lap, smiling up at her.

Chapter 20

WITH A SMALL cry of relief, Grace dropped to her knees and wrapped her arms around Evan, pulling him close.

"Mom," Evan said, his voice muffled by the squeeze, "I couldn't find you or Grandma, so I came over here."

Grace untangled her arms from her son and sat back on her heels. She ran her hand along Evan's cheek. "Oh, sweetie. I am so sorry," she said, glancing over at Kathleen with an apologetic look. "Mommy went for a walk."

Kathleen registered her stepdaughter's guilt and brushed off the incident with a wave of her hand and a smile. No one needed any more drama today. "Evan, this was the right thing to do. Just come over here to Ryan's."

"Okay," Evan nodded, going back to flipping the pages of his book, unaffected by the semi-drama going on around him.

"Let's get you back to the house, little man," Grace said, ducking her head to meet Evan's eyes.

"But," Evan protested. "I'm not even done with the book."

He held it up to show he was only half-way through the pages.

Kathleen inched forward in her chair and craned her neck at Ryan. "I'm sure Dr. Gordon won't mind if you borrow it for the afternoon."

Ryan, who had been sitting back, stood up and helped Evan to his feet. "Of course, buddy. Keep it as long as you want."

Kathleen smiled at his willingness to befriend Evan. His kindness and generosity warmed her heart. Ryan was the sort of son-in-law any woman would want. And the kind of man young ladies like Grace should be noticing.

Her stepdaughter, however, was busy whispering into Evan's ear, no doubt trying to get the child to leave the picture book behind.

"Ryan," Kathleen clapped her hands together, signaling the end of the discussion, "I have the perfect solution. Why don't you come over for dinner tonight? Evan can borrow your book until then."

"Awesome!" Evan yelled, pumping his fist in the air.

Grace stood up straight and raised an eyebrow, clearly not entirely comfortable with sharing a meal with Dr. Gordon.

But it was done. Kathleen looked expectantly at her neighbor, waiting for his reply.

Ryan hesitated, scuffing one loafer on the wood floor, then accepted with a wide grin. "That sounds great. I'd love it. It sure gets old cooking macaroni and cheese from a box." He chuckled at his own joke.

Grace turned to look at him curiously. "Aren't you going to bring your wife?" She gestured a finger to a picture on the coffee table. Ryan and a woman were hugging happily on top of a ski slope, snowflakes drifting across their smiling faces. Grace frowned at the picture, then at Ryan.

Kathleen drew in a sharp breath. She hadn't mentioned

Lori. Anyone would assume he was still married, with all of the photos still up around Ryan's house. But who was she to tell someone how long to grieve?

"I would," Ryan said, his smile intact, meeting Grace's gaze straight on. "But we're not married anymore."

Kathleen could see that his response startled Grace.

It took her stepdaughter more than a moment to regain her composure. "I-I'm sorry," Grace said in a loud whisper. Her cheeks immediately flushed pink.

"Maybe I should have explained." Kathleen shrugged and broke the silence, trying to smooth things over. "I didn't think..."

"Don't worry about it." Ryan's cell phone started humming. "Excuse me," he said, grabbing the black case. He punched in some numbers and waited for the call to connect. "Sorry," he apologized. "Work."

Kathleen herded Grace and Evan out the door. "See you tonight. Let's say six o'clock?"

A thumbs up from Ryan was more than enough confirmation. He was talking animatedly about a patient with a broken leg when the screen door closed behind them.

Evan tugged at her sleeve. "Grandma, I'm hungry."

"Well, I'll take care of making breakfast. French toast, waffles, eggs? Whatever you like." Kathleen rubbed his head and winked.

Evan whooped and ran toward the cottage with Grace close behind.

As she followed along the path connecting the two houses, Kathleen began to plan the rest of the day.

She had twelve hours.

Half of a day.

It would take Kathleen at least that long to talk some sense into Grace.

Chapter 21

AFTER A BREAKFAST of fluffy, golden waffles topped with whipped cream, maple syrup, and maraschino cherries, Evan announced he was ready to swim.

Grace peeked outside. The storm clouds had cleared, leaving behind a bright blue, cloudless sky. Rays of sunlight sparkled on the still-damp grass. On the lake, a small fishing boat trolled slowly along the shoreline.

"Go ahead and get changed, sweetie," Grace said with a smile. "I'll be ready in just a minute. I need to help Grandma clean up the dishes."

Evan jumped up and down in delight. Grace couldn't help but giggle as her son ran to the bedroom, almost knocking over his chair in excitement.

"Now that's a happy boy," Kathleen said, smiling broadly as she carried her plate and silverware to the sink.

Grace stood up and stacked the remaining plates, feeling a pang of guilt that she hadn't included Kathleen. She cleared her throat and walked over to the counter where her stepmother was washing the breakfast dishes.

"Are you going to come down with me and watch Evan swim?" Grace asked. "He'd love it if you did."

Kathleen looked up from the sink and smiled. "Thank you, but I think I've had enough swimming for one day." She touched the back of her head for emphasis and smiled. "Besides, I think I might need a release from my doctor to go near the lake or the Sailfish after getting this lovely gash on my head."

Grace felt the breath catch in her throat and a rush of emotion washed over her. For the first time in what seemed like forever, she felt no anger or resentment toward her father's second wife. Aside from Evan, Kathleen was the only family she had in the world. Maybe, Grace thought, it was time to let go of all the hurt and pent-up frustration.

If for no one else, for her father. He loved Kathleen, and she could have died this morning. After being struck by the sailboat boom, she was lucky to be walking around the cottage and making breakfast for Evan. It was a miracle they were having this conversation.

Surprising herself, Grace reached over and patted her stepmother's hand. "I'm glad that you're okay. We all are. Thank goodness Ryan was home."

For a moment, Kathleen said nothing and Grace withdrew her hand. "I'll go check on Evan," she said, taking a step away from the counter. "We'll be down by the dock if you need anything," she added, thinking that perhaps Kathleen wanted to be left alone. Maybe she needed to rest.

But Kathleen turned, her eyes glittery with tears. "Thank you, Grace. It means so much to me. I know that things haven't been easy for you—since your mother died. I loved her, you know. She was my best friend."

Unable to speak or reply, Grace looked away, unsure she wanted to listen to much more. Her legs felt weak and her stomach churned with anxiety.

The mention of her mother brought back a multitude of

emotions. It was because Kathleen stepped into her father's life so quickly—seemingly without thought or remorse—that Grace had never accept her as a part of the family.

Though she didn't know for sure, Grace suspected Kathleen had everything to do with Henry's sudden move to Upstate New York. It was a way to have her father's undivided attention, to erase his former's wife's memory, and start fresh.

"Please know that I'd never, ever try to take your mother's place," Kathleen continued. "But I am here for you. If you want to talk about anything, I'll listen. If you want to ask me questions, I'll answer all of them. And I'll help with Evan in any way I can," she continued. "You've been working full-time, raising Evan by yourself. And now we've lost Henry."

Grace swallowed the lump in her throat, wanting to run and hide like a child. She forced herself to stay and listen, hoping she was almost done talking. Grace was an adult, and this was Kathleen's house. What was more, this talk—this confession or apology—whatever it was, did take courage on her stepmother's part.

The least she could do was hear her out. But she didn't have to believe her.

"I know that it's not the best of circumstances, but I'm so glad that you're here. Your father would be, too. He loved you so much." With a small smile, Kathleen wiped at her eyes.

"I loved him, too," Grace whispered. She was afraid of bursting into tears if her stepmother said another word. "Evan's waiting," she added, gesturing toward the lake. "I need to get him down to the dock."

"Of course," Kathleen replied with a small smile.

WHAT TOOK YOU so long?" Evan asked, looking up at Grace when she knocked on his bedroom door.

"Oh, you know, adult stuff. I was talking to Grandma Kathleen," Grace replied. "But I'm done now, so let's go."

Not waiting another second, Evan ran full speed out of the room, burst through the door of the cottage, and headed for the lake.

"Wait for me," Grace cried after him, breaking into a jog. She hadn't even changed into her bathing suit.

Evan made it to the end of the dock in less than thirty seconds, then plunged in feet first, never breaking his stride.

After a huge splash, he came up for air, a huge grin on his face. "Yahoo!" He yelled. "Come in, Mom, the water's great!" Even demonstrated by laying on his back and kicking, splashing Grace's toes and legs.

"Oh, sweetie, I can't. I never changed clothes. I don't have my bathing suit on," she laughed. "You were too fast for me."

Evan pretended to pout, but soon went back to swimming. He dove to the bottom, picking up stones and making them skip, then practiced cannon balls and flips off of the neighbor's wooden float, making Grace call out a grade of one through ten.

The air warmed considerably as the sun rose in the sky. Grace wished for the hundredth time that she'd put on her swim suit. She could ask Kathleen to come down and watch Evan while she changed, but Grace didn't want to chance continuing the morning's conversation with her stepmother.

After another half-hour of sitting in the sunshine and watching Evan swim, a bead of sweat trickled down Grace's neck. She was roasting in her long-sleeved shirt and shorts—and it was becoming more unbearable by the minute.

When she finally couldn't stand it any more, Grace stood up, brushed herself off, and dove in. When she broke the surface, Evan clapped and yelled.

"It's about time, Mom."

Grace splashed back at her son playfully. They swam and dove, enjoying the cool water against their skin. Her t-shirt and shorts hung heavy on her body. If the neighbors had been watching, they probably thought she was crazy.

But Evan was happy—and in this moment—Grace was, too. She had nothing to worry about but enjoying the time with her son.

Chapter 22

RYAN CLOSED THE door behind him, set down his brief-case, and pulled off his tie. After shrugging off his sport coat, he sank into the nearest chair by the window and put his feet up.

He was through at the office, had put in a full, produc-tive day, and was home at a decent hour. His staff had nearly fainted away when he walked out of the office at five minutes to five.

One of the nurses teased about Ryan having a hot date, but he quickly squelched the idea when he told her that his dinner companion—yes, a female—was Henry Mason's widow, Kathleen. Of course, he didn't mention that Evan and Grace would be there, too.

Ryan strode around restlessly, absentmindedly picking up mail and checking his iPhone. He looked at the clock, al-most positive that the hands were stuck on twelve and five.

Try as he could, he couldn't get Henry's daughter out of his mind.

She was striking, with her dark hair and clear, bright eyes.

Grace was smart, educated, and well-spoken. Ryan could understand now why Henry had talked nonstop about his lovely daughter. When she smiled, which hadn't been often since her father's funeral, her entire face lit up, and the sight made Ryan's heart beat a little faster.

It was the distance that she put between herself and others—especially Kathleen—that intrigued Ryan. Clearly, she was upset about her father dying, but there was more there, bubbling under the surface. Unless he was completely mistaken, under Grace's brave exterior, the confident, together, I-don't-need-anyone-else attitude, there existed a pervasive sadness and acute loneliness. An open wound or injury that had never been healed.

If only Henry were here. He would explain everything.

As he stared out the window at the lake, Ryan wondered about Evan's father and searched his brain to recollect any comments Henry or Kathleen had made about Grace's husband.

He had even checked her hand. She wasn't wearing a ring.

Ryan folded his arms. He wasn't used to feeling this way, especially after just meeting someone for the first time. After all, dozens of people—good friends, coworkers, even his patients—had tried to play matchmaker without any success.

He'd gone on a few half-hearted dates with the prettiest girls around town. Ryan always came up with an excuse not to see them again. Ryan just wasn't interested. He was married to his work. And he told himself that was enough.

This feeling about Grace would pass.

It was fleeting, an infatuation, like he was fifteen years old and Grace was the cute new girl in his science class.

Except that this was not high school.

And Grace was probably one of those women who hated men. It would figure that she was divorced or separated. Maybe her husband had cheated on her.

It happened so often these days. He heard story after story from his patients about marriages breaking up. An affair, sometimes multiple affairs, or a simple lack of caring about the other person caused the split.

Ryan shook his head.

He needed to get outside, to breathe some fresh air, and clear his head. He would see Grace in an hour, enjoy the meal Kathleen prepared, talk with Evan, and that would be it. He would politely and permanently forget about Grace Mason, her issues, and her big, beautiful smile.

Slipping on his swim trunks and grabbing a towel, Ryan headed for the dock.

The wooden planks creaked under his footsteps. The dock was wide enough for two people to fit easily on the end. He and Lori had sat there many nights, the first month they lived in the house, counting the stars, dangling their toes in the dark water. Until he got too busy with work.

Some days he half-expected to find her there, waiting for him.

At the end of the dock, Ryan shielded his eyes with his hands from the sun beating down. He took a deep breath. Without another thought, he threw down his towel and dove.

The water felt slippery and cool against his skin. Under the surface, strands of seaweed swayed and fish darted away from the sudden movement.

As he swam, kicking hard toward the surface of the lake, he pushed thoughts of Lori out of his mind.

The last thing he needed was another failed relationship.

He couldn't handle another broken heart.

Ryan stretched his arms out, scooping at the water. He felt sure the lake, being around it and in it, helped wash away whatever feelings were left, bit by bit.

Chapter 23

GRACE STOOD AT the kitchen window, washing blueberries for a pie her stepmother was baking for the impromptu dinner with Ryan. Where she was standing, she could see Ryan's house and dock perfectly.

She watched as he dove off the dock, into the water. He was athletic and graceful, with long, sinewy muscles like a triathlete.

Grace strained to see where he would surface. It seemed like forever before he came up for air. Finally, she saw his head and arms pop out almost 20 yards away.

She had been holding her breath and standing on her toes, watching Ryan. As she relaxed and went back to her work at the sink, concentrating on finding and plucking off the tiny stems, she didn't notice that Kathleen had crept up behind her.

"Ryan's a good swimmer, isn't he?" her stepmother asked.

Grace jumped and let out a shriek.

Kathleen smothered a giggle. "I'm sorry, I thought you heard me."

With a frown, Grace felt her face grow hot. She struggled to get her composure back. Kathleen, undoubtedly, had seen her gawking out the window at Ryan. "What are you doing sneaking up on me like that?"

With an amused smile, Kathleen continued to watch over her shoulder. "I didn't. I just came to see if you were finished with the berries. I need to get that pie in the oven."

Grace wiped her hands dry on the towel and folded it carefully by the sink. "Just finished up." She raised an eyebrow at her stepmother. "I wasn't watching him, by the way."

Kathleen nodded and took the washed and cleaned berries. "All right. If you say so." She began rolling out the dough on the counter.

Grace leaned back and looked at her thoughtfully. Her stepmother had the distinct look of being up to something.

"Kathleen, you aren't trying to set me up with this Ryan guy, are you?

Kathleen stopped rolling. "What makes you think that?" Her voice hid the slightest hint of teasing.

"I don't know," Grace said, pursing her lips. "How about inviting him over to dinner tonight? Or telling Evan to go over there anytime?"

"Well, for your information, young lady," Kathleen replied. "I have no intention of fixing you up. I was only trying to be nice. He rescued me and the sailboat this morning."

This, she admitted, made sense.

Grace shrugged her shoulders. "Okay. Well, good." She turned and looked back out the window. "Because if you were trying, I'm not interested. Evan and I live in Mississippi. We're going back to Mississippi in a few days."

"Of course," Kathleen murmured, intent on arranging the pie crust in the pan.

While her stepmother worked, Grace snuck another look out the window. Ryan had disappeared. His towel was gone, too.

"You're not his type, anyway. At least I don't think so," Kathleen said casually, pinching at the dough.

Grace's chin jerked up. She blinked, absorbing this detail.

Seeing her reaction, Kathleen smiled brightly and hurried to correct herself. "Oh, I don't mean it like that. He prefers blondes, I think. His wife was blonde. And you're not interested, right?"

"Right," Grace agreed as Kathleen sprinkled sugar over the blueberries.

Her stepmother reached over and turned on the oven. "We've got another thirty minutes until dinner. Why don't I get the grill going? You can make the salad and Evan can set the table."

With that, Kathleen whisked out the door, closing it gently behind her. Grace looked at the empty kitchen.

"Fine," she muttered to herself. Her stomach was churning. Why did hearing about Ryan and his wife bother her? It shouldn't. She was perfectly happy with it being just she and Evan. It had worked that way since he was a baby.

Evan's dad was gone. Now her father was gone. It seemed every man she depended on disappeared.

No, Grace didn't want anything to do with men. She didn't need anyone else to let her down.

Chapter 24

E VAN SET THE table, placing knives and spoons haphazardly around the plates, mismatched cups to the right of each setting. Grace smiled while he carefully folded the napkins in half, setting them to the side of each fork.

"I'm done, Mom," Evan announced with flourish.

"Thank you, sweetie," said Grace, tossing the large green salad. "Good job. Dinner won't be long now."

"Hello! Anyone home?" Ryan called through the screen door. He was dressed in freshly-pressed khakis and a navy polo shirt, his hair still damp from his swim in the lake.

"Hey Dr. Gordon." Evan scampered to let him in with Kathleen following close behind.

Ryan handed over two bottles of wine and kissed Kathleen on the cheek. "Dr. Frank's wine. I remembered Henry saying that these were some of your favorites."

"Riesling and chardonnay. Lovely choices, Ryan. Thank you," Kathleen said, glowing with pleasure.

Ryan waved at Grace and smiled, making a dimple appear on his right cheek. "I thought white wine would be best, since I spilled punch on you the other day."

"Don't worry about it," Grace felt the corners of her mouth tug up. "I'm pretty sure that I overreacted."

"I'll be on my best behavior, I promise," Ryan winked.

Grace couldn't help but giggle. He was charming and funny, no wonder Kathleen and her father liked him so much.

"Do the honors?" Ryan asked, presenting one of the bottles.

Grace expertly unwrapped the covering over the top of the bottle, rummaged through a drawer near her hip, and found a corkscrew. The cork popped, making a hollow noise. Evan laughed at the sound.

"New Year's Eve," Ryan joked.

Kathleen brought out three glasses and Grace poured. The wine was mellow and sweet, warming her core.

"Mmm." Grace nodded her approval.

Ryan seemed to relax. "Can I help?"

"We're almost done. Have a seat."

Grace sipped the wine, looking at Ryan while he talked to Evan. He was animated as he spoke, talking about the lake and fishing. Evan was nodding with the rhythm of their conversation, asking questions about sunfish and perch and what was best to use as bait.

Grace got up to refill glasses. Over bites of bread and corn, Ryan asked Grace about living in the South.

"Well, we're near the ocean, which is great. It's warm most of the year, even in December. We never have snow."

"Never!" Evan chimed in.

Kathleen laughed at his reaction. "Well maybe you'll have to come back to the lake in the winter sometime. I'm sure there'll be lots of snow here."

"Absolutely," Ryan added, looking straight at Grace. "So, Kathleen says that you're a teacher. Do you like it?"

Grace chewed slowly, not used to answering so many questions. She gave the simplest answer. "I do. I love the kids and being in the same school with Evan." She reached over and tousled her son's hair.

"What grade do you teach?"

"I have kindergarten this year and it's so much fun. The kids' innocence and openness makes it great. They're at the age when they're not caught up in being rich or poor. They don't care about appearances or who's wearing the most expensive tennis shoes. They're just there to learn and have fun."

"Grace, didn't you think about teaching at a college?" Kathleen asked. "Henry mentioned that you'd be really good at that, too."

Ryan waited for her answer. He took a sip of wine and smiled across the table.

Grace blushed. "Oh, I don't know. It was just a silly thing I'd talked about. You know, one of those things you think you want to do when you're little."

It was a weak excuse. The truth was harder. She'd given up on getting her master's degree after Evan was born.

Grace changed the subject. Any topic away from her life would be better. "What about medicine? Why be a doctor?"

"I ask myself that sometimes." Ryan wiped his mouth carefully with a napkin. "No, really, I think that it comes down to a few things."

Kathleen nodded, and Grace assumed she'd heard the story before.

"We grew up with nothing. Dirt poor. My dad was an alcoholic, in and out of rehab. My mother ran off when I was thirteen. We didn't have a lot to eat most of the time."

Grace tried to conceal her surprise. For a moment, she was sorry she'd asked. But Ryan didn't seem upset by it, and Evan ate vigorously, ignoring the adult conversation.

"Anyway, my dad didn't think too much of school. But I was good at it, a natural, the teachers said. Tests were easy for me. I was lucky. Because we didn't have anything, I was given grants for college. I won scholarships because of my grades.

Worked full-time to have money for books and to eat."

Ryan took another swallow of wine.

"The day I went off to college, my dad sat me down. He said some awful things, and I'll never forget them. He was drunk and mean. He said, "You'll be back. Maybe not tomorrow or the next day, but you'll come home. You'll never make anything of yourself."

Ryan cleared his throat self-consciously, as if he was unsure about continuing the story. "So, I went away and never looked back. Failure was not an option. We never talked again. I went on to med school and he died the day before I graduated."

The room became completely quiet. Kathleen had stopped eating. Grace sat back in her chair and blinked at Ryan. He was so open and honest. She couldn't help but admire his drive and tenacity.

"Sorry." Ryan moved his plate away toward the center of the table. "I didn't mean to put a damper on dinner."

"I had no idea." Kathleen cocked her head and looked at Ryan like she was seeing him for the first time.

"It's not a secret, but this isn't something most people know." Ryan looked at Grace. "Too much information?"

Kathleen interrupted before Grace could form an answer.

"Ryan, it's wonderful what you've done. You've helped so many people."

Grace felt a pang of worry. *Please don't say anything about my father.*

Kathleen continued talking anyway. "I know that you would have helped Henry—if you could have."

Ryan sat back in his chair. He frowned and then smiled crookedly, looking down at his plate. "Of course."

Chapter 25

KATHLEEN DUG INTO the earth with a small shovel, chasing away earthworms and an occasional slug. The morning sun was warm on her shoulders. Her broad-brimmed hat shielded her face, though she didn't care much about protecting it from wrinkles now. Time and gravity had done their job, she thought ruefully.

She had risen with the sun, bound and determined she'd attack the stray weeds choking her marigolds, snapdragons, and salvia. Still, it was later than she wanted when her eyes finally opened. She, Grace, and Ryan had stayed up later than she'd anticipated.

Yes, it had been a good night, Kathleen thought. Henry would have enjoyed it more than anyone. He would have tried to outdo Ryan with funny stories, making everyone laugh until their sides hurt. Henry was a favorite at dinner parties and church suppers. They had done so many outings with other couples. Kathleen wondered if she would be included, now that he was gone. Surely, Henry's absence might make her friends feel strange.

How empty she felt walking into the kitchen. It was her first thought this morning, standing in the center of the room, by herself, surrounded by quiet. Kathleen felt the walls close in on her. The feeling of claustrophobia was overwhelming. She could breathe better outside.

Henry would have been out with her this morning, too. Maybe not helping, as gardening wasn't his favorite thing, but he would have been nearby, reading the newspaper under a shade tree, talking about this or that.

In another few days, Kathleen would be by herself. Grace and Evan would leave and go back to their lives in Mississippi.

Despite the pleasant conversation last night, she was sure her stepdaughter was already counting the days until she could leave. And Kathleen would be alone.

Alone. The word sounded scary to her, and she wasn't one to be frightened. There were certainly enough people around, friends and neighbors, if she needed them. Kathleen dug harder into the earth, her hands snatching at the weeds and tossing them to the side of the garden bed. She sat back on her heels and surveyed the plot of land. Kathleen hadn't been happy with the way things were growing. Maybe she needed a change.

The neat rows of red and yellow suddenly looked all wrong to her. Everything was even and straight, even the flowers had grown to virtually the same height. The mulch was kept from sliding out into the walkway with smooth black edging.

She reached around for her water bottle. It must still be in the house, she thought. Her lips were dry and she longed for a swallow of water, but decided it could wait just a few minutes more.

Starting in one corner, Kathleen tugged at the marigolds. The ground was soft and pliable; the plants came up easily, roots and all. The snapdragons looked a little wilted, too. Kathleen dug around them. She worked steadily, plant by plant, until she had cleared the entire garden and all that was left was brown dirt, broken up.

She sat back on her heels, a little shakily. She was hot, maybe too hot. What time was it anyway? A bead of sweat trickled down her neck. Her tongue was dry and thick. She looked at her watch. It seemed to float off her wrist.

Kathleen heard voices inside the house. Grace and Evan were up and about. She tried to call out. She couldn't form the words with her mouth. Kathleen stumbled and tried to catch herself falling.

The earth was soft and warm when her cheek hit the ground.

Chapter 26

GRACE WAS BREATHING so hard by the time she reached Ryan's office, a person would have thought she'd run the whole way. It was enough that she'd practically carried Kathleen all the way up the steps and into her car, calling for Evan to bring the keys right away.

About the time she was ready to run back to the house, Evan bounded up the driveway, waving the keys in the air. "Why are you yelling?" His face was flushed too.

"Grandma's not feeling so well."

"I'm perfectly fine," Kathleen retorted. She opened her eyes and blinked several times after Grace picked her off the ground.

"No, you're not," Grace argued. "We're going now!"

That was good enough for Evan, who climbed into the back seat and slammed the door in time for Grace to take off, tires squealing, in the direction of town.

The Mercedes her stepmother owned was old, vintage somewhere around 1980, faded silver, with paint peeling off the sides in small strips. The engine clanked loudly as they came to a stop sign, then hesitated and jerked when Grace pressed the accelerator.

"Should have taken the rental," Grace said under her breath, but loud enough for Kathleen to hear. "Have you considered trading in this car for something a little more modern? It's going to quit before we get there."

Grace, finally able to speed up, kept pushing the car to go faster. A twenty-five mph speed limit sign flashed by the window.

"Slow down, you're going to get a ticket." Kathleen leaned forward, checking the odometer. She made a clucking noise with her tongue and sat back again, gripping the handle of the door as Grace made a sharp turn.

"If I get a ticket, I'll pay it."

The color was returning to Kathleen's face, Grace noticed, trying to keep at one eye on the road.

Wide-eyed, Evan was glued to the window. "Do you see any police cars?" he asked. "I'll bet they'll start their sirens if they see Mom blow by them this fast."

"Evan, really, it'll be okay," Grace said, turning to look at her son in the backseat. "I'm not going to get a ticket." She was so busy talking that she almost missed the sign pointing into the driveway of Ryan's office.

"This is so unnecessary." Kathleen heaved a sigh and looked up at the ceiling of the car and started to open her door.

"Kathleen, please," Grace protested. "I'm coming around to help you."

"I feel fine. Leave me alone." Her stepmother's tone sharpened as she climbed out the car herself. She slammed the door twice to get it to stay closed.

Evan ran ahead and grabbed Kathleen's hand while Grace hurried behind them, looking up at the office. It was small and neat, tucked behind a modest line of trees and flowering plants.

Inside, the office was bright and sunny, with skylights cut in the ceiling to catch the sun's rays. A pretty receptionist sat behind the front desk and greeted them politely when they walked in the door.

"Can I help you?"

Kathleen stepped forward talking in an octave higher than her normal voice, "Actually, no. We're just here to say hello to Dr. Gordon."

"No. We're here to *see* Dr. Gordon," Grace interrupted. "For medical reasons. It's an emergency. My stepmother isn't feeling well."

Kathleen shot her a glare and sunk into a chair in the corner of the room.

A familiar voice floated through the door. It was Ryan. "Can you call these folks back? I need to talk to them about some labs." He raised his eyes from the paperwork and noticed Grace. "Oh, hey. I didn't realize you were here."

Grace drew in her breath. He was looking straight at her, expectantly. His eyes were more blue today. She hadn't really noticed the scar on his chin before.

"Grace…what's wrong?" Ryan asked.

"It's about Kathleen. I found her outside—after she tore out the entire flower garden near the back door. It's a mess." Grace realized she was rambling. "Anyway, I think she passed out from the heat."

Ryan listened patiently and shot a concerned look at Kathleen. "C'mon back. Follow me." He waved an arm in the direction of the hallway and started walking quickly. "Can you pull Kathleen Mason's chart, please?" He said quietly to one of the nurses as he passed her. "Room three. Just give me a second." Ryan held open the door and shooed them inside.

Grace walked over to Kathleen and offered an arm. After hesitating, her stepmother grasped hold and pulled herself up. She wasn't steady, Grace noted. It was good that they were here.

The door clicked shut behind them. Evan knelt down and started playing with small trucks he found in the corner basket of toys.

Before they could sit and get settled, Ryan opened the door. "Ready?"

Kathleen started to protest immediately. "This really isn't necessary. Please, it's nothing."

Ryan held up a hand. "If this is a waste of time, then I'll cook dinner for you. How about that?"

Kathleen sat up on the table obediently and let Ryan look in her eyes and throat. He took her temperature and listened to her heart. Swinging the stethoscope around his neck, he stepped back and looked at Grace.

"You say you found her outside. She had fainted?"

Grace nodded. "One minute she was working in the garden, the next, she was laying in it. I was terrified, with everything that's happened." Her voice trailed off and she looked over at Evan, who was still playing, making beeping car noises every now and then.

Ryan made a note in the chart.

"I was just taking a nap." Kathleen said, not convincingly.

"She was not." Grace looked at Ryan pleadingly. "Is she going to be okay?"

"She's dehydrated. Probably could have been heatstroke if you wouldn't have found her when you did. She's lucky to have you and Evan around."

Grace felt a pang of guilt. They were only going to be in town for another week. Pressing her lips together, she watched as Ryan turned to type notes into a small laptop computer sitting on the counter.

Evan glanced up. "Cool. What's that?"

"It's where I keep my doctor notes."

"But, you're not wearing a white coat." Evan said curiously. "I thought you had to."

Ryan shook his head and laughed. "Nah. Just gets in the way."

Grace watched them carefully. Evan really seemed to like him. And not wearing the white coat was a nice touch. He wasn't pretentious. A welcome relief in a man.

Ryan frowned and scribbled some notes on a piece of paper and handed it to Grace. "Make sure she drinks enough water and stays out of the sun. Call me anytime you have a concern. My number's at the bottom."

Grace glanced down at the paper, folded it up and nodded. "Thanks."

Ryan bent down and shook Evan's hand. He kissed Kathleen on the cheek. "Be more careful. Drink water and get some rest."

Grace wondered if her stepmother would listen. She also wondered why Ryan Gordon watched her walk all the way down the hall and out the door of his office.

I'm not his type, she reminded herself. *And I'm leaving.*

Chapter 27

KATHLEEN STARED AT the array of colors set before her like a rainbow. She fingered the edges of the samples, debating on one, then another. She pulled out a celery green, deep red, sunny yellow, and a robin's egg blue. They were all pretty, she thought.

But none were quite right.

"Can I help you?" A friendly, ruddy-faced salesman stepped up next to her, looking over her shoulder. "Trying to find a color?"

"Yes, thanks," she replied. "I'm not quite done."

The young man was trying to be helpful. "Sure thing. Just let me know if you need anything." He walked away, whistling like Henry would when he had a song stuck in his head.

She concentrated on the palette of hues, then shut her eyes. What would Henry say about changing things? Would he care? Why was she so worried? It was her house now. Hers alone. Grace was leaving, she'd be a thousand miles away and back in Mississippi by the time anyone got around to painting.

Kathleen focused on the rose and pink. She was drawn to their warmth. The colors looked happy and alive, like flushed cheeks on a child.

A voice interrupted her thoughts.

"Can you believe it? The Millers cancelled. Just like that. Changed their mind. Said they weren't ready." A man dressed in white from head to toe was talking to the salesman. He was carrying several cans of paint and nearly dropped them on the floor when he reached the counter.

Kathleen turned her head to get a better look.

"It's a whole week's worth of work. I have other jobs scheduled tight through July and August, but nothing I can move around." The man twisted his cap in his hands, looking at the young salesman.

"Sorry, man. It's a tough break. Can't say that we've had anyone in asking for help." The salesman paused awkwardly. "I'll let you know."

The man nodded. "Thanks. I appreciate it. Anything I can do with all of this paint? It's custom-mixed and I think I'm stuck with it. Not much call for this color."

The salesman shook his head. "You can leave it here for now. Someone might want it. But we'll have to settle up at the end of the month."

Kathleen took a step toward the two men. "You're a painter?" Of course he was, she thought, as soon as the words were out of her mouth.

"Yes, ma'am."

"I heard you say you had a job cancelled this week?"

"That's right. Do you know the Millers?"

Kathleen laughed. "No. It's just that I was thinking...I need someone to paint my house. As soon as possible," she said suddenly, wondering where her sense of urgency had come from.

"Tell me about the house," the man said.

Kathleen described it in detail, the windows and doors,

square feet. The house had been painted only two years before. It was in good shape, with no peeling or chipped parts. The man listened intently, nodding his head until she finished talking and caught her breath.

"What do you think?" she asked him, feeling slightly off kilter.

"I'll do it," the man said. "We can start today. This afternoon. I have a crew of men who can finish it by Friday."

Kathleen felt a rush of excitement. "Great."

"Do you have a color in mind?"

Kathleen hesitated. "I've looked at these, but they're not quite right." She pointed down to the rectangles of color on the counter by her hip. "I want something fun. Something splashy. Uplifting." She smiled to herself. It was unlike her and she knew it. It felt good.

"How about something similar to this one?" The painter leaned past her and picked out a swatch of paint. "I have tons of it and I'll give it to you half-price."

His voice was hopeful, but not pushy. She looked down at the color in his hand. Kathleen's eyes widened.

"Sounds perfect."

Chapter 28

FOR THE THIRD time that day, Grace picked up the book and flipped through the page. It was a thriller by one of her favorite authors, guaranteed to keep her turning the pages. She had brought several novels like it for reading on the plane to Mississippi.

For some reason, she couldn't focus on a single sentence. The words seemed to dance in front of her eyes, swirling and jumping until she had to look away. Her thoughts kept drifting back to her stepmother and Ryan.

From the dock, Dr. Gordon's house was in perfect view. That afternoon, she had plenty of time to study it. The yard was well-kept and mowed, though the landscaping was not as lush and colorful as Kathleen's.

The porch overlooking the lake was wide and open, just the right size for entertaining and sipping wine. Ryan, however, was at work, and wouldn't be home for hours. It was a shame, she thought, being the perfect day for a late-afternoon picnic.

Grace bent her head and looked down at the open pages.

Just as she finished reading the first line, she heard the sound of tires on the gravel behind the house.

Her initial reaction was to jump up and see if it was Ryan. No, it was probably her stepmother, back from town. She wondered what had been so important that Kathleen spent the entire day away.

The sliding glass door moved behind her. Evan's voice called out. "Mom. Mom!" he said louder.

"Right here." Grace shifted to the edge of her chair and looked over her shoulder.

"There's some guys in a big white van."

Grace wrinkled her forehead.

"Are they in our driveway?" She caught herself. "Grandma's driveway?"

"Uh-huh." Evan nodded his head vigorously.

"What do they look like?" Grace got up from the chair. She put her book down, closing it on the chapter she was reading. There wasn't any sense trying.

"They've got white on and they're carrying cans of stuff."

Grace stifled a laugh at the mental picture she was getting. "Okay, okay. Let's not panic. I'm sure they're at the wrong house. Let's go talk to them."

Grace walked through the open door into the house and through to the screen door leading out to the driveway.

"Hi there!" She said to the group of men, who seemed to be setting up to work. "May I help you?"

The man, who seemed to be in charge, looked at another man, and then back at Grace. "We're here to paint."

"Um. What?" Grace said. "You must have the wrong place."

"Miss Kathleen talked to me today in the paint store. She gave me a check as a down payment. She picked out the color. And it's not tan. Or brown." His voice was calm and he held out the check. It was made out to Moore Painting for one thousand dollars.

Grace started to stutter. "But…" She threw up her hands. "Okay, okay. Never mind."

"Didn't mean to surprise you. It was kind of a last minute thing for us, too." His voice was apologetic.

"No problem." Grace touched Evan on the shoulder. "C'mon, let's go inside. We'll work this out with Grandma when she gets home."

"I want to watch." Evan said stubbornly.

Grace stopped and patted her son on the shoulder. "I guess that's okay. Just stay out of the way, okay? I'll be inside if you need me."

Evan sat down on the grass happily. The workers started talking amongst themselves and there was the sound of cans opening and ladders being stretched tall. Grace tried to ignore it. She walked over to the refrigerator and grabbed a Diet Coke, popping open the lid. The soda went down her throat soothingly. She swallowed, took a breath and tilted back the can again.

"Wow!"

Grace heard Evan exclaim from outside. She almost choked on the soda. What could be wrong now?

Curiosity got the best of her. She walked back outside. The men stopped talking. Evan was laughing and pointing at the house. Grace turned to look.

There, along the strips of khaki, was the brightest pink she'd ever seen in her life.

Chapter 29

GRACE WATCHED AS Ryan pulled in his driveway minutes before Kathleen was due to arrive. It would be impossible for their neighbor to miss the new paint color, and she hoped he'd walk over for a closer look.

After hearing his truck door close firmly, Grace heard Ryan let out a long, low whistle. The sound sent a delicious chill along her bare arms, and she hurried to meet him at the front door.

"Evan," she called out to her son. "Dr. Gordon's coming over to look at the paint job. Do you want to say hello?"

Her son's pounding footsteps were the answer.

"Wow!" It was all Ryan could manage as he walked over to Kathleen's yard. His eyes were wide with surprise, but his mouth held a hint of amusement. He began to walk back and forth, surveying the paint job, and shook his head a few times—either from amazement or disbelief.

Grace stepped out of the house. "Hey there. 'Wow' is about all that Evan's been saying."

"I've never seen anything like it!" Ryan grinned and locked eyes with Grace, holding her gaze. "We won't be able to miss that one, even from the middle of the lake."

The chug of Kathleen's Mercedes interrupted the conversation. The diesel engine was distinct. There was no way her stepmother could surprise anyone while driving that vehicle.

Grace stepped closer to Ryan as they waited for Kathleen. Today, he was wearing a light blue polo shirt which exactly matched his eyes. His skin, from being in the sun so much, had turned golden brown.

Carrying bags on both arms, Kathleen rushed over. "Well, what do you think?" Her voice was excited. Grace could tell she was pleased.

"Grandma Kathleen, your house is pink!" Evan shouted.

"It's very, very pink." Grace echoed, turning around slowly, her eyes leaving the house. She wracked her brain for something positive to say to Kathleen. Her stepmother would want to hear something good. "The white trim is pretty."

When she turned from the house, her eyes widened even more at the sight of the changes in Kathleen. She'd had highlights put in, a subtle effect, and her hair was cut into a smart, stylish bob. Her stepmother was dressed in a linen pantsuit the color of persimmons, with adorable matching sandals gracing her feet.

"Your hair looks wonderful," Ryan said, making Kathleen flutter her eyelashes.

"And the new clothes. They're very cute," Grace added, still in partial shock from the transformation. "When did you...? You decided to do all of this today?"

"Why not?" Kathleen laughed and raised her arms in a playful shrug, making all of the shopping bags crinkle and rattle.

"Here, let me take those," Ryan said, gesturing toward his neighbor's packages. "Evan, want to give your grandma a hand?"

"Thank you," Kathleen nodded, allowing him to take all of her new treasures. Evan was given one small bag to carry to the cottage while Ryan took all of the rest. Grace couldn't help but notice that the muscles in his arms flexed nicely under the weight of Kathleen's purchases.

While her stepmother made her way to the cottage, Evan skipped beside her, leaving Ryan and Grace alone, both still looking at the bright pink against the soft tan of the house.

"I'm a little worried." Grace said aloud.

"Worried?"

"Maybe concerned is a better word." Grace turned to face him, wrinkling her forehead. She shifted her weight from one foot to the other and tried to think of a good explanation for Kathleen's behavior, none of which had been terrible.

"Okay, so maybe she likes pink. A lot." Ryan raised his eyebrows and cocked his head toward the cottage.

"It's not even that. It's just a feeling," Grace struggled to explain. "And I don't think that my stepmother usually acts like this. Not according to my father. She doesn't sing at funerals or parties, she never takes the boat out by herself. Kathleen plans everything, keeps several appointment books, meets her friends from church for breakfast Wednesday mornings, and has her hair done every Thursday afternoon."

Ryan listened, never taking his eyes off Grace's face. When she finished talking, he extended his hand and touched her arm.

"We both have to remember that Kathleen's a grown woman. And Henry's not here anymore," he said softly.

"I know that," Grace answered stiffly. She knew, but she couldn't shake the feeling that Kathleen wasn't thinking clearly. She might do something else, something crazy. And what if she wasn't here to help?

As if reading her mind, Ryan put both hands on Grace's shoulders. "Listen, you don't have to worry. I know that you have to leave soon, but I'm not going anywhere. And I'll keep an eye on Kathleen." He let his arms drop back to his sides. "I promise."

Chapter 30

THE NEXT MORNING, Kathleen was gone again. Grace discovered it when she walked into the kitchen to make coffee. A note on the counter left few details, saying only that she would be back later in the day and to call her cell phone if they needed anything.

By the time Grace woke Evan and made toast, bacon and eggs, it was mid-morning.

"What do you think about going to the playground?" Grace suggested while Evan ate his breakfast. Red Jacket Park in Penn Yan was close and right on the water.

"Great," Evan said as he finished off the last forkful of eggs.

As he ran to get his shoes, Grace cleared the table and drank the last of her coffee. Her eyes fell again on Kathleen's note. She didn't mention anything pressing the night before.

It was possible that Kathleen's strange behavior was due, in part, to their visit. Had they overstayed their welcome? Was it overwhelming to have a child in the house? Perhaps Evan reminded her stepmother too much of Henry and it was becoming difficult to have him around.

They would go back to Mississippi early, Grace decided, and allow Kathleen to get back to a normal existence. She was probably feeling stressed out, and rightfully so. Her life had been turned upside down. Henry was gone. Kathleen was a widow. And here she was stuck with Grace and Evan twenty-four seven, forced to be cheerful and entertain.

Driving away from the cottage, Grace punched in the number for the airline. Evan dug out his Nintendo 3DS and was playing intently beside her.

After a brief recording, an operator answered. After reciting her confirmation number and itinerary, Grace asked about catching an earlier flight.

"Still Rochester to Biloxi, Mississippi?"

"Yes, and anytime of day is fine."

"Please hold while I check on those flights."

Jazz music filled her ear as Grace drove toward Penn Yan. It was a gorgeous outside and it looked like the entire community had taken the day off to enjoy the weather.

There were people out fishing, kids jumping into the water off of floating docks, and sunbathers galore. She hadn't even broken out her bikini once. Her legs were so white they'd probably scare the fish. Grace giggled a little to herself at the thought.

The music clicked off abruptly and the operator's smooth, peasant voice came back on the line.

"I'm so sorry, ma'am. All of the flights on those particular days are sold out. Is there another day that I could check for you?"

"No. Thank you so much." Disappointed, she hung up the phone.

Grace tapped on the wheel. She would fix the situation with her stepmother. She owed it to Henry. Going to a hotel was too obvious—Evan would complain to no end—and her father would come back from the dead and strangle her if she pulled that stunt.

A heart to heart discussion was out of the question. The last thing either one of them needed was a few hours in front of the campfire trying to work out all of their differences from the past. Some things didn't need to be messed with. Or talked about. Too much time had gone by, there was too much emotional distance between them, too many unanswered questions.

On this, Henry would disagree. It had always been his wish that she and Kathleen could be friends. She had lost count of the number of times he'd urged her to reconcile with her stepmother. Make love not war, he always said.

In turn, Grace would change the subject. Tell her father about school, the children in her class, or something new going on with Evan. And after a while, Henry gave up.

The solution had to be subtle.

Grace glanced back at Evan, who had closed and put away his Nintendo 3DS. Red Jacket Park was in view and she could tell he was excited. Grace counted at least a dozen other children running and jumping in the wide open space.

It struck Grace, then, that *space* might be exactly what Kathleen needed.

Grace could keep busy with Evan outside. They'd take a few more day trips, run errands and stay out of the cottage. She could water the flowers, check the mail, and go for walks with Evan. She'd even ask her son to be a little more quiet, especially at night. And there would be no more inviting Ryan Gordon over for dinner.

Kathleen didn't have to feel stressed out; she certainly shouldn't feel like she had to leave her own house.

Satisfied with her new plan, Grace parked under a shade tree and slid the keys into her purse.

"What are you going to do first?" she asked Evan. Her son was already unbuckled from his seatbelt, eyes on the silver slides and see-saw. Some families played in the water several hundred feet away. She watched them, smiling and laughing, splashing around, knee deep in the lake.

While Evan ran toward the jungle gym, Grace walked over to the giant swing set. She had a perfect vantage point from the center wooden seat. She sat down, grabbed hold of the heavy, linked chain, and pushed her feet against the dirt. Her tennis shoes made marks on the soil.

Shading her eyes and swaying gently, Grace watched Evan talk to some other boys his own age. After an animated discussion, he joined the group in a game of tag on the field next to the playground.

Grace backed up and swung a little higher. She looked up at the sky, enjoying the feel of the wind on her cheeks as she floated back and forth. She savored the funny feeling in her stomach when the wooden seat came closer to the ground. Her hair caught in her lips and tickled at her face.

"I didn't expect to see you here!"

A familiar voice made her almost fall off the swing. She skidded to a stop, kicking up clouds of dust in the process.

"Well, hello," Grace coughed and stood up, brushing off her shirt and shorts. Her cheeks began to burn.

It was Ryan Gordon, dressed in running clothes and a baseball hat, grinning down at her.

Chapter 31

RYAN HAD SEEN her, at a distance. Grace seemed dreamy, lost in thought, when he approached. Her dark hair shone in shades of chestnut and amber, the ends of it curling up. Her cheeks were flushed a healthy pink, like she'd been laughing at something wonderful, and her eyes were closed so tightly he could see her thick lashes on her cheeks. She was blissfully peaceful.

The grass, green and soft, hid the sound his running shoes would have made. When she looked up at him, startled, he realized he didn't have a reason in the world to interrupt her solace.

Ryan could see the surprise in her eyes and quickly searched his brain for an excuse to be standing just a few feet away, watching her on the swing.

"Sorry if I startled you. Next time, I'll make a little more noise."

Grace's eyes fluttered open and she stood up quickly, making the swing bang against her leg before it settled in place. "Oh, Ryan." He cheeks tinged a darker pink, the color of carnations in bloom. "Hi, how are you?"

"I'm great. Just out for a quick run. How's Kathleen?"

"I'm not sure," Grace furrowed her brow. "She left early this morning to run a few errands. She was gone before Evan and I woke up."

Ryan nodded.

Grace heaved a sigh. "I wanted her to rest today."

"You know, I've thought about what she's been doing. Change is hard on people. Maybe it's her way of dealing with your Dad being gone. Some people go a little crazy and paint their houses pink," he paused and winked.

"Right," Grace smirked and rolled her eyes. "It happens all of the time."

"All that I'm trying to say is that it's okay if she acts a little off. She's getting used to life without Henry, testing her boundaries. It's got to be weird."

"It is," Grace agreed, her voice barely above a whisper.

Ryan stepped closer and bent down to look into Grace's eyes. "I miss him too. Really. And I care."

"Thanks for saying that."

Grace sat back down on the swing, keeping her eyes trained on Evan.

Ryan shifted on his feet, trying to think of something else to say. He didn't want to leave, but Grace hadn't invited him to stay.

"Well, I've got to get back to my run," he said finally.

Grace looked up, shielding her eyes with one hand. "Shouldn't you be at work?"

"I'm off early today. One of those perks of being your own boss, I guess." Ryan grinned. "Besides, I wanted to get out on the lake for a while this evening—especially before the weather changes."

"Oh?" Grace blinked up at the sky.

"Yeah, someone said something about a big storm front moving through tomorrow," Ryan added. "I'm a closet weather geek, in addition to being a doctor."

Grace shook her head and muffled a giggle. "I'm not so sure you should make that public knowledge. It might ruin your single-guy doctor image."

Ryan snorted with laughter. "I didn't realize that I had a reputation to destroy. I'll tell the office to stop ordering me t-shirts from The Weather Channel for my birthday."

"I think someone's trying to get your attention," Grace said, tilting her head toward the monkey bars.

"Hey, Dr. Gordon," Evan yelled. He waved, hanging upside down. Ryan grinned and waved back, an idea forming.

"I actually stopped to see if you'd let me take Evan out on the boat or the wave runner. It seems like he'd love it." He wondered why he hadn't thought of it before.

Grace twisted her lips to the side, considering this. "I'm sure he'd love that. He has to wear a life jacket, okay? I think Kathleen only bought him two or three," she smiled.

"Oh, I'm all about safety first," Ryan grinned. "Tell Evan I'll see him back at Kathleen's in an hour or so."

He turned and began jogging, picking up speed, and reaching his stride when he reached the concrete.

Anyone else Ryan would have dismissed, written off and forgotten about. But there was a little tug at his heart, just at the very edges when he looked at Grace. An off-kilter zap of attraction he couldn't deny.

He was a doctor—obviously he could analyze and rationalize human nature—even his own. For years. he'd studied the way people interacted, communicated, and loved. And despite what everyone wanted to believe, it wasn't conscious or rational. Ryan could attribute it to simple chemistry and the laws of nature.

He ran faster, pounding the pavement beneath his feet, and for a moment, he wondered if Grace noticed the same connection. In the past few days, she'd opened up, actually flirted a little, and joked with Ryan. Grace was a different person when she let herself laugh and smile. She was beautiful and alive.

Yes, whatever existed between them was real. Undeniable.

He was certain that Grace felt it, too.

Chapter 32

THE PAINTERS HAD made remarkable progress in just two days. Half the house was pink now; enough so that it looked like it had been dipped in frosting on one side.

The trucks were pulling out of the driveway when Kathleen heard a knock at the door, sharp and loud.

It was Ryan, all smiles and bursting with energy. "Hey there. I ran into Grace earlier—at the playground—and I offered to take Evan for a ride on the wave runner. She said it was okay with her."

Kathleen rose from the sofa and hurried to open the screen door. She motioned Ryan inside. "Yes, Grace mentioned it. She made a run to the library to get a few books, but she's not back yet."

"Should we wait until she gets back?"

"No," Kathleen shook her head. "Let me call him. He's been dying to see you." She paused and cupped a hand around her mouth. "Evan! Ryan's here!"

The sound of running footsteps thudded through the house. Evan skidded to a stop in the kitchen, breathing hard.

"Hey Dr. Gordon," he exclaimed, barely containing his excitement. He turned to Kathleen, already starting to kick off his tennis shoes. "Grandma, where's my life jacket?"

Ryan held up the blue and red vest.

Waving and blowing kisses, Kathleen watched them speed off into the distance, a spout of water arcing off the back of the small machine. For a moment, she wished she had taken a picture of the two of them, faces glowing, not a care in the world.

The house quiet, Kathleen puttered around the kitchen, wiping up a spill on the counter and setting the table for dinner. With both Grace and Evan gone, there was no sense starting supper now, she thought.

She went through her checklist. Kathleen had picked up fresh corn, beans and berries from the farmer's market stand. She had prepared vegetables and steaks for the grill. It could be ready within twenty minutes.

Kathleen stretched her arms over her head and sighed. The house was too still. She walked outside onto the porch and sat in one of the chairs, propping her feet against the railing.

She sighed deeply, taking in the perfect view of the lake. Henry had always been sure there was something special about the lake, something magical. Kathleen didn't doubt it.

How many amazing sunsets had they watched together over the years? How many evenings had they fallen asleep and woken up to enjoy the first moments of morning together. They both loved the sound of water, gently lapping against the shoreline. It was the most soothing sound in the universe, they had decided.

Kathleen missed Henry. She missed their conversations, the way he laughed, the way her head felt on his sturdy shoulder. Kathleen missed everything about him.

She sat under the big maple tree that perched in the corner of their property. The shade it provided in the summertime was worth all of the leaves she would have to rake in the fall. Hummingbirds flitted to and from her feeder, filled with sweet red nectar. Several birds darted to a nearby suet stand, chirping and flapping their wings. As they did, hundreds of leaves rustled and shifted against each other.

Just this Spring, Henry had nearly persuaded Kathleen to let someone trim the larger branches of the tree. She had argued it would ruin its natural beauty.

Today, the tree sat as it always did, its heavy limbs reaching up into the sky, draping over the left side of the cottage roof.

Dusk began to fall over the lake, etching traces of silver along the hilltops. She checked her watch, and scanned the horizon, wishing that Ryan's wave runner would suddenly appear. Kathleen shivered in her shorts and t-shirt. It was getting late. *Wasn't Grace due back any time now?*

As the wind picked up, branches overhead began to creak from the pressure. The air, now unseasonably chilly, forced Kathleen back inside to grab a wrap or jacket.

She clicked on the remote, and caught a glimpse of a meteorologist from the local television station. After pressing the mute button, Kathleen went straight to the bedroom and slipped on a warm cardigan. She rolled up the sleeves and buttoned up the cable-knit sweater. It was one of Henry's favorites.

Her eyes fell on the dresser, to the container holding her husband's ashes. She ran her fingers along the decorative edge, wishing for a miracle. Some way to turn back time, erase the past, and bring her husband back.

I miss you, Henry. I don't want to be alone.

Kathleen closed her eyes, one hand still resting on the urn.

If she prayed hard enough, maybe he'd come back. If that was too much, he could send a message. A sign.

Kathleen sank to her knees, feeling the weight of the universe pressing down on her shoulders. It was all too much to bear. She wasn't strong enough. She couldn't make it. Not one more day.

Putting her face in her hands, she began to sob. She hadn't cried—really let go—since the doctors told her that Henry had passed away. She was too busy keeping it all together for Grace and Evan.

Then, Kathleen heard a voice.

Soft at first, then louder. More insistent.

The voice was calling her name.

Chapter 33

Kicking off her shoes by the doorway, Grace noticed that the house was strangely quiet. She set down her stack of books on the table and glanced around.

No Kathleen in the kitchen.

No eight-year-old sprawled on the couch, nose buried in a book or magazine.

Even the television, flashing pictures across the room, didn't make a sound.

"Hello? Anybody home?" Grace asked, pulling off her light jacket.

Thunder rumbled in the distance. Lightning flashed, and for a few seconds, everything was as bright as daytime. The table was set. A small pile of dishes were stacked to the side of the sink.

"Evan? Where are you?" Grace called out as darkness descended on the cottage again. She inched her way toward the living room, half-expecting her son to jump out from behind the sofa and scare her.

"I'm in here." Kathleen answered from the bedroom.

Thunder boomed again, closer this time. Grace jumped

a little at the noise as her stepmother appeared, closing the bedroom door behind her.

"Evan's with Ryan. They're out on the wave runner." Kathleen said, her eyes darting toward the lake.

Grace swallowed, trying to remember her conversation with Ryan. He'd mentioned a strong storm front, but she was certain that it was predicted to come through the region tomorrow, not tonight.

Both women jumped when the lights flickered. Another crack of lightning illuminated the lake.

"I'm sure they'll be back soon." Kathleen added, pulling up the sleeves of her oversized sweater.

"I hope so," Grace replied, pacing the room.

"It was clear when they left," Kathleen said, gesturing out at the dock. "It only started clouding up a few minutes ago."

Grace cupped her fingers around her eyes and leaned closer toward the window, looking for anything familiar. She squinted into the darkness, willing Ryan's wave runner to come into view.

Finally, she heard the faint chug of a small motor, and a bright blue and red life vest caught her eye.

"It's them!" Grace shouted, then breathed a sigh of relief and turned to look at her stepmother.

Kathleen didn't answer. She stood there, eyes closed, hands clasped together under her chin. Her lips moved slightly, as if in prayer.

Rain began plinking against the window. It hit slowly at first, then faster, beating out a staccato rhythm.

Grace bit her lip and grabbed her windbreaker. "You stay here," she ordered Kathleen. "It's starting to pour."

Without waiting for her stepmother to protest or argue, Grace pushed on the screen door and burst outside. She gasped. Rain pelted her skin, prickling her pores as she ran toward the shore. In a matter of seconds, Grace was soaked through to the skin.

As she made her way down the steps, the big maple overhead swayed dangerously. Grace paused for a moment, raindrops splashing on her cheeks and forehead. She watched the branches overhead twist and bend. The limbs whipped wildly, thrashing the cottage rooftop, causing twigs to fall around her feet.

A shower of leaves followed, the greens and browns tumbling end over end, urging Grace forward. She grabbed at the slippery rail, needing to steady herself. The wind howled, angry and defiant, the cry of a wolf pack.

It would be okay, Grace told herself, inching forward. The tree had stood there a hundred years or more, it would probably make it another few hours.

Evan was there, on the dock, peeling off his life jacket and soaked cotton shirt. He didn't look frightened, though Grace sensed that the ride back to Kathleen's cottage was a little bumpier and wilder than he'd expected.

It didn't matter. Evan was all right.

A few steps more down the gravel path and her son was in her arms. "Thank goodness you're safe!" Grace exclaimed, hugging him tight and kissing his head.

Evan waited the requisite moment or two to squirm out of her grasp. "Mom. Quit it!"

But Grace wasn't about to let go. She held Evan close, waiting until Ryan finished cranking the boat onto its stand. He ran over and wrapped an arm around Grace.

"Let's get Evan inside," Ryan said, his mouth close to her ear. "Kathleen's probably worried sick."

Grace nodded and began making her way back to the cottage, Evan held tight to her side. Halfway up the path, a white light brighter than anything Grace had ever seen arced across the top of the cottage.

Thunder roared again, and Grace watched in horror as half of the ancient maple tree fell directly on top of the roof of her stepmother's house

Chapter 34

RYAN FOUND KATHLEEN cowering in a corner by the refrigerator when he burst through the door of the cottage. He'd sent Grace and Evan to his house, not waiting for a reply or argument. He wanted them out of danger as soon as possible.

After making sure Kathleen wasn't seriously injured, Ryan examined the thick, wet tree that pierced the corner of the ceiling. Rain poured in, gushing and splashing through the hole.

Ryan grabbed a bucket from under the sink and centered it under the biggest leak. Looking at the damage, he guessed that most of the tree limbs were still in the attic. He needed to check the roof, too, but getting Kathleen out of danger was his first priority, as the rest of the tree could fall any time.

As he took Kathleen's elbow, Ryan was amazed that she escaped relatively unscathed. His neighbor was like a cat with nine lives, with all that she'd been through the past few days.

He helped Kathleen grab a few items from the house. As they crossed the lawn, carrying clothing, a few bags, and some toys for Evan, Ryan noted that his neighbor was remarkably unfazed despite the circumstances.

As he ushered Kathleen inside, Grace called out to both of them.

"The power's out," Grace said. "I wasn't sure where to find your flashlights." She was perched uneasily on the corner of a chair, a towel over her shoulders, hovering over Evan.

"Sure thing," Ryan said. He grabbed a few candles from a cupboard, placed them in holders, and set them in the center of the kitchen table. He rummaged around in a drawer for a lighter or book of matches.

"Any luck?" Grace asked.

Ryan produced a book of matches, folded the packet back, and struck one thin strip against the tiny black surface. A flame burst to life, and Ryan hurried to light the candles. Once glowing, the tapers cast a circle of warm light around the room.

Evan, not the least bit upset, entertained himself with a deck of cards Ryan had left on the kitchen counter. Kathleen had already made herself at home, wrapping up in a thick jacket, and was humming to herself, flipping through the newspaper.

"You're so calm," Grace said, leaning toward her stepmother. "Are you okay?"

Kathleen looked over the corner of the newspaper and shrugged. "Well, I think so. After all, there's not much any of us can do right now." She rustled the section of pages noisily and gave a pointed look to her neighbor. "Isn't that right, Dr. Gordon?"

Ryan, unwilling to be inserted in the discussion, changed the subject entirely. "Sure. And, um, I think the rain's about stopped. I'll go out and take a better look."

Grace flashed a smile in his direction

Ryan grabbed a flashlight and stepped outside, closing the door behind him. The sky had cleared, revealing a beautiful sunset. The lake shimmered and shined, looking like gold and silver ribbons of silk rippling in the wind. A few birds swooped down in the distance.

As he walked toward the cottage, swinging the spotlight back and forth, he wished once more that Henry was there. His neighbor would joke and make light of the situation, quipping how Kathleen had planned it all—schemed with Mother Nature to get a new roof on the cottage.

Right now, by himself, Ryan couldn't think of a single funny thing to say. The hole, gaping and wide, spanned three or four feet across on his neighbor's roof. He needed a large tarp, some rope to tie it down, and more than a few helping hands to get it all in place.

Ryan stepped inside and jotted a few things to remember down on a piece of paper.

Kathleen had made a peanut butter and jelly sandwich for Evan, who was curled up on one corner of the couch. Grace sipped a tall glass of water.

"It's not as bad as I thought," Ryan said carefully. "I'm going to call in a few favors to some contractor friends. I'll see if I can get some folks over to start fixing things in the morning."

He paused. "Please stay tonight. And as long as is necessary to repair the damage."

Ryan saw the relief flood Kathleen's face. "Thank you. You're sure it's no trouble for us to stay? We can go to a hotel."

"I insist. Evan and Grace can take the spare bedrooms. You can have my room. I'll sleep on the couch."

Kathleen started to protest.

"No, it's fine." Ryan was firm. "I insist. I wouldn't feel right about it, otherwise. There's plenty of space." It was true. The house was much too big for Ryan by himself.

Kathleen smiled her appreciation. Grace looked exhausted but grateful, stroking her son's hair.

Evan seized at the lull in conversation. "Can I sleep with Grandma tonight? We're supposed to go on a bike ride tomorrow. And maybe see the Mennonites with their horses and buggies."

Grace paused, a little surprised at his request, but smiled and swiveled toward Kathleen. After the evening's disaster and chaos, if that's what made Evan comfortable, then that's what he should do. "It's okay with me." She raised an eyebrow at Kathleen.

Her stepmother slid an arm around Evan's shoulders and squeezed. "Sure, sweetie. I'd love that." She looked up at Ryan. "Dr. Gordon? There's just one more thing. A small favor, and I promise that I am done asking for the night."

"Anything," Ryan replied with a wink. "Name it."

Kathleen pressed her fingers together, looking hopeful. "Would it be too much for you to go and get Henry?"

Chapter 35

SINCE LORI HAD left, Ryan had spent many nights sleeping stretched out on the couch. Somehow, it seemed easier than resting in his bedroom. He often fell asleep with the Discovery Channel or the History Channel on. He'd wake up hours later, searching for the remote to click it off.

Now though, it was almost morning and he was too comfortable to move even a few inches. It was infomercial time and all he could do was cover up his head to block out the noise and light.

This morning, though, something else was different. Ryan opened one eye. For one, there was a big pink bag sitting next to the fireplace, toys scattered in the corner of the room, and a leather suitcase by the door. Rubbing the sleep out of his eyes, sure he was imagining things, Ryan blinked a few more times. The bag and toys were still there.

Ryan stretched his arms above his head, pulling the pillow over his face. "Maybe it was all a bad dream," he said, murmuring into the pillow.

Slowly, painfully, the reality came back. The storm had

come through, a tree had fallen on Kathleen's cottage. Ryan had not only offered up his house, he'd asked Kathleen, Grace and Evan to stay as long as was necessary.

Ryan scratched his head thoughtfully and sat up straight, letting the comforter fall off of his chiseled chest. How long had it been since other people had slept in his house? He couldn't remember the last time.

One by one, he placed his feet on the hardwood floor. Slivers of light peeked through the blinds. Ryan walked to the front of the house and stood by the window, letting the heat of the morning sun warm his bare chest and arms.

It was time to make coffee, his brain was screaming out for it. This morning, though, he resisted for a few moments, taking in the healthy green of the grass and the deep blue of the lake. Along the bank of his neighbor's lot, under the shade of a weeping willow, a lone fisherman cast his line, hoping for a bite.

Ryan rubbed his eyes. What a change from just eight short hours ago. Evidence of the night's storm was everywhere— broken branches strewn across the yard, lawn chairs upended, a roof torn apart—but the calm Ryan felt inside his heart was remarkable and strong.

A family was safe inside the four walls of his home. A mother, one grown daughter, and her young son had trusted him, gone to sleep under his watch, and were resting peacefully.

For the first time in a long time, he had a purpose—and it wasn't about being a doctor, keeping appointments, or prescribing medicine.

It was much, much more.

Kathleen trusted him. Evan looked up to him.

And Grace, whether she knew so or not, needed him as much as he needed her.

Ryan belonged.

Chapter 36

THE SOUND OF banging and power saws woke Kathleen with a start. She clutched at the sheets, wondering where she'd fallen asleep. Scenes from last night flashed through her mind, black and white, like a silent movie. The vision of the tree crashing through the ceiling played over and over, until she forced her eyes open.

Kathleen shook herself awake. She was staying at Ryan's. She was safe.

The clock next to the bed said almost eight-thirty. It wasn't like her to sleep this late.

Quietly, she slipped out of the bed, careful not to disturb Evan. He had begged to sleep with her last night. Grace hadn't seemed to mind much, and with little discussion, took Ryan's bedroom.

Kathleen felt warm and happy looking at her grandson. His chest rose and fell with deep breaths under his t-shirt. One arm was behind his head, his legs were curled up, snug tight against his belly, and his face was a picture of peace and contentment.

Oh, to be a child again without a care in the world. Kathleen sighed. Those days were long gone, though she had much to be thankful for now, even with the accident last night.

The container with Henry's ashes sat on the dresser by itself. It was the last thing Kathleen had looked at before she closed her eyes to sleep. Somehow, having Henry there with her was a comfort.

It was silly, she knew—asking Ryan to go back and get him last night—but she couldn't have slept without Henry just a few feet away. Her neighbor did as she asked without a moment's hesitation. Maybe it was time to let her husband go, but Kathleen was hanging on, even if for one more day.

A chainsaw sputtered, then started outside, whirring and buzzing as it cut through giant branches and stumps.

Evan stirred, rustling the covers and blinking his eyes. He sat up quickly, throwing the sheets back, wide-eyed. Kathleen covered her mouth to keep from laughing out loud.

"Where am I, Grandma?"

"We're at Dr. Gordon's house, dear."

"Oh, yeah," Evan looked thoughtfully at Kathleen, and then brightened, extending one finger toward the sky. "I remember now! There was a big storm, and there was lots of lightning… and that giant tree fell on the house!"

"That's right."

The sound of machinery intensified. Evan slapped his hands over his ears to block out the noise. "What is that?"

"Some men working outside, I think. Dr. Gordon called some men to take the tree apart and haul it away." Kathleen said. "They'll leave a few logs and branches so we can have a big bonfire. Would you like that?"

"Cool. I mean, yes ma'am." Evan bounced off the cot, running a hand through his disheveled hair. "Where's my mom?"

"Still sleeping, I hope." Kathleen wondered how anyone could be sleeping through so much noise, but there had been a lot of excitement. Maybe Grace was just worn out.

Evan sat up straight, hair askew, and pointing every which way. "Let's go look at the house. I want to see where the tree busted up the roof!"

Kathleen smiled and motioned toward the backpack in the corner.

"There are some clothes in there. Why don't you get dressed and I'll make you some breakfast. Then, we'll check out what the workers are doing."

"Okay," Evan replied, already grabbing at the bag, unzipping, and pulling out clothes. He had his t-shirt over his head by the time Kathleen closed the door behind her.

The living room and kitchen were empty. A full pot of coffee sat on the counter. Ryan had written a note.

"Hi everybody. Help yourself to anything in the house. Nothing is off-limits. I'll be home after six o'clock. There are bicycles behind the garage. Feel free to use them."

His name was scribbled at the bottom.

Pouring herself a cup of coffee and mixing it with creamer, Kathleen stirred thoughtfully.

Several boxes of cereal were set out. She chose one and poured out two bowls, splashed on some milk and gathered a few spoons from a drawer. Evan came out the door, dressed and ready.

"There's a Mennonite farm up the hill that I'd love you to see. They have horses and sheep and chickens. There's a blueberry patch where we can pick our own berries. They have several children, and I've heard there's a new baby lamb, just a few days old," Kathleen said, pausing to take a breath. "What do you think?"

Evan nodded in agreement, his hand constantly moving from the bowl to his mouth with scoops of cereal.

"We'll have to ride bicycles, uphill some." Kathleen hoped her legs would carry her. It was steep and winding. She could always walk the bike part way.

"Sure, no problem," Evan said, making a muscle and

feeling his bicep. "Can I have more cereal then? I'll need the energy."

Kathleen poured more and hesitated. "Do you think your mom wants to come?"

Evan shook his head, unconcerned. "Nah, she'd probably like to read or something."

"There are only two bicycles. You two could go instead." Kathleen questioned him hesitantly, wanting him to say no, selfishly wanting time with him for herself. Grace had him all of the time, and he was leaving soon.

"No. That's okay."

Kathleen breathed a little easier. He had made his choice. "We'll leave her a note then."

A few minutes later, breakfast dishes cleared, grand-mother and grandson made their way to the back of Ryan's garage. Two shiny mountain bikes were waiting for them, one slightly smaller than the other, both with wide seats and rearview mirrors attached. Adjusting the seat to Evan's height, Kathleen pronounced them ready to go.

"Do you want to look at the hole in the house first?" The saws and grinders seemed to get louder and louder.

"I can kind of see some of it from here," he said. "Maybe let's go later? All that noise is giving me a headache."

Kathleen smiled. "Me too."

"Don't we need helmets?" Evan questioned. He looked around curiously.

Kathleen felt a pang of uneasiness. Grace would certainly insist on one. But, they'd be back in no time. "It'll be okay. We'll be careful."

After searching, unsuccessfully, a few moments more, the two pedaled away, toward the Mennonite farm on the top of the hill.

Chapter 37

G RACE HAD BEEN awake for hours, but resisted any movement. As daylight broke, she lay motionless in the great bed, absorbing the sounds around her—workers outside banging tools and talking amongst themselves, the sound of cars driving by on the main road, then Ryan up, getting ready for work.

Before he left for the office, Ryan made a pot of coffee, and the nutty aroma filled the house. Undertones of cinnamon and hazelnut tickled her nose as Grace drifted in and out of a light sleep. It had been ages since she'd really slept in.

Kathleen had knocked and peeked inside the room, letting Grace know that she and Evan had made plans for the day. "I've got him. We've got lots to do. You go ahead and rest," she whispered and closed the door behind her.

Wandering out into the living room in her pajamas, Grace surveyed the house with different eyes. With no one around, she could be more inquisitive, stare at things up close and touch them.

Grace poured herself a cup of coffee and put the mug

in the microwave. While she waited for the timer to ding, she wandered around the kitchen. Without thinking, she opened a few kitchen cabinets. She found Ryan's stash of coffee—a collection that rivaled her stockpile at home in Mississippi. Grace counted half a dozen bags of ground coffee. Hazelnut, Vanilla, Ethiopian, Columbian, Peruvian, and one package of an Organic Rainforest blend.

Grace smiled and ran her finger along one of the labels. It was something else she and Ryan had in common—something other than Henry and Kathleen. She couldn't exist without her morning coffee. For Ryan, it certainly seemed the same way.

Other cupboards revealed a few bowls, a mixer, and one cookbook. None of the drawers revealed any deep, dark secrets. Silverware was neatly stacked in a tray, next to a pizza cutter and some sharp steak knives.

Grace put her hand on the last cabinet in the room. She stopped herself and shook her head. What was she doing? This wasn't her house—it wasn't her stepmother's house—and it certainly wasn't her place to be snooping around.

What did she expect to find, anyway?

Grace knew she should be doing something productive, like working on her lesson plans for school. They'd be expected in a few weeks. The outline and notes were in the pink bag by the door, but Grace couldn't motivate herself to touch it.

Instead, she kept searching. Grace couldn't seem to help herself. She was looking for clues. A connection. Some insight into Ryan's current life and past relationship. What had happened? Who was to blame? How did it fall apart?

The photo on the ski slope caught her eye again. Grace picked up the picture and held it by the corner of the frame, examining the faces. His wife had to have been very young when she left. She had a smile a mile wide, as some would say. They were laughing about something with goggles on their heads and there were snowflakes in their hair and on her eyelashes. Ryan was happy, you could tell. There was a glow about them, something special. She wondered what had happened. Who left who and why?

Grace set the photo back down. There were drawers in the table the picture sat on. Pulling at the bottom drawer, Grace found a few photo albums. They were carefully labeled and marked. She ran a hand along the edges, debating about opening the pages. Certainly, Ryan wouldn't mind that much, would he?

There were college photos, graduation, and several pictures of Ryan in scrubs when he must have been a resident. His hair was shorter and he was clean shaven. Another photo was from medical school graduation, then a shot of him and his wife in front of the clinic he owned now in town. They were holding hands and smiling into the camera. He was in a navy suit and tie, she in a pale pink silk dress that flowed below her knees. The sign beside them was the same as the one she saw when she took her stepmother to his office. Ryan Gordon, M.D. Then, below that line, Family Practice.

The telephone rang. Grace stopped and shut the album, placing it carefully where she found it, inside the drawer. Surely, it wasn't for her. Someone would leave a message. Grace glanced around for the phone. It wasn't on the charger.

Ring, ring. Surely it would stop. Why didn't he have an answering machine anyway? The telephone rang eight more times and then, finally, silence.

Grace looked out the window. The pounding and banging at her stepmother's house had stopped for a few minutes. The tree that had fallen on the roof was all but gone, the pieces of trunk and branches neatly stacked. The workers were taking a break, guzzling soda and eating doughnuts under the shade of another tree closer to the lake. Grace didn't want to talk to them either. She was restless though. The phone started ringing again.

"Fine. Fine, I'll get it." Grace muttered to herself and cleared her throat. "Uh, Gordon residence?"

Chapter 38

RYAN WASN'T HAVING the best of days. It was only eleven o'clock in the morning, but he'd already seen fifteen patients, admitted a child to the hospital for croup, diagnosed a case of chicken pox, examined a broken toe, and extracted a small hook from the eyebrow of a man who wasn't very happy to have his fishing expedition interrupted.

The last patient had come in, pole still in hand, spots of blood on his shirt. He was in his eighties and had lived on Keuka Lake all of his life. He was worried about leaving his boat unattended at the Morgan Marine, fearful that someone might take his catch for the day. His friend, who'd driven him to Ryan's office, made him leave the ice chest full of small mouth bass, his bait, and their cold drinks.

"They'll keep an eye on your boat," Ryan reassured him. He knew the owners at Morgan. They were good people, honest, and straightforward. He'd purchased his Larson LX, his boat trailer, and all of his supplies from the family since he moved to Penn Yan.

Ryan glanced up at the clock, wishing the hands would

move a little faster. He was anxious to get home. Though he tried to keep focused on his work and patients, his mind kept drifting back to Grace, Kathleen and Evan in his house.

Mostly, he thought about Grace—the way she looked just before bedtime, her hair disheveled, her eyes closing with a desperate need to sleep. He'd walked by her more than once just to be close to her, overcome by an urge to wrap her in his arms and tell her that everything would be all right. He wanted to be close enough to inhale the scent of her skin, which always carried a faint, fresh hint of baby powder.

"Thanks, doc," the fisherman stood up from the table when Ryan finished. They shook hands, and Ryan stepped out into the hallway. Every room was full with charts in the bin outside every door, and the waiting room was stacked with people. He could hear at least one cranky baby fussing. His staff was used to the hectic pace. He was one of only a few physicians in town.

Ryan chugged along at a good clip, stopping occasionally to look up information on the computer or take a phone call from a colleague who needed a consult.

From all account, his reputation was good. He was patient and kind and spent just enough time with each patients—so much so that most of them felt like friends. The small break room was overloaded with brownies, candy and treats. Ladies from church were constantly baking pound cakes and cookies. Someone's grandmother always brought him freshly canned peaches and tomato sauce in the summertime.

What was more, there were hugs and kisses on the cheek for every loaf of homemade bread, pint of strawberries, and crate of apples. His staff often joked that if Ryan ate all that was brought in, he'd gain fifty pounds in a month. He shared all of it, pressing plates of goodies into the nurses' hands at the end of each day.

He had bent down to speak to one of his oldest patients, Miss Ella, when he saw the black buggy owned by one of the

Mennonite families outside of town flash by the window. It was not unusual to see the horse and carriage around town early in the morning, but most days, the families spent in the fields, harvesting sweet corn, vegetables and berries. Ryan assumed one of the family's children was sick and turned back to focus his attention on his elderly patient.

The sound of heavy work boots in the waiting room distracted him again, and one of his staff members came running to the back to find him. She knocked quickly on the door and opened it after waiting a beat.

"Dr. Gordon, I'm sorry to interrupt, but I think you'll want to see this *right* away. I've got them coming back to the room you use for minor surgery." His staff member waited for a nod, which he gave her, and the girl disappeared from the doorway.

Ryan frowned and stood up from his stool. His worker was young and relatively new to his practice, but she had proven capable, with a good head on her shoulders. Knowing this, and that his staff was well trained in what to do in case of an emergency, Ryan excused himself from the room.

"I'll be back just as soon as I can," he told Miss Ella and patted her hand.

Ryan strode to the back room quickly, pausing to wash his hands at the sink. Scrubbing up a soapy lather, he heard the door to the hallway open.

Kathleen being carried in by one of the Mennonite farmers, Adam Shenk, and Evan was being carried by his wife.

"Dr. Gordon," his neighbor fluttered her fingers and attempted a wide smile.

"I thought we'd had enough excitement for one day," Ryan said, trying not to frown as he took a quick look at Kathleen. Her face was deathly white, though, and there were smudges of dirt and blood along both legs. Her ankle, swollen almost twice its normal size, had turned purple and red.

"I'm fine, dear," Kathleen said in a weak voice. "It's my

grandson that you have to worry about."

"Adam, thank you for bringing them in," Ryan said, and gestured for the farmer to bring his neighbor toward the rear of the office. Evan was behind Adam, asleep in the arms of Adam's wife. She held him close, rocking him from side to side. He looked small and fragile in the woman's grasp.

"Hey buddy," he said gently, quickly examining Evan's face, arms, and legs for cuts, broken bones, and bruises. His clothes were dirty and ripped in places, but Evan himself looked relatively unscathed. Ryan breathed out a sigh of relief.

"I'll follow you both to the back room. It's the largest in the building," Ryan explained. "I'll see both of them in there."

He motioned for his nurse. "Could you call Mrs. Mason's stepdaughter?" he asked quietly. Grace needs to know that her son is here. Please tell her that there's been an accident, but it appears that they're both going to be fine," he added. "And tell the rest of the patients that we've had a small emergency and that I'll be running a little behind. Thank you."

"Yes, Dr. Gordon."

Ryan hurried inside the surgical suite. The door closed with a click behind him. Adam hesitated, his burly hands laced on his suspenders. Evan was still sound asleep and Kathleen was resting on the exam table, head to one side, with her eyes closed.

"Doc Gordon, we had to bring them on in." He spoke with a clipped Pennsylvania Dutch accent. "You can see her ankle is in bad shape. And this little one," Adam said, gesturing at the sleeping Evan, "ran almost a mile back to our house to find us."

Ryan raised his eyebrows. No wonder Evan was worn out.

"They had just left the farm," Adam continued. "Miss Kathleen had brought the little one up to see the new baby lamb. They were on bicycles. They had been gone twenty minutes when this one came running back, yelling at the top of his lungs."

"Again, I can't thank you enough, Adam. It was a fine thing to do for Miss Kathleen and Evan. Grace, his mother, should be on her way any moment."

Ryan slid off the stethoscope from around his neck and touched Kathleen on the forearm. Her eyelids fluttered open at the touch.

"So, Kathleen, can you tell me what happened?" He listened to her heart and lungs, then took a closer look at her ankle, prodding gently. She shifted slightly on the exam table, wincing in pain.

His neighbor met Ryan's eyes and then looked away sheepishly. "Well, we were heading home from Adam's house. We had just finished seeing all the farm animals and visiting with the children," Kathleen took a deep breath. "We had borrowed your bicycles, and I decided we should have a race."

Ryan stopped examining Kathleen's foot, his fingers frozen in mid-air. "What did you say?"

"A race," Kathleen said, a look of regret on her face. "I thought it would be fun. You know how fast you can get going down the hill from Adam's place?"

Ryan shook his head in disbelief. Kathleen looked away in dismay.

"Continue." Ryan said sternly, straightening up. He put his hands on his hips. He noticed that Adam and his wife were silent, their eyes never leaving Kathleen.

"So, we started down the hill and got going pretty fast, and a truck came whipping around the corner out of nowhere. I went off the road one way, and Evan went off the other, into a ditch. Luckily, his side was soft dirt."

"And the side you fell onto?"

"I didn't exactly fall." Kathleen rolled her eyes and paused. "I think I flipped over the handlebars and hit my ankle on some rocks."

"You're lucky you both weren't killed," Ryan said, scolding her gently.

Evan started to stir, lifting his head off the shoulders of the farmer's wife. She stood up, whispered to him gently and slid him into the chair, where his head bobbed and rolled for a moment. He looked up at Ryan, confused, and promptly fell asleep again.

Adam and his wife, Lydia, made a quiet exit, Adam shaking Ryan's hand on the way out. Kathleen murmured a word of thanks as they left.

Ryan walked over to Evan and squatted down. He ran a hand along his arms and touched his dirt-lined face. He probed his legs and moved his ankles. "It seems like he's okay."

Turning to Kathleen, "Let's get an x-ray of this ankle and get you fixed up."

"What should I tell Grace? She's going to be furious." Kathleen's voice trailed off in a question.

"Why don't you try the truth?" Ryan didn't mean to be smart, but it was his only answer.

Kathleen pursed her lips. "You don't understand Grace. Things are...well, she's not going to like it."

"Probably not," Ryan agreed.

"She has a hard time with relationships." Kathleen said. "Especially since her mother died. Maybe she'll tell you about it. It's been complicated...and there's a history there...between Henry, me, and Grace's mother. We were friends once, all of us, a long time ago."

"And it's complicated for Grace now, because...?" Ryan asked.

"It's not something she'll share with me," Kathleen replied.

Ryan thought about this. How could he get someone to open up when they built barriers as high as the Great Wall of China. He'd had glimpses of Grace's personality, her fun and sweet nature, but those were few and far between. Ryan couldn't help his attraction to his neighbor's stepdaughter. He felt an overwhelming urge to fix what was ever wrong, but unlike medicine, this couldn't be fixed with bandages and prescriptions.

"I think—with your permission—and Evan's," he said slowly, "that I'm going to ask Miss Grace out on a real date."

Kathleen clasped her hands together in delight. "Finally!" she exclaimed in a whisper, smiling from ear to ear. "I've been hoping and praying..."

"Shh!" Ryan said, putting a finger over his mouth. "Don't tell anyone. She might say no."

His neighbor pursed her lips. "She'd better not. Someone will need to talk some sense into that girl."

"You," Ryan chided, "are in no shape to be arguing with anyone."

Kathleen sighed a little. "How about an apology?"

Ryan raised an eyebrow. "What do you mean?"

"I'm sorry," Kathleen said and put her hand on Ryan's arm. "I owe you two new bicycles."

Chapter 39

YOU DID WHAT?" Grace looked incredulously at Kathleen. "I can't believe you talked Evan into doing something so hair-brained. You are supposed to be the adult" Grace began pacing back and forth in Ryan's living room.

Kathleen was sitting on the couch, her leg in an air cast, propped up on the overstuffed ottoman.

Ryan was out by the grill, cooking steaks and burgers. Evan was by his side, chattering away, helping marinate the meat.

Grace heard them laughing. They were both doubled over, mouths wide open. They obviously couldn't hear the conversation inside, so Grace continued with her lecture.

"You're lucky to be alive."

"I think I heard that somewhere else today." Kathleen remarked.

"Listen, I know that you like to make jokes, but I am not being funny."

Kathleen raised herself up on the seat a little higher. He chin raised, she looked at Grace with narrowed eyes. "I've had about enough of you preaching at me. The child is perfectly fine. Evan was having fun."

Grace pursed her lips. Kathleen continued.

"I wanted to spend some time with him before...you have to leave." Kathleen's voice cracked a little. She turned away and looked at her hand.

Grace once again felt a tinge of guilt. Her stepmother was never very emotional. Was she just trying to shift the guilt away—or simply make her feel bad? After all, it was she who cooked up that ridiculous scheme. What was a grown woman doing racing down gigantic hills with an eight year old?

Ryan and Evan burst in the door, steaks and burgers steaming and smelling heavenly. "Soup's on." Ryan was flushed from the heat. He wiped at his forehead with the back of his hand. "Who's ready to eat? I'm starving."

Grace walked away from Kathleen to the stove. She was pretty sure that if Ryan and Evan had overheard their conversation, she would know from their reaction.

She reminded herself that Evan was safe.

Kathleen hadn't meant for anything to happen.

She was trying to have fun.

Grace clicked off the water boiling the corn and lifted the pieces carefully on to a plate. Ryan set the plate on the table, hurrying to help Kathleen to the table. Hobbling awkwardly, Kathleen settled into the seat at the end. Grace tried not to watch and smiled brightly at Evan. He looked back at her with a puzzled expression.

"Why are you so mad at Grandma?" He asked her pointedly.

Grace tried not to look surprised. So they had heard some of it.

Ryan tried to hide a smile.

Grace opened her mouth. "We were just having a minor disagreement. I'm not angry, sweetheart. Really." It was not very convincing.

Evan looked at her skeptically. "You sure seem like you're mad." He started munching on his ear of corn.

The room was quiet then, except for the occasional crackle of ice melting in the glasses and the clink of silverware.

Grace felt her face flush. She hadn't done a very good job at hiding her anger. Her father would be disappointed with her holding a grudge against his wife for so long. He would be urging her to forgive, if she couldn't forget.

"I'm sorry, Kathleen," Grace finally said. "And I am sorry, Evan and Ryan. I was scared that something terrible had happened to you, honey."

"Aw, Mom," Evan laughed. "I'm fine."

"Apology accepted," Kathleen smiled and patted her lips with a napkin.

"Good, then everyone's happy," Ryan said and tried to change the subject. "How was the farm? Tell me all about it, Evan."

The mood lightened and shifted then. Evan was animated, describing the animals, the children, and the huge barn full of hay. Ryan seemed to be hanging on every word, laughing at the description of the cats chasing mice in the barn and the chickens pecking at the ground. Evan told how he was able to pet the baby lamb, just a week old, and how its coat was as soft as a fleece blanket.

Dinner was finished then, and Kathleen sat helplessly at the table as Grace cleaned up the dinner dishes. Ryan grabbed some pills from the counter and doled out two to Kathleen. She swallowed them with some water and watched Grace work.

Grace was trying hard to ignore her, but felt her eyes staring at her from across the room. Her back prickled at the thought. Grace loaded the dishwasher in a flash. She couldn't get out of the kitchen and away from her stepmother's stare fast enough.

"I guess I'll go to bed," Kathleen announced, her mouth forming a yawn. "Ryan, can you help get me into the bedroom?"

"Gladly." He sprung to her side and lifted her easily, helping her hobble to the room.

"Good night all." Kathleen called out.

Evan ran over and planted a kiss on her cheek. Grace forced herself to answer. "Good night," she said, watching her stepmother. The sun was starting to set on the top of the hills. The sky was turning pink and red.

"We're going swimming!"

She heard Evan come up behind her. He had already changed into his trunks.

"You are?" Grace felt surprised. Why had no one asked her?

Ryan came back into the room. "Your stepmother's all settled. The medicine I gave her will help her sleep and ease the pain. She'll feel better in the morning and hopefully some of the swelling will go down by then. I propped up her ankle with a pillow."

Grace nodded. "Good. Thank you." Ryan was being so wonderful about taking care of Kathleen. She wondered if he thought she should be the one doing the scurrying around, fetching the medicine, and helping her stepmother to the bedroom.

She'd have to talk to Ryan abut getting someone in to help out when she and Evan left. Grace thought about asking now, but changed her mind. She wasn't in the mood to discuss it.

She ran her fingers through a strand of hair. "I hear you're going swimming?"

"If it's all right with you, we will. It's a perfect night for it." Ryan looked hopeful. "Want to come?" Evan didn't wait for the rest of the conversation. He grabbed his swim goggles off the table and bounded out the door.

Grace paused, considering the look on his face. She felt the urge to run and get her own bathing suit, but stopped herself.

The sound of tires rolling by startled both of them. Grace looked out the window. "The contractor just pulled up to Kathleen's house."

She bent her head in the direction of the man driving up in a blue truck. "I think I'll go talk to him and see when he thinks the repairs will be finished. I want to make sure everything's going on schedule."

Ryan didn't say anything. He looked hurt.

"You two go on and have fun," Grace said, trying to smile.

Ryan didn't return her smile. His gaze was steady and unwavering. Ryan waited a beat, and then answered. "I wish you'd change your mind and come with us. The house will be fine. They'll do a good job."

It was Grace's turn to be silent.

"You know, it's a perfect night. The water's warmed up and the sunset's gorgeous," he added. "While you're still here, you should try having some fun."

Ryan walked past her, out the door. He grabbed a towel and slung it over his shoulder.

Grace blinked back surprise. Ryan hadn't said it in a mean way, but the truth of his words stung just the same.

Chapter 40

RYAN WOKE TO the sizzle and smell of bacon and eggs. He was again, sleeping on the couch, which faced the window looking out over the water. His blankets were twisted around his ankles and his shirt was pulled half-way up his chest. The coffee pot bubbled and shook.

"I took the liberty of sampling from your collection. Is chocolate macadamia nut okay?"

Ryan kicked off the covers and hoisted himself up to look over the back of the couch into the kitchen.

Grace was bustling around, her hair up in a ponytail. She had showered and dressed. She actually had an air of happiness about her, he decided.

"Sure," Ryan said slowly. "What's the occasion?"

"Since you're so nice to let us stay here, I decided I could return the favor and cook for everybody."

"I'm not going to argue with that." Ryan jumped up from the couch, straightening his shirt. "I'll just duck into the bathroom and be right out to help set the table."

Grace was humming a little bit to herself, flipping over what looked like French toast and bacon in two separate pans.

After running a comb through his hair, Ryan decided he had a few minutes to shave. A few strokes later, his chin was visible again. he leaned over the sink.

Did he like this girl? Was she sending him a signal that she might actually be interested? It had been so long since he had felt any kind of attraction to anyone, it took him by surprise. Grace seemed to ignite him and infuriate him all at the same time. He was probably reading it all wrong. No, he'd have to play it cool. She was leaving, wasn't she?

Back in the kitchen, Evan had woken up and Kathleen was hobbling slowly to the table, looks of suspicion on both of their faces.

"Hey everybody! Good morning." Ryan went over and tousled Evan's hair. He pulled out a seat for Kathleen, who slid in as gracefully as she could.

"Morning," Kathleen replied. She looked rested and cheerful.

"Who made breakfast?" Evan asked with a look of concern on his face. His brows were knitted together.

Ryan shook his head. "Not me."

Evan looked from Kathleen to Grace and back to Ryan. "Mom?"

Grace turned around. She had been piling plates high with food. "Yes?"

"Can I go to the office with Dr. Gordon tomorrow? He said it would be okay," Evan asked breathlessly. "We can see patients together, he's going to show me how his stethoscope works—"

"Wow," Grace glanced over at Evan, who had his hands pressed together in a prayer position. Her son was so hopeful there was no way she could say no. "That's a great opportunity for my little guy. Are you sure?" she asked Ryan.

Ryan rubbed his hands together in anticipation and winked at Evan. "Definitely. It'll be a guy's day. He'll be my assistant."

"So I can go?" Evan pleaded.

Grace nodded. "Sure, honey." She motioned at Ryan and mouthed some additional instructions, just in case. "Just call me if I need to come and pick him up, okay?"

Ryan grinned. "We'll be fine, Mom," he joked.

This brought a laugh from Evan and made Kathleen giggle.

"Well, before we eat, I have an announcement." Grace looked proudly at everyone, turning from the stove. "The contractor says the roof will be done in three or four days. They're going to work through Saturday so that we can move back in on Sunday."

Kathleen clapped her hands excitedly.

"Good news!" Ryan tried to be excited, not feeling true enthusiasm as much as he should have. Selfishly, he was quickly getting used to the idea of having an extra three people around.

"That's not all, that's not all." Grace made a shushing noise, holding her finger to her lips. "The contractor's also taking me to dinner."

Ryan watched her wink at her stepmother and stopped smiling. *Surely she was joking.*

"What?" Kathleen's mouth gaped open a little bit. Sneaking a look at Ryan, and then recovering, she said, "What I mean is, that's great, dear."

"Dad was always bugging me about dating someone," Grace shrugged. "I thought, well, what the heck. You never know."

"You never know," echoed Ryan. Pangs of jealousy swept over him. He felt almost sick.

All at once, Evan got up from the table, knocked over his

glass of milk, and sent his fork flying across the table. Ryan caught it in mid-air.

"You didn't ask me if it was okay." Evan pushed back his chair and ran outside.

Open-mouthed, Grace stared after her son.

"I'm going to talk to Evan. And I'm not hungry," Ryan announced, walking toward the door. "I just lost my appetite."

"What in the world?"

Kathleen let out a heavy sigh. "Let them go. Ryan will talk to him."

"But, I'm his mother. I need to explain," she said, wiping a hand across her forehead. None of this was going as she planned.

"Give him a few minutes to calm down," Kathleen said. "And in the future, it's probably better not to spring something like this on him at the breakfast table."

Grace hung her head. Kathleen was right. How could she have been so foolish?

"And, just to be clear, your father wanted you to date and find someone nice who would treat you well. He didn't mean with some guy you've known for ten minutes."

"Someone like Ryan?" Grace said slowly. She traced the edge of the table with her fingertip.

"What's wrong with Ryan?" Kathleen asked, defending him.

"There's nothing wrong with Ryan. He's perfect."

"Well, now, after your little announcement, Ryan might not be so interested." Kathleen retorted.

Grace winced. Again, her stepmother was correct.

"Maybe," Kathleen said carefully. "I had hoped maybe you'd hit it off, but obviously that's not going to happen."

"Probably not," Grace agreed.

Kathleen spoke again. "Give Ryan a few minutes to get your son calmed down and then talk to Evan about it, at least.

He's sensitive, like your father was."

"Okay," Grace said, nodding. "I will."

"Good," Kathleen replied, pushing back from the table. "And, I guess...have fun tonight."

Chapter 41

GRACE WAS SURE her night ranked right up there with the worst date in history. Her clothes reeked of cigarette smoke, her eyes stung, and she'd had one too many glasses of cheap wine.

The contractor seemed nice enough at first. True, he wasn't really her type, with his slicked back hair, faded jeans, and hiking boots, but Grace tried to keep an open mind about the situation. She'd agreed to the date, the least she could do was give the guy a chance.

When the conversation turned to sports and fishing, Grace's mind went on autopilot, detaching from the loud restaurant. Her thoughts drifted to Ryan, and she pictured him on his back porch looking over the lake.

She had been stubborn. She'd hurt his feelings, and Kathleen's too. Evan had refused to talk about it, though he'd hugged her before she left the cottage.

"So," the contractor was saying. "You been to the Sprint Cup Series?"

Grace swallowed and tried to recall what her date had

been talking about. NASCAR? Grand Prix?

"At Watkins Glen," he prompted her, looking a little perturbed that she hadn't been paying attention.

"I haven't ever been to a race," Grace explained, "but I've heard that the gorge is beautiful for hiking. I'd love to bring Evan."

"That your boy?" The contractor asked and took a swig from his beer.

Grace nodded and sat up straight. "He's eight. And very smart. He's a really good kid."

Her date shrugged and downed the rest of the bottle. "Never was quite sure about the whole family thing. It kinda ties you down, doesn't it?" He snickered a little. "Me? I like taking off at the spur of the moment. Vegas. Atlantic City. Anywhere I can play craps and a little blackjack. You been there?"

Grace stiffened. "No, I haven't." She reached for her water and took a sip. Was this guy for real? She didn't mind hearing about NASCAR, but divulging that gambling was his favorite past-time was beyond bizarre. She needed an escape route, and fast.

Thankfully, the waitress stopped by the table, interrupting the already stilted conversation. Without asking, her date ordered a round of shots. "Give us a couple of Kamikazes," he snapped.

The girl scribbled down his request without a smile and disappeared into the kitchen of the restaurant.

Grace raised an eyebrow. This guy was crazy—a little mean—and desperate enough to see if she'd stay and get drunk.

"Listen, thank you for inviting me tonight. But, actually, I have to go." Grace stood up from the table, folded her napkin and put it next to her empty plate. Thank goodness they hadn't ordered anything to eat yet.

The contactor didn't move from his chair, didn't offer

to walk her to her car, or ask if there was anything he could do. He just stared at Grace, frowning, with both arms folded across his chest.

"I-I'm not feeling well." Grace pressed a hand to her stomach. It wasn't a total lie. She did feel sick, her head ached, and she wanted to get home—back to the cottage, anyway—as soon as possible.

"See ya around, then," the contractor said finally.

Grace gathered up her jacket and purse, flashed a tight smile, and walked out of the restaurant. She inhaled deeply and shook her head in relief. It was all she could do to walk—not run—to the rental car.

Her hand shook as she tried, unsuccessfully, to unlock the door. Finally, after hitting several other buttons on the key fob, the doors clicked open. Grace slid inside and shrunk down in her seat, relieved to be alone again.

After starting the engine, Grace eased into traffic, pointing the car in the direction of Kathleen's house. The headlights coming in the other direction were starting to look fuzzy. Grace blinked a few times, slowing down to look at the street signs. Now where was the turn she wanted?

Blue and red lights flashed behind her. Grace glanced in the rearview mirror. Surely, the policeman didn't want her to stop? There were only two cars on the road, though. Grace slowed down, pulling the car next to the curb. Breathing hard, she smoothed her hair and dug in her purse for a piece of gum, but came up empty.

The police officer was standing outside her window. Slowly, she pushed the button to roll it down about a half-inch. He leaned in to talk.

"Yes?" Grace managed to squeak out. She reached over and turned off the engine.

"License and registration," he barked. He seemed annoyed at her resistance to rolling down the window, but didn't ask her to lower it more. She tried to focus on his face. It was yellow and fuzzy around the edges from the street light glowing behind his head.

"It's a rental."

The officer stared at her like he had never heard anything so ridiculous. "Check the glove compartment for the registration. You do have a license, don't you?"

Grace fumbled again through her purse for her wallet, dumping half the contents out on the seat next to her. "It's in here somewhere." Her favorite lipstick and three pens fell into the space between the center console and the seat.

Out of the corner of her eye, Grace saw the lights of another vehicle flash behind her. Great, she thought. Just what I need. Another police officer.

A familiar voice called out. Grace strained through the haze of her mind to think who it might be.

The officer had turned around and was talking to someone. That someone, Grace thought, was slapping the policeman on the back and telling a joke. Both men chuckled at the punch line.

"Uh, miss?" The officer's face was back at the window.

Grace looked up from her searching.

"Doc here says he can vouch for who you are. He says he can drive you home, if you're not feeling well."

Grace started to protest, and then thought better of it when she took a mental tally of how much she'd actually had to drink. The officer's face floated into two faces, then back together. Grace shut her eyes.

"Slide over, little missy." Ryan Gordon's face appeared at her window, and before she could protest, he was already opening the car door.

Chapter 42

GRACE CLIMBED OVER the seat, jamming her elbow into the dashboard in the process. Tears welled up in her eyes, but she fought them back, squeezing her hand on the bruised skin.

"Ouch." Ryan cranked the car and put it into drive. "Why don't you get buckled up? he added, looking over at her in concern.

"What are you going to do with your car?" Grace managed to ask, wrenching the seatbelt over her middle and clicking it locked.

"Left it," Ryan gestured across the street. "We're right across from my office. I was working late, and I saw your little incident going on down here, and decided to take pity on you." His tone of voice was teasing and light.

For once, Grace decided to leave it alone. Her head was hurting too much. They drove in silence for a few minutes, leaving the outskirts of town. It was darker and lights inside the car were starting to do strange things. Grace looked outside at the trees whizzing by.

"I feel sick," she muttered, clutching her abdomen.

"What?"

"Sick. I feel sick," Grace murmured feebly. This was an understatement. She felt as if she'd chugged a gallon of poison, not white wine.

Immediately, without another question, Ryan pulled the car over on the side of the road.

In a matter of seconds, Grace opened the door, leaned over and emptied the contents of her stomach on the pavement. It was all alcohol, and her throat burned when she finished.

It happened so quickly that she hadn't realized that Ryan was standing beside her, holding on to her arm. Carefully, and gently, he wiped off Grace's face with the edge of his shirt, then smoothed the hair from her face. With a firm grip, he guided her back into the vehicle, propped her up against the seat, and shut the door carefully.

"Feel better?"

"Yes," she murmured. Grace was mortified. The last time she had gotten sick in front of someone was in college, and later, when she was pregnant with Evan. Not that her son's father had been there to wipe her face—or even stay in the room. He was already gone.

Grace looked over at Ryan, trying to focus. She needed to be grateful, even if he did see her throw up on the side of the road.

"Why are you...?" Grace stopped, trying to regain her train of thought.

"Why what?" Ryan took his eyes off the road to look at her for a second. "Need to stop again?"

"No. Thank you." Grace whispered. "Why are you being so nice to me?"

Ryan turned the car slowly onto another street and eased the car forward a little faster. Grace rolled down the window. The air felt good and clean on her face. She inhaled deep, gulping breaths, trying to get oxygen into all parts of her body.

"You're Kathleen and Henry's daughter, for one." Ryan said. "And, I couldn't just leave you there to get a DUI. They might have put you in jail for the night, just for fun. The guys around here take drinking and driving pretty seriously."

Grace let her chin drop. What had she been thinking? Without Ryan's help, she certainly would have had a lot of explaining to do.

Ryan brought the car to a stop outside Kathleen's house. He put the keys in his pocket. Grace watched him, but didn't protest. She could always find the keys tomorrow, after she slept off this nightmare of an evening.

"Do you need some help getting into the house? You can hang onto my arm." Ryan held out his hand to Grace. His eyes were soft and seemed to reach out to hers, twinkling brightly in the moonlight. Grace had a hard time looking away.

"I think I can make it, but I'd like to come right back out. I really think I could use some more fresh air. Want to sit on the dock after I get cleaned up?" Grace asked, hesitating before she looked up at him.

Ryan nodded and winked. "I think someone needs to keep an eye on you."

"Give me just a minute." Grace slipped into the house. It was silent, and both bedroom doors were closed. There was a light on in Kathleen's room, but she didn't want to disturb her or talk about her night.

Grace eased into the bathroom, shrugged out of her dress and heels, washed her face with ice cold water, and brushed her teeth. It took only a few minutes, but she felt one hundred times better.

Ryan was waiting for her by the steps. "Hello again," he smiled and began walking next to her toward the dock.

Grace, still unsteady, hoped her feet wouldn't give out. One foot slid a little on the stones.

"Let me give you a hand." Ryan asked again.

Grace let him take a few fingers first, and then her palm touched his. She closed her eyes. His touch made her knees go a little weak. Did he feel her tremble? Maybe he'd think it was just the alcohol. She stole a glance in his direction. He was looking at the sky.

The moon came out from behind a cloud and illuminated the lake. Millions of stars twinkled overhead, the water shimmering beneath.

Grace sat down on the wooden planks and took her sandals off. Dipping her toes in the water, she leaned back and looked at the night sky, bracing herself on her hands. She exhaled, blowing the air out between her lips.

Ryan sat down beside her, leaving a big gap between them on the edge of the dock. "Beautiful, isn't it?"

"Amazing," Grace agreed.

"Better than the date?" Ryan laughed.

"You should have told me that guy was such a jerk," Grace chided him.

Ryan raised his eyebrows. "As if that would have mattered?"

"You're right." Grace laughed. "I can be stubborn." She splashed at the water with her toes. Sitting down made her feel better. Her head was starting to clear, like smoke floating away from a fire.

"Stubborn is an understatement," Ryan elbowed her gently.

"You could say that." Grace looked over at him. "He was late, I was early, he was dressed like a biker, and I was over-dressed. He drank too much, I drank too much, and we have absolutely nothing in common."

"Well, now you know," Ryan said, smiling broadly.

Grace rubbed at her forehead, wincing. "And now I have a terrible headache."

"Want something for it?"

"Sure. That would be great." Grace leaned back for a better view of the night sky reflecting off the lake's surface.

Ryan stood up. "It'll just be a minute. I'll bring a non-alcoholic beverage to go with it." He leaned down, as if he was ready to whisper a secret in her ear. His face was so close she could hear him breathing.

And he kissed her, with lips slow and soft. Grace melted into the warmth of his hands in her hair and on her face. It was delicious and unexpected and all together perfect.

A fish jumped and splashed the water near the dock. The sound broke the moment and they both caught their breath, looking down and away from each other.

Ryan stammered something unintelligible about Tylenol and being right back.

Grace grinned at him in the moonlight and watched him disappear into the dark near the bottom of the steps. She turned back around and faced the water.

Grace was alone again with her thoughts. Her head was spinning. It was a good thing she was sitting because she probably would have fallen down in all the excitement. She decided the best thing to do was stop thinking.

The water had never looked so inviting. It was muggy, she was hot and Ryan was gone. Without another thought, Grace stripped off her pants, slipped her shirt over her head and stood at the edge of the dock.

Poised and still, she raised her arms above her head. Taking a breath, Grace leaned forward and dove in.

Chapter 43

R YAN HEARD THE splash behind him, but thought it must have been one of the neighbors' kids throwing a rock or a ball into the water, although it was kind of late for that. Bounding up the stairs, he thought about Grace and her date, secretly glad it didn't go well.

He wondered about kissing her, but from the way she leaned into him, it had been the right choice. He hadn't been wrong that Grace felt something, too.

After rummaging through his cabinet for Tylenol or Advil and coming up only with two empty bottles, Ryan decided to try Kathleen. He'd noticed a light on earlier.

After he knocked, his neighbor came to the door on her crutches, dressed in her bathrobe and slippers, peering at him curiously over her reading glasses.

"Ryan," she said. "Is anything wrong?"

"I need some Tylenol for a patient," he quipped. "I usually have an entire pharmacy at the house, but I'm all out.

"Come on. I'll find you something." Kathleen propped open the door and motioned for Ryan to come inside.

"It seems your daughter indulged a bit much tonight at the local tavern and decided to drive home. Some of our friends at the Penn Yan P.D. were offering to assist her when I intervened," Ryan explained. "It was nothing. They were doing road checks across from the office, she was tired, and I offered to drive her home."

"Oh really?" Kathleen's eyes were wide. "Thank you. I thought I heard her come in a little while ago."

"She did," Ryan said. "She's down on the dock now getting some fresh air." He paused to look at Kathleen. She seemed relieved that her stepdaughter was home and safe.

"Good. Thanks."

"Do you mind if I grab her some water or something else to drink?" Ryan asked.

"By all means," Kathleen sat down in one of the chairs in the living room, propped up her ankle on a nearby ottoman, and grabbed a book.

Ryan opened the refrigerator door and looked inside, selecting an ice cold Diet Coke. As he shut the door, Kathleen looked up.

"And...I have to ask. How did the date go? Did she say?"

"Yep," Ryan answered. "Not so well." He tried to keep the happiness out of his voice. "I don't have many details. Don't really want them either."

"That's too bad." Kathleen met Ryan's eyes. "About the date, I mean." Her lips curved into a small smile.

"Right, too bad." Ryan echoed. They were both glad it was over. On his way back out the door, he stopped and glanced back at Kathleen. "Maybe I shouldn't have told you about her getting stopped by the police. Promise you won't say you know?"

"Promise." Kathleen crossed her fingers and held them up, a wry smile on her face. The low light from the lamp illuminated half of her face, hiding enough of it that Ryan couldn't read what she was really thinking.

She didn't say anything else and went back to the page of her novel, thumbing at the top corner.

"Need help with anything at all before I go?" Ryan paused at the door.

"Thank you, but I can manage. I'll probably be in bed by the time you come back up." Kathleen didn't look up from the book. She settled down further in her seat.

"All right. Give me a shout if you need me."

Ryan let the screen door close behind him. Peering out at the dock, he didn't see Grace waiting there. "Great." He muttered to himself.

In a few steps, his eyes adjusted to the black of the night. Her shoes were still there, sitting next to a mound of something lumpy. He squinted, trying to see what it was. He cracked open the Diet Coke and was about to take a swallow when he heard a voice.

"Hey, so you did come back." Grace called out to him, splashing the water with her hands.

Stepping onto the dock, Ryan leaned to the right. His eyes adjusted, and he could just make out her head and shoulders in the lake.

"Guess you'll need a towel."

"Oh, I hadn't thought about that," Grace giggled.

Ryan sat her Diet Coke down on the dock next to the pile of clothes. "Headache better?"

"Much. The water is therapeutic. My dad always said there was something magic about this lake. Something in the stardust, especially when it's summer," Grace tilted her head back, looking at the moon hanging low over the water. "Maybe he was right."

"There's certainly is something wonderful about it," Ryan agreed. "I can't imagine ever leaving."

"I can't believe I stayed away this long," Grace started to say, then stopped herself.

She swam a few strokes, kicking the water hard. Grace

was a strong swimmer. She dove down and Ryan lost sight of her for a minute until she burst to the surface, breathing hard.

"You could come in," Grace urged. Her voice sounded soft and low.

Ryan thought about it, resisting the temptation to rip his clothes off and dive in after her. She seemed strong and fragile all at once—the wrong move and she'd be frightened away again. "Maybe."

Grace backstroked away from him, the water frothing at her feet. Crickets sang to each other all around them. It was an orchestra of sound filling the air. A lone owl swooped from the trees, flapping his great wings.

"Why so long? Why did you wait to come here?" The words slipped out of Ryan's mouth before he could stop them.

Grace stopped swimming and treaded water, looking up at him. Ryan searched, but couldn't see her eyes. "I-I can't...I don't want to talk about it."

"It's fine. Sorry I asked," Ryan said, regretting it. In an instant, the air had changed from warm to cool around them. Hadn't he and Grace just made a connection? He thought he'd broken through her shell, just a little, with the kiss on her soft lips.

"This is a small town," Grace said, her tone taking on a slight edge. "Certainly, you must know all of the little secrets. And big ones too."

"No. Your father and Kathleen didn't share anything like that with me." Ryan said. It was the truth, but that didn't seem to matter to Henry's daughter.

Indeed, Grace didn't reply. She began to swim back toward the shore, pulling through the water in smooth, even strokes.

When she came close to the end of the dock, Grace paused, treading water. "Ryan, could you please shut your eyes so that I can get out?"

"I'll get you a towel," Ryan offered.

"No thanks. You've been very kind and I really appreciate it, especially you bailing me out. Can you turn around, please?"

Ryan folded his arms across his chest and put his back to Grace.

The water dripped as she climbed up the ladder. Scooping up her clothes, her shoes, and the Diet Coke, Grace walked away from him, shaking the dock from side to side, almost breaking into a run.

The sound of her footsteps on the wooden planks echoed off the water's surface. He could hear her feet swish over the thick grass.

Ryan's heart sank at the sound.

"Grace?" Ryan called out, finally opening his eyes. There was no answer. He turned around. The dock and the yard were empty. Grace was already gone.

Chapter 44

KATHLEEN WAS UP early to see the sunrise. She was determined to enjoy it, with the morning's vibrant pinks and purples streaking across the morning sky. She was managing better with her swollen ankle and foot. It was still bruised, awkward, and cumbersome, but Kathleen was determined not to let it slow her down too much.

Ryan checked his cell phone for messages. "You're sure there's not another thing I can do for you?"

Kathleen laughed. "I'm not helpless, Ryan. Thank you, though, for warming up my coffee and fixing me some toast."

"It's the least I can do."

"You've opened up your house and let us stay here. Henry would love you for it. I won't forget it."

Ryan waved her compliments away. "You'd do the same for me."

"Of course," Kathleen nodded.

Evan ran out of the bedroom, tennis shoes in hand, long, white shoelaces flying.

"Hey sport. We're almost ready to go." Ryan looked at his

watch. "Actually, we've gotta run. Kathleen, you have my cell phone number and the office number, right?"

"I have it all memorized. Speed dial." Kathleen grinned and pointed at her forehead.

"Good." Ryan smiled and motioned for Evan to follow him. "Ready champ?" He grabbed his keys from the hook on the wall.

"Is Mom still sleeping?" he asked his grandmother under his breath.

"I think so, sweetie. She didn't feel so well last night, so I think she needs to rest a little while longer," Kathleen explained. "But, as soon as she gets up, I'll remind her that you're working with Dr. Gordon today. I know that she'll want to hear all about it tonight."

A dark, worried look crossed Evan's face as he kissed Kathleen and hugged her tight, almost seeming like he didn't want to let go. For a moment, Ryan wondered if Evan really wanted to hang out with him at the office and play doctor-in-training. But when his grandmother released him, he followed Ryan to his truck and slid into the seat next to him.

As they sped off toward town, Ryan talked and asked him questions about school and his hometown. Evan mumbled responses and kept his eyes toward the window.

"What's on your mind? Did you want me to take you back to the cottage?"

Evan turned his head, his eyes filled with tears. He shook his head.

"I'm worried about my grandma. And my mom is acting weird."

Ryan frowned and gripped the steering wheel. He was surely intuitive for an eight-year-old. His heart went out to him.

"What's Grandma going to do without Papa around?"

"I'm here. I can help her."

Evan didn't answer. He rubbed his knees.

"Don't you think I can?" Ryan asked, frowning.

"Yes, but you're not her family."

"That's true, but I feel like she's almost family. She's kind of been like a second mom to me," Ryan said slowly. "Are you worried because she had the accident and hurt her ankle?"

Evan nodded his head furiously.

"Do you think she needs someone with her, in the house? To make sure she's all right?"

The eight-year old wiped away a stray tear. "She needs us."

"You and your mom?"

"Yes." Evan said firmly. "School doesn't start until August. We don't have to go back to Mississippi right now."

Ryan considered his words. He turned the corner and pulled into the office parking lot. Driving into the end space, Ryan stopped the car and put it in park. They sat, silent, the only sound the blowing of the air conditioner.

After a minute, Ryan said. "Evan, if you want me to, I'll try to talk to your mom about staying for a while longer. If she won't, I can probably have someone come look in on your grandma a few times a week until her ankle heals. How does that sound?"

"Good." Evan managed a small smile. "You'd do that for me?"

"Of course, buddy. Give me a couple of days to work on it."

"But we leave in a couple of days."

"Don't worry," Ryan reassured him. "I'll figure something out."

As he opened the door and stepped out of the truck, Ryan hoped he could come up with a viable plan—and fast.

A plan that included Grace staying, too.

Chapter 45

PROPPED AGAINST THE counter, balancing on one foot, Kathleen hunted for coffee. She hesitated and picked a bag of ground beans. She was pouring the water into the carafe when Grace walked in from the back bedroom.

"Good morning," Kathleen said, taking in Grace's red-rimmed, blood-shot eyes. She was moving slowly, as if she'd just finished running her first marathon minutes before. "Did you get some good rest?"

"Yes, thank you for letting me sleep. I needed it," Grace smiled weakly and turned her head, looking for Evan.

"Today was the big day," Kathleen reminded her. "He went to the office with Ryan this morning. You just missed them."

Grace rubbed at her temples, squinting up at the kitchen light. "That's right. I knew that. Was he excited?"

"I think so. Ryan made sure that I had his cell phone and office numbers all memorized in case Evan decided that playing doctor's helper wasn't for him."

"That's good," Grace said carefully and sank into the

nearest chair.

Kathleen flicked the button on the coffee pot. "So, how was last night? Did you have a good time?"

"It wasn't at all what I expected," Grace wrinkled her forehead and put her chin in both hands. "In fact, it was quite the debacle. Apparently, our contractor likes to drink—a lot—and gamble away his paycheck."

Kathleen scrunched up her nose. "Oh, Lord. I'm sorry to hear that. I had no idea."

"Me neither," Grace shrugged and feigned indifference. "We had a few drinks, never ordered dinner, and I decided to leave before things got any worse."

"Oh dear," Kathleen said and blinked. She swallowed a long list of questions, a few of which included her stepdaughter being stopped by the Penn Yan Police Department and being rescued by Ryan Gordon.

Henry, had he been alive, would have launched into a lecture about drinking too much and then driving home. He would have chided Grace for not calling, and reminded her that Evan needed his mother alive.

Today, though, it seemed useless. And she'd promised not to say a word. It was clear Grace was hurting. She was a grown woman, she'd clearly learned her lesson, and didn't need to be lectured.

"Well, what do you have on the agenda this morning? You only have a few days left." Kathleen tried to sound upbeat.

"First, I'm going to grab a hot shower," Grace said, standing up from the table. "I think, after that, I might feel almost human again."

Kathleen smiled at the comment.

Grace didn't seem to notice. "And If you don't mind," she said, pouring herself a cup of coffee, "I'm going to head to the college and poke around the library. I'd like to see where Dad worked."

"Good idea." Kathleen said, pleased that her stepdaughter had taken the initiative to see the campus. "He'd like that."

She watched as Grace made her way toward the shower, steaming coffee mug in hand. Her stepdaughter's impromptu trip to Keuka College couldn't have come at a better time.

Kathleen was expecting an important visitor.

Chapter 46

THE KNOCK ON Ryan's front door was firm.

"Kathleen?" A voice called from outside.

"Tripp, come on in," Kathleen said. "I'm here in the kitchen."

The screen door groaned as it opened. The man in the dark suit, shiny shoes and silk tie looked out of place in the comfort of Ryan's house. His smile was broad and his eyes twinkled as he peered around the kitchen and then spotted Kathleen at the table. Tripp Williams had been her family's attorney for as long as she could remember.

"Morning." His thick, overstuffed briefcase found a place on the counter. Tripp adjusted the tie around his neck, tiny beads of sweat forming on his shiny forehead. His eyes widened in surprise when he saw Kathleen's air cast under the table. "Whoa! You trying to take up mountain climbing or something?"

Kathleen chuckled. He never missed a detail, and always had a great sense of humor.

She gestured for her attorney to sit down. "Just dumb

luck, I guess. I was riding bicycles with my grandson and I swerved. Somehow I ended up over the handlebars, ahead of the wheels, and in a ditch."

Tripp whistled long and low. "And your grandson?"

"He's fine, really, thanks for asking. Evan has a few scratches. You know how kids are. They can bounce back from anything."

"That's the truth." Tripp rubbed his chin. "And how are you bouncing back from Henry being gone?" He said the words delicately, as if Kathleen would break into pieces if he talked too much.

"Oh, I've been so wrapped up with Grace and Evan visiting, then the tree fell on the house, and now this ankle…" Kathleen's voice trailed off. She always thought about Henry. She missed him terribly. "I'm fine."

"That's good to hear," Tripp nodded. "But you've had a lot happen in the past few weeks, and I'm sure it can be overwhelming. Give it a while. Time fixes a lot of things."

Kathleen didn't say anything, but wished that would work when it came to her relationship with her stepdaughter. Nothing seemed to be making it better.

Tripp cleared his throat. "So, where are Grace and Evan? I saw them at the memorial service, but didn't get a chance to speak to them."

"Grace's gone off to the college to explore a little. And Evan's at work with Ryan Gordon. He's going to see if he likes being a doctor," Kathleen smiled.

Tripp leaned on the counter with one hand, his other in his pants pocket. "Well, that's something. Good for him. Ryan always was a stand-up guy. Shame about his wife, too. Always thought they'd have a bunch of kids."

Kathleen nodded. "We were hoping the same. Things do get a little quiet around here, with Grace in Mississippi with Evan. Some little ones running around would be great."

"You'd never be bored," Tripp chuckled. "Has Grace

thought about being here—you know, permanently—with Evan? Surely she could find a job."

Kathleen looked down at the floor and back up at Tripp. Pursing her lips, she exhaled. "I'd love it, but I'm not sure she's giving it much thought right now. She has a lot on her mind, as well, with her father passing away."

Grace and Evan relocating had been what Henry wanted more than anything. Over the years, though, it seemed that the idea had slowly faded from his mind. It was like a dream that he gave up over time; it slipped out of his grasp, bit by bit.

The attorney's visit was one way for Kathleen to give Grace the option of staying once she was gone, no strings attached. Henry and she had been trying to finalize the papers for months. They had never finished.

It had fallen on Kathleen to complete. Tripp's legal assistant had been working tirelessly at Kathleen's urging to get her will and trust revised. Henry's name had to be removed, the paperwork reprinted, and signed.

It was all hers now, to do with whatever she wanted. There would be no changes to the intent of the documents, she explained. She just needed to get it done. *Before anything else happened.*

The papers spelled out the trust exactly as she remembered it. All the property and money went to Grace. She could sell the cottage or pass it down to Evan. Kathleen shuddered at the idea of strangers living in the house she and Henry loved so much. She realized she was daydreaming when Tripp cleared his throat.

"So, are we ready to review the papers and get them signed?" Tripp prompted.

"Yes. Sorry, my mind's just wandering a bit." Kathleen apologized. Did he have other clients like this—ones with messed up relationships with their kids? She wasn't about to ask.

"It's fine," he said, waving a hand in her direction. "This

is a lot to digest." Tripp grabbed the briefcase he had set on the counter. "Maybe this will help. Once Grace sees it all, she might come around."

Kathleen nodded, hoping he was right.

Tripp grabbed for the stack of papers. "Okay, let's get down to business then. It should only take a few minutes to go over this."

Tripp was a big man. He slid out a chair and sat down. The seat creaked under his weight. After thumbing through files, he found the one he was looking for and slid it out of the pile.

"Here it is."

It was a thick file, wrapped in a manila folder, with Henry and Kathleen Mason typed on the edge. Kathleen caught her breath as she looked at it. There was Henry's life, what he had left, inside the confines of about three inches of paper. It was hard to look at.

Tripp opened the papers, smoothing out the sheets for Kathleen to review.

One by one, she signed or initialed, right next to the places where Henry's name would have been.

Chapter 47

THE CAMPUS WAS quiet, with dew wetting her shoes as Grace walked from the sidewalk into the grass, cutting a direct path to the new library. The small sign on the glass of the door listed the summer hours.

She was early. The building didn't open for another hour.

Inside, the library was still dark. Grace cupped her hands around her eyes and looked in.

The building was brand new, yet built in the style of the other structures on campus. Its bricks were dark red, trimmed in white stone, with tall windows framing each wall, letting the light shine in on the hardwood floors. Rows of books were carefully stacked on shelves and new computers lined tables in the back.

"Thinking about breaking in?"

Grace nearly jumped out of her skin at the sound of an unfamiliar voice. She whirled around in surprise, almost tripping over her own feet in the process of getting away from the door window.

"Sorry I frightened you."

Grace was breathing hard. She clamped a hand to her chest, looking at the stranger. He stuck his hand out. He had a friendly face and nice eyes, and was wearing an official badge bearing the university logo. She offered her hand and he gripped it and shook it vigorously.

"Mark Jensen," he said, grinning. "I work on campus. They tell me that I'm in charge of a lot of things around here," he joked. "Most days I still feel like a student, though."

Grace smiled, talking in a rush to explain herself. "Nice to meet you. I-I'm just looking around."

Mark Jensen, who she estimated to be around forty-five, stood looking down at her, eying her curiously. Grace suddenly remembered she hadn't introduced herself.

"I'm Grace. Henry Mason's daughter. Visiting from Mississippi." She blurted out, her face getting red. Everyone knew her father.

"Ah, yes," Mark Jensen replied. "We were all so sorry to hear about Henry. He was a real gem. It was a nice service at Garrett Chapel," he added, turning to face the library. "Everyone here misses him."

"Thank you."

"So, I'm guessing that you might like to look around inside?"

"Love to." Grace wondered about her luck of running into Mark Jensen, especially when he produced a huge set of keys. He jangled them in his hand until he found the one he needed.

The lock clicked open with one turn. He pushed on the door. Grace walked inside, careful not to brush up against his arm.

The air was cool and still inside. Grace gasped at the beauty of the building. The ceiling reached three stories up, with circular hallways curving around each floor. There were paintings on walls, carefully hung, and memorabilia from the town and lake.

"How wonderful this place is. I love libraries and college campuses. Dad loved working here. He talked about it all of the time." Grace wished she'd stop chattering so much and wished Mark Jensen would stop looking at her so intently.

"It's been a great addition to the campus. The donation was very generous."

"He was a good man." Grace's eyes misted up. "He loved books."

"He certainly did."

Their conversation was interrupted by the sound of the wooden doors opening again. Footsteps echoed and Grace turned to look. A tiny woman, carrying a stack of magazines was walking slowly from a back hallway.

"Why good morning, Dr. Jensen. You're here early. Looking for anything in particular?"

Grace glanced at Mark quickly. A doctor? She was more impressed. Certainly not a serial killer. At least this lady knows who he is. Grace started to relax a little.

"No, ma'am, just giving a tour to this young lady here. This is Grace Mason. She's Henry Mason's daughter."

The tiny woman peered at Grace over her glasses. "Oh, my goodness. How wonderful! So nice to meet you." She mumbled something to herself and went back to stacking.

Grace wrinkled her forehead.

Before she could speak, Mark bent down and put his face close to Grace's ear. "She's the sweetest, hard working lady, but she's a little forgetful. Well, actually, she's a lot forgetful. But, she volunteers here and has been a librarian for forty years," Mark whispered. "Folks have to go around and re-stack the books she's just stacked. But no one has the heart to tell her it's time to retire."

Grace stifled a laugh, but wondered about the lady's reaction to her father's name. Surely he didn't know *everyone* on campus.

"Well, it was nice to meet you, Grace." Mark said. "And what is it that you do?"

"I'm a teacher's aide. Elementary school."

Mark nodded. "Excellent. No wonder you're a book lover." He smiled warmly at her. "You don't know do you?"

Grace stopped smiling. "Know what?"

"About your father?"

Grace's heart started beating faster. What in the world was he talking about?

"Your father donated the money to build this library."

"Yes, I knew that..." her voice trailed off.

Mark Jensen nodded. "That's not all. He named it after you and Evan. Your son, right?"

Grace reeled back in surprise, unable to speak. She tried to comprehend what he was saying. He pointed up to the inscription on the wall.

Sure enough, it spelled out not just Mason Library, but the *Grace and Evan Mason Library*. She stared at the words in awe, looking at the shape and shadows between each word. She was immortalized, at least her name was, in flowing silver letters.

Her father was amazing. Even in the afterlife.

Mark Jensen patted her shoulder, seeming to read her mind. "He was a very generous man. I liked him a lot. You should be proud."

Grace nodded, speechless.

"I'm sorry we had to cancel the dedication ceremony. The college is looking at rescheduling it in a few months," Mark said. "It seemed...too sudden to hold the ceremony after Henry's passing. Would you like to come back for the dedication?"

"Of course," Grace said.

"If you'll call or email with your address, I'll personally make sure that you and your son are on the VIP list—being that your names are on the library and all." Mark winked and slipped a business card out of his pocket.

"Thank you."

"It's been wonderful meeting you. But, I'm afraid that our chance encounter has put me a bit behind schedule. I've got to be on my way, now, as some people are expecting me in my office. Take care now."

"You too." Grace waved goodbye and looked down at the card.

It read, "Mark Jensen, Ph.D. President, Keuka College."

Chapter 48

RYAN AND EVAN came in the door around five o'clock, carrying bags from the local farmer's market. As they unpacked the groceries, Ryan noticed that Kathleen had managed to limp out and talk to the contractors, who were packing up their tools and heading home.

Grace was outside, reading a book on the porch swing facing the lake. She waved hello immediately. After folding down the corner of a page, she put down her novel and helped set the dinner table as Ryan threw thick, juicy steaks on the grill. Evan shucked corn, chattering and shouting above the roar of boat motors.

Ryan split his attention between Evan and the water, where everything was turning golden in the melting sunshine. Water skiers and children in tubes zoomed by, being pulled by ropes more narrow than his little finger. Sailboats drifted into the shadows and out of sight, getting one last chance to catch the wind before nightfall.

Dinner was loud and noisy, with everyone talking and telling stories about their day. The vegetables were cooked to perfection, and Kathleen and Grace praised Ryan's grilling skills.

"You've spoiled us, now," Kathleen exclaimed. "We can't move back to our house and miss your culinary skills."

"The steaks are delicious," Grace agreed, "everything is."

Ryan boasted about Evan's office skills. "You should have seen your son today, Grace. He's a natural."

Evan looked at his mother proudly. "I got to take blood pressure, listen to heart beats with a stethoscope and look in people's ears. It was cool."

"That's great, honey." Grace said, nodding enthusiastically. "It was really nice of Dr. Gordon to take you with him."

"The patients and staff loved him, of course," Ryan added. "He can come back and work with me anytime."

Evan beamed.

"And how was your day, Grace?" Kathleen asked pointedly. "Did you enjoy the college? See much of the campus other than the library?

Ryan turned to look at Grace more closely. Her eyes seemed to darken a little at the question. Under her cheerful exterior, he sensed that something was wrong. He tried to make eye contact, but she wouldn't look at him.

"It was interesting." Grace answered. "I met Mark Jensen out at the college today."

Ryan chimed in. "Good guy. He's done a lot as the new president of the school. A real go getter. Your dad thought the world of him."

"He's very nice." Kathleen nodded in agreement. "So what did he have to say? Did he give you a mini tour?"

"Kind of," Grace looked down at her plate and played with her green beans, turning them over with her fork. "Maybe we should talk about this after dinner."

Kathleen frowned. "Well, whatever for? I'd like to hear about your afternoon. Wouldn't you Evan?"

Grace's son chewed thoughtfully and shrugged.

"Did something bad happen?" Ryan asked, trying to think of what might have upset her. The staff on the campus was so helpful and nice, he couldn't imagine anyone offending her or treating her rudely.

Grace took a small sip of water. "Actually, he showed me the sign, in the library. The one they were going to unveil at the dedication," She met Kathleen's gaze, smiled tightly, and raised an eyebrow. "I was a little surprised—and thrilled—of course."

Kathleen flushed red. A hand flew to her cheek. "Oh, sweetie. I didn't tell you. I meant to, but with everything that happened. Your father's heart attack, and then the funeral..."

"And they cancelled the dedication," Grace added.

Ryan wiped his hands with a napkin and set it on the table. He wasn't following the conversation, but he certainly didn't like where it was going. The room had gone from relaxed atmosphere to heightened tension in less than thirty seconds.

"Grace, you want to fill the rest of us in here?" he asked.

"We're talking about the college library" she replied. "The new one that was just built. My father donated the money for the construction and there was supposed to be a ceremony."

"Right," Ryan prompted her to finish the story.

"So, it's named after Evan and me."

After a beat of total silence, Evan looked up at his mother. "After me? Cool? Where is it? Who did that Grandma?" His eyes twinkled excitedly.

"Your grandfather did, sweetie," Kathleen chimed in.

"That's wonderful," Ryan nodded. "I'll bet no one at your school has a building with their name on it, Evan."

"I want to see it," Evan piped up. "Can we go tomorrow? And maybe Grandma can take a picture of it."

"Sure, honey," Kathleen reached over and patted him on the leg. "Why don't you take your plate to the sink? The adults are going to sit and talk for a few minutes. You can read your book or play in the yard while it's still light outside."

"Okay," Evan got up from the table, stacked his silver-ware, and left it on the counter. After looking outside at the darkening skyline, he disappeared into his room.

When the door closed almost all the way behind Evan, Kathleen straightened up and put her hand on the table. "Grace, I am so sorry that I didn't tell you."

Ryan looked from one woman to the other.

"I just wish I would have known sooner," Grace pressed her lips together as a tear slid down her cheek.

"Grace, you were sent the invitation," Kathleen drew in her breath. "The name part, the unveiling of the sign inside the library, was supposed to be a surprise. Your father thought it would be a nice gift for Evan and you to have. Always."

The entire room was quiet again, except for the sound of the lake sloshing against the shore and a few birds calling to each other in the distance.

"We were going to tell you. Henry was going to tell you, because you weren't speaking to me. He hoped it would be a truce, kind of a peace offering," Kathleen explained. "And then he died before he could."

"You took him away from me," Grace said evenly. "You took my father away from me and from Evan."

"Grace! How could you ever say that!" Kathleen gasped and shrank back in her chair as if someone had struck her across the face.

"I don't think that's fair," Ryan said in a low voice.

"You've always hated me. Ever since—" Kathleen broke off and burst into sobs.

The bedroom door burst open.

Evan had been standing there, the entire time, listening to the conversation. He wiped away his own tears with the back of his hand. He straightened up and looked at Grace.

"You ruin everything. You said you weren't mad at Grandma. You lied." Evan stomped his foot and shook his head.

"Oh, sweetie," Kathleen turned to try and comfort him.

"Evan…" Grace started to get up from the table, but Ryan beat her to it.

He knelt down and folded Evan into his arms. "It'll be okay."

"NO!" Evan shouted, wiggling out of Ryan's grasp. He ran from the room.

The sound of a lock snapping into place reverberated through the kitchen.

"We need to talk." Ryan said to Grace, motioning for her to come outside.

Without a sound, she followed him.

Ryan took a deep breath. His mind raced. Ryan wanted to shake Grace, to inject some sense into her, and comfort her all at the same time. She was hurt, and crying, too, like a little girl lost in the woods who couldn't find her way home.

Grace wasn't angry. She had quietly asked why she hadn't been told about the dedication. This time, it seemed like the fault lay with Kathleen.

This argument, this feud that had been going on for so long, needed to stop. Somehow, someway, there had to be a solution.

It needed to end now, tonight.

Chapter 49

KATHLEEN WATCHED AS Ryan led Grace by the arm out the door. The screen door fluttered back and forth in the breeze and then closed with a click. The dinner dishes could wait, she decided. Evan was more important. Someone had to talk to him.

Shifting her weight to her good leg, Kathleen reached for the cane she had been refusing to use. She was tired though, the day had drained her. Bracing one hand against the table and pushing up, she swayed upward and stood. If this is what it's like to get old, she thought grimly, just kill me now. That's what Henry would have said.

Kathleen hobbled over to the door Evan had closed and locked. She knocked gently and called out to him. "Evan. Evan, open up."

"No." His voice was firm and defiant.

"It's only me."

"No, it's not. Mom and Ryan are there, too."

"They went outside. I promise. Cross my heart."

Silence. Kathleen held her breath and waited and pressed

her ear to the door, listening for acknowledgement.

"Come on, Evan, let me in." Kathleen thought for a moment. "I need to get something. My toothbrush."

"It's in the bathroom."

"Darn it, you're right." She snapped her fingers and smiled. Her grandson wasn't going to be fooled that easily..

"Well, how about I just need to sit down? It's pretty uncomfortable leaning against the door on one leg. You don't want me to fall over, do you?"

Kathleen thought she heard him sigh. The bed creaked loudly and there were footsteps toward the door. "Are you sure Mom is outside?" Evan said, distrust in his tone.

"Positive. She'll be outside for a while," Kathleen said, hoping it was true.

"Okay." Evan unlocked the door and slowly opened it a crack, peering through the opening up at Kathleen. His eyes were swollen and red.

"Let me in," Kathleen said.

Evan pulled open the door and stepped back, turning to flop on the bed, stomach first.

"I hate Mom," he said, muffled, into the pillow.

"What did you say?" Kathleen carefully set her cane against the dresser. She leaned over Evan, stroking his hair.

He rolled over on his back and stared at the ceiling, looking small on the big bed. He clapped his hands on his forehead. "I said," Evan paused dramatically, rolling his eyes back, "I hate Mom."

Kathleen sat down, folding her hands in her lap. She watched him as he stared at the ceiling fan, refusing to meet her eyes.

"Everyone feels that way, once in a while."

Evan glanced at Kathleen curiously, and then looked away quickly. "Even you?" He laced his fingers and slid them behind his head, stretching out.

"Oh, sure, I'd get really angry at my own mom sometimes. But we always made up. After all, she was the only mom I had."

Evan slid his knees up and rolled his head to one side. Kathleen felt like Evan was sizing her up. At least he was listening, she thought.

"What's bugging you about your mom?" Kathleen asked, trying to sound innocent.

"She said something to make you upset." Evan pouted. Kathleen tried not to smile at his bottom lip poking out. She'd never been able to resist that look, but held back from touching him now because of his outpouring. Kathleen was afraid to move, fearing he'd stop talking and shut her out.

"And she doesn't want to stay here." Evan rolled on his side. He cast his eyes down on the comforter, picking at a piece of lint.

"And you still do?" Kathleen said carefully. "You want to stay here?"

Evan shook his head vigorously. "Uh-huh." He started to tear up again.

"I'd love for you and your mom to stay," Kathleen said and patted his leg, "but it's not my decision."

They were silent, together, thinking. Kathleen's heart ached at his confession. She probed a bit more, deciding she needed to be fair.

"Wouldn't you miss your friends and your house? What about the school you go to? Wouldn't you miss all of it?"

Evan's eyes were thoughtful, as if he were chewing and digesting Kathleen's words. It was a while before he answered. The blades of the ceiling fan hummed above them as they cut through the air.

"Not really," he said, slowly and honestly, without much emotion. "I don't like my house, there's no lake there. There's not much to do, no yard to play in, and only a few kids my age around us. Just old people."

Before she could help it, Kathleen winced at the comment, hoping Evan wouldn't notice. He saw her shudder and smiled.

"Not you, Grandma," he said frankly. "I mean the ones in wheelchairs that sit and fan themselves on their front porches all day. They'd never race down a hill!"

They both laughed.

"Well, what about the school?" Kathleen asked. "You're going to be in the third grade. I can't believe it."

"No, it's nothing special. It's big and loud and hot." Evan stuck out his tongue. "The air conditioning quits all the time and when it rains, the water leaks through the ceiling. Besides, Mom doesn't like it much. The principal is always asking her out. Gross. He's fat and bald." Evan made a face and stuck his finger in his mouth like he was gagging.

Kathleen tried not to laugh. She didn't doubt it. She tried again. "What about your friends? Wouldn't you miss them?"

"I guess so. I have a few that I play baseball and soccer with. But I miss you more. I'd miss Ryan too."

Kathleen leaned over and hugged Evan close. "You're sweet to say that." She heaved a sigh, thinking about his words. "We still have a few more days together. Maybe I can send you a ticket and you can come up and visit at Christmas time, when you're on winter break."

Evan nodded, but Kathleen could see it didn't do much to soothe the ache in his heart.

Chapter 50

T HE PORCH SWING creaked as Grace sat down. She braced her feet on the floor and swayed back and forth, watching Ryan's face.

"I know that you want to help," Grace began. She didn't need her father's friend to try and fix things. He might make things worse, and she was confused enough. "And I'm not sure that this involves you."

"In any other circumstance, I would agree," Ryan argued, his tone stern. "But this is about more than just a disagreement or lack of communication." He paused and ran a hand through his hair. "I'm living with the three of you in my house, and not that it gives me a right to inject my opinion, but I see some of what's going on and I care."

Grace turned toward Ryan and propped her elbow on the back of the porch swing, looking into his eyes. "I know," she said softly.

Ryan cleared his throat. "Okay. Well, yes, I think that Kathleen should have told you. If I would have known, I would have reminded her to fill you in about the details of the dedication. But she didn't and she's human. She's lost someone and is hurting too."

Grace rubbed her bottom lip and drew back from Ryan a few inches. She looked at the long, thick planks of wood beneath her feet. Her eyes stung with tears. It was her father. Her blood, Evan's grandfather. It meant more to her. It hurt more.

Ryan hesitated. "Please. Let me explain."

Grace looked up at him. He was so hopeful she'd listen, so convincingly honest in his feelings, and so damned handsome. Grace felt herself melt a little. Ryan cared—he really cared about her and Evan.

Ryan sat down on the porch swing next to Grace. He eased back and shifted in the seat. He locked his eyes on Grace.

"Your parents are special to me. They were there for me when my wife left. I was in denial; paralyzed when she filed for divorce. All I could do was work and sleep. Your father cut the yard, brought me the mail, and your stepmother cooked for me more than a few times. Basically, they got me living again—interacting with the world like a human, not a robot."

Grace searched his face. "What happened? With your marriage?"

"I was married to work, basically. I put all of my energy into building my practice and didn't leave any time for a personal life. I was focused on my patients, keeping up with my charts, making sure that the office ran smoothly," Ryan explained. "Lori—that was my wife—tried to tell me. She finally decided that she'd had enough and left."

"It must have been quite a shock."

"At first," Ryan admitted. "I was stubborn and hard-headed about the break up. I thought that she'd come back. When she didn't, I was angry for a long time," he added. "I spent a lot of time talking to Henry about it. I even went to a few counseling sessions. Eventually, after a lot of soul searching, I realized that I was mostly to blame."

Grace inhaled at the confession. It took a lot of bravery to share things so personal and deep.

"If I had to do it over again, I would do it all differently. I would be a better husband and partner. I would have paid attention to the little things," Ryan said. "I would have been better about admitting my faults and listening to the people who loved me. And I would have argued less and practiced a lot more forgiveness."

"So, she did try to tell you?"

"Only a million times," Ryan said with a rueful smile. He reached out and gave Grace a playful poke.

Grace grinned. "Well, I know that you have to be a hot commodity, being a single doctor and all." It was said in a teasing way, but she wanted to know what he'd say. Surely, he'd had the opportunity to date whomever he wanted. He was gorgeous, smart, and available. "I'll bet you have women beating down your door and burning up your cell phone," she joked.

"Maybe, maybe not." Ryan rubbed his chin. "For a long time, I wasn't ready for any sort of relationship. If I did meet someone, she wasn't the right person, or it just didn't work out."

"I understand that," Grace said. "Evan's father bolted out the door and out of the country as soon as he found out I was pregnant."

"Nice guy," Ryan said, rolling his eyes.

"Didn't make me want to jump into any other relationships, either." Grace bit her lip. "I couldn't handle getting hurt again."

"I understand that."

"My mother never got to see Evan. She died before he was born."

Ryan reached over and squeezed Grace's hand. His touch was warm and secure. She was sorry when he pulled his hand away.

"So, do you want to tell me about Henry and Kathleen? What happened after your Mom died?"

Grace took a deep breath. Ryan had shared so much with her. She could do the same. It might help him understand about staying away from Henry for so long.

"Kathleen and my mother were best friends since grade school. They did everything together. They even went to the same college and opened up a small business together. They had a cute little dress shop in town. It was really successful," Grace explained. "That was how they both met my father."

Ryan nodded, prompting her to go on.

"Apparently, Kathleen was immediately smitten and flirted to beat the band. My mom wasn't interested—she was dating someone else at the time—so she didn't pay him much attention," Grace said. "When my mother broke it off with her boyfriend, my father was there, waiting in the wings, swooped in, and asked her out."

"How did that go over between the two of them? The women?"

"Well, knowing that Kathleen really liked Henry, she said no," Grace laughed. "Apparently, my father asked her out a dozen times before he wore her down and she finally said yes. I think it took him all of six months."

Ryan grinned. "That sounds like Henry."

"It caused a bit of a rift between my mother and Kathleen. They both liked him. Kathleen said that she saw him first—this is all coming from my mother—I certainly wasn't there," Grace said and shrugged. "But it did strain their friendship. Eventually, they put it behind them and my mother asked Kathleen to be the maid of honor in her wedding."

"And she did?"

Grace nodded. "Kathleen got married, too, shortly after that. It was the first guy she'd met and talked to after my father finally got my mother to agree to a date. Not, probably, the smartest move, but at the time, it must have helped her heart stop hurting a little bit."

It was Ryan's turn to agree. "Yes, I think so."

With a large sigh, Grace rubbed her cheek, thinking carefully about the story her mother recounted. She hoped that it wasn't a problem to share it with Ryan. He cared about Kathleen, he was a doctor, and of all people, Ryan would understand.

"So, shortly after Kathleen got engaged," Grace continued, "her fiancé started beating her."

Chapter 51

IT WAS A slap at first, then a black eye. A year later, a broken rib or two. He'd always promise to stop," Grace continued. "He'd apologize and say it would never happen again. At the time, it wasn't quite as easy or acceptable to get a divorce, especially in Mississippi. Even now, there's a one year waiting period to end your marriage. Her husband made sure that she knew that."

Ryan set his jaw and shook his head. Grace watched his expression go from intent and interested to disgusted at the details.

"So Kathleen was trapped. She had quit her job at the shop to stay home so she didn't have much in the way of pocket money. My mother tried to help her as best she could, but she was pregnant with me and had bouts of intense morning sickness—the sort that lasted all day."

Grace paused and took a breath.

With understanding, Ryan added, "So it wasn't like your mom could just come to the rescue every time Kathleen needed help."

"No, that finally fell to my father," Grace explained. "He could never say no to anyone who needed it, and my mother wouldn't have wanted him to."

"Did it cause more problems? With the husband?" Ryan asked.

"Things didn't get any better. If he saw my father, he'd pretend nothing happened or he'd fly into a rage and my dad would have to drag him off somewhere and get him calmed down—a bar, the bowling alley. Anywhere other than his house."

"Didn't she ever call the police?"

Grace drew one leg up and set her foot on the edge of the swing. "It wouldn't have done any good. Kathleen's husband was an attorney—a defense lawyer whose clients were among the bottom feeders of Biloxi and the gambling world."

"So he had connections? The police, other lawyers, some judges, maybe?"

"Exactly," Grace confirmed. "And he held that over her head like a blanket, threatening to smother her with it. According to my parents, he was charming and handsome, well-dressed, with money to spend, but underneath it all, he was one of the most cruel men they'd ever met."

"Sounds like it."

"By then, several years had passed. I was growing up and only occasionally heard about Kathleen. I knew that they were trying for a baby. My parents talked about it a lot after dinner when I was supposed to be in bed," Grace cocked her head and cupped a hand around her ear. "I could hear them through the vents. For some reason, and I didn't understand it at the time, Kathleen always lost the baby."

Ryan rubbed his hands down his pant legs and looked out on the lake. Grace was certain he understood. He was silent, listening, taking in the awful story.

"One day, Kathleen saw my mother and me in the grocery store. They hadn't seen each other in a while, maybe six or seven months. Both of them hugged, and I remember thinking that when my mother stepped back, I had never seen Kathleen look so different. She was round and glowing. Happy."

"So she was pregnant and pretty far along? In her last trimester?"

"I think so," Grace agreed. "I was in high school and I remember my mother remarking that it was a little late for her to be having a baby. Both women were in their late thirties. But she tried to be happy for Kathleen. She stopped talking about it when I asked too many questions."

Ryan moved his hand closer to Grace, rubbing one finger along the smooth white paint. His face bore a thoughtful, pained expression. Realization about his neighbor's secret life.

Grace swallowed hard. "The last thing that happened was that my father went away on a long business trip. I remember it being important, because it was to a big city, like Philadelphia. He had promised to bring me home some souvenirs, a miniature Liberty Bell, something like that so that I could show my history class."

In the distance, birds called out to each other over the lake, swooping and diving in the morning sun. Chipmunks chattered and fussed over nuts, scampering to hide them in the nearest tree.

Grace smiled at their antics. She didn't want to remember the next part. It had been years since she'd shared it with anyone. To say the words out loud made them real. And that made the pain of losing her mother worse, even now.

"So the ending of the story isn't a happy one," she continued. "My mother got a phone call in the middle of the night. It was Kathleen. She was hysterical, crying, screaming into the phone. I can see myself standing in the doorway of my mother's bedroom, half-asleep, but wondering what all of the fuss was about."

Ryan tilted his head toward Kathleen's cottage.

"My mother bundled me up in a coat. I was still in my

pajamas, and I think that my mom had rushed out of the house so quickly that she still had her slippers on. In the dark, along the highway near the ocean, we drove to where Kathleen lived. It was the night of a full moon, and all of the stars were out, glittering and reflecting on the waves. It was so beautiful, and I felt safe snuggled next to my mother, lying down with my head in her lap."

Grace caught her breath and made herself slow down. Her heart was beating so fast that her chest began to ache with the pounding inside. She dragged her toes along the planks under her feet, willing herself to continue.

Ryan slid an arm around her shoulders and squeezed. "You don't have to finish now. We can talk later," he said. "Or not."

The story needed to be finished. Grace drew some strength from the warmth of Ryan's arm around her. She didn't know what it meant, other than it was a kind gesture between friends, and for right now, that was enough. She was lucky to have it.

"I don't remember the rest very well," Grace admitted. "There was a big truck with a huge, loud engine that was directly in front of us. My mother was worried because the man wasn't going the speed limit and was driving pretty erratically. I know that he was carrying a big load of tree logs, because that's what the police and rescue squad people told me later. The doctors and nurses said that I was lucky to be alive," she said.

Ryan jerked with the realization of what Grace was saying. His fingers gripped her shoulder, drawing her closer. She could feel his breath, warm on her neck.

"The man swerved and lost control of the semi. The logs hadn't been secured and a few slid off. My mother didn't have time to get out of the way. She was killed instantly, and I would have been too, had my head not been in my mother's lap."

"Jesus Christ," Ryan muttered under his breath. In a state

of shock, he drew his hand away from Grace's shoulder and stopped the swing. He stood up and began to pace back and forth on the porch, arms crossed on his chest. "I had no idea. I can't imagine how horrible that must have been for you."

"I don't remember much. I was in and out for a while. The rescue squad had to cut me out of the vehicle, but I don't have a memory of that, either."

Ryan turned to face Grace and leaned against the house. "So, you blame Kathleen for losing your mother? Is that what this is about? All of the tension between you?"

The air felt heavy and muggy then, hard to breathe. Grace didn't reply at first. She knew it was how she'd felt for a long time, holding in untold amounts of anger, brimming, overflowing, spilling out of her in endless supplies.

Somehow, after almost ten days of living and breathing in the same house, of watching her son interact with her mother's best friend, some of the regret and sadness had slipped away.

"Until now, yes, I think so. I couldn't bring myself to forgive her. I did blame her. I wasn't even twenty and my mother was gone," Grace said, her voice catching. "If Kathleen never would have made that phone call, if she never would have married that terrible man. If she never would have gotten pregnant..."

"Maybe, despite everything that had happened to her, she still was hoping for a little happiness," Ryan said.

"It's true. She didn't have much joy in her life," Grace agreed. "But everything changed for her after my mother died."

"She lost the baby?"

"Yes," Grace said and looked up at Ryan. "She did. And I can't imagine how that must have felt. She filed for divorce soon after. It was granted after a year. Her husband, surprisingly, didn't put up a fight. I think he found someone else in one of the casinos. Someone younger and very foolish."

"And Henry was there for her?" Ryan pressed his lips

together in a straight line.

Grace nodded. "All of the time. He took care of me, got me well, and I was busy applying to college and going out with my friends, trying to forget that my mother was really gone. If I didn't stay in the house—if I stayed out of her bedroom—and away from everything that reminded me of her, I was able to get through the day," she said. "I didn't even realize what was happening right in front of me."

"Kathleen and Henry?"

With a shake of her head, Grace struggled to continue. She dabbed at the dampness around her eyes. "They came in the house one night, much later. I think I was on the phone or doing homework. I didn't pay much attention to them, how happy they looked," she said and winced. "I was so wrapped up in being sad about my mother."

"And then what happened?" Ryan asked gently.

"They told me they were getting married and moving to Upstate New York. That my father had been offered this wonderful position at Keuka College. They were thrilled and talked non-stop about it...until they realized that I wasn't answering either one of them," Grace said. "I ran out the door and over to a friend's house. I think I stayed there for about a week."

They both watched as a duck swooped down and landed on the water, wings fluttering and then folding gently against its body. Ripples of water fanned out from where it lay.

"Have you ever talked to Kathleen about this? Does she know this is how you feel?" Ryan asked.

Grace pressed her lips together and thought about this. "She should know," she said finally. "How couldn't she? If she wouldn't have called my mother and we hadn't been on the road—"

"No one could have predicted that," Ryan argued, cutting in. "I think if she'd known there would be an accident, if she could predict the future, she never would have asked your mom to come and help her."

With a begrudging nod, Grace agreed. "I know. I see that now. I guess that I've always been waiting for her to bring it up. For her to apologize. But she's never said a word."

Ryan rubbed his cheek with his palm and wrinkled his brow. "Well, maybe she thinks you won't listen. You haven't exactly made it easy to have a heart-to-heart," he said. "You might have to make the first move. Tell her you'd like some time to talk about everything. Clear the air."

Grace folded her arms, hugging them to her chest. He was right. Ryan was the voice of reason, the logic to her conflicted emotions. Grace memorized the look on his face against the backdrop of trees and blue sky. He smiled at her, then reached over and smoothed a stray hair, tucking it behind her ear. His hand rested on her cheek for a moment.

"Thank you for telling me about your mom. It must have been hard to share that. I can't imagine what you went through," Ryan said.

"It still hurts a lot," Grace admitted.

"I understand, now, why you've got so much tied up inside you. So many painful memories, so much confusion about the past," Ryan said. "I know now why it's so hard to be around Kathleen."

A thick lump began to grow in Grace's throat. She didn't want to start crying in front of Ryan. It had been a long time since she'd shared this much about her family with anyone. She was suddenly exhausted, but somewhat relieved at the same time.

"This is just my opinion, and you can take it or leave it, but I think Kathleen needs a second chance," Ryan added. "Everyone does."

Grace sucked in a deep breath. She had all of twenty-four hours before she and Evan had to leave. *Would she have the strength to go through with it? How would she bring it up? What would Kathleen say?*

She felt Ryan's gaze. He was watching her closely, looking

for any reaction.

"You're right," Grace replied, raising her eyes to meet his.

He smiled when she answered, his whole face lighting up with her response. "Good."

"I'll talk to her. I promise," she replied, "before I leave."

"That's all I'm asking."

Ryan stood up then and steadied the porch swing. He turned to leave, but then seemed to reconsider. Before Grace realized what was happening, he reached down and kissed her cheek.

"I really care about you, Grace," he whispered. "I want you to be happy."

With that, Ryan walked away, his loafers making a brushing sound against the wood of the porch steps.

Chapter 52

KATHLEEN'S EARS PERKED up when she heard her grandson's voice change from sweet to strained and upset.

"Tomorrow? Why does it have to be tomorrow?" Evan said, his voice cranked up to a whine.

There was a soft response from Grace, likely explaining why it was time to leave. A moment later, Evan ran into the living room, away from his mother and their conversation. He was breathing hard and flushed, eyes red-rimmed. Without stopping to look at Kathleen, Evan launched himself, face-first, onto the couch. He gripped the nearest pillow, pulled it to his chest, and buried his face.

Grace rushed out after him, apologizing. "I'm sorry, Evan. It's how I planned the trip. Wednesday is when our plane leaves. Don't you miss home?"

Evan raised his head and inch and gave his mother a stony look. "No. I like it here," he sputtered. "I don't want to leave. Ever!"

Kathleen blinked, unprepared for Evan's outburst. She held herself back from going over to the sofa and comforting him. It was up to Grace to handle the situation right now, though it pained her not to step in and help.

"Evan," Grace said sternly and put her hands on her hips. "Go to your room until you can cool off."

"But Ryan promised to take me on the wave runner." Evan sat up straight and recoiled at Grace's response. His eyes were big and watery, tears threatening to spill over.

"I'll think about it." Grace replied. "The bedroom," she commanded again.

Evan stormed out of the room. He grabbed for the handle of the door and slammed it shut behind him, making the windows shake. There was the sound of the bed creaking and shoes kicked off onto the floor.

Her stepdaughter was visibly shaken. Grace bit her lip, staring at the bedroom door.

"He'll be okay," Kathleen said after a beat. "Why don't you take a few minutes and get a breath of fresh air? Take a walk or run down to the store?"

Grace pressed her fingers to her temples. "I think I will," she replied. "That's a good idea."

"I'll stay here and listen for him," Kathleen offered. "By the time you get back, maybe he'll be feeling better. He'll be back to his sweet self and can spend some time on the wave runner. I know that he'd hate to miss that."

"I know," Grace agreed, letting her hands drop to her sides. Her shoulders slumped a little. "He just never talks to me like that. I-I'm shocked."

Kathleen inhaled and nodded, encouraged that Grace was actually sharing her feelings. She had to be careful. Everyone was so emotional. She just wanted to be supportive.

"He loves you so much," Kathleen said. "I think he's had a hard time with all of this, too, even though he didn't know his grandfather very well. Death is scary for anyone, but especially so for children." She paused. "You know, he's probably afraid that he's going to lose you, too."

This made Grace wince. She blinked and looked at the bedroom door. "You're right," she murmured. "I didn't think about that."

Kathleen kept quiet and watched as her stepdaughter weighed these ideas.

"I think I will go out for a few minutes. I'll run to the store and pick up some milk and fruit," Grace said, picking up her purse and keys. "You're okay with watching Evan?"

"Of course. Take all of the time that you need," Kathleen said.

Grace managed a small smile and thanked her. She slid on her sunglasses and cast one last glace at Evan's door.

K ATHLEEN LISTENED TO Grace turn on the car and pull out of the driveway. The familiar sound of tires on gravel brought back memories of Henry leaving early in the morning. She hadn't had time to miss their routine, but would have plenty of time to think about it when Grace and Evan left.

Evan. She wanted badly to comfort him and tell him everything would be okay. Kathleen cocked her ear, listening for a sound from the bedroom where Evan had locked himself inside. A few minutes ago, she had heard some banging around, perhaps in one of the closets. She assumed he was looking for a toy or a book to read and hadn't wanted to ask for help.

Clouds had started to gather, gray and dark, outside the kitchen window. A slight breeze was playing in the curtains and Kathleen thought for a moment that it might be best to close all of the windows because it might rain. Reaching for the sill, she pulled gently to close the glass. Turning the latch, she locked the window in place, closing off the flow of air from the outside.

There was still no sound from Evan. She expected him to run out after Grace had left, asking for a piece of toast or fruit, complaining that he was hungry. Or, maybe he'd want to play cards or have Kathleen watch him swim. Kathleen took a few steps toward the door, her bare feet making no sound on the floor. She rapped her knuckles lightly on the door.

"Evan. Evan?" Kathleen listened for an answer. She knocked again, more firmly this time. Kathleen placed her hand gently on the doorknob. "Evan, I'm going to come in now and talk to you. Just warning you that I'm coming in."

Kathleen turned the knob ever so slightly, thinking it would be locked, but it gave way easily and she pushed the door open, peering inside.

The room was dark and the bed covers were rumpled. One pillow was on the floor and the other, under the comforter. From the sight of the bumps on the bed, Kathleen thought for a moment that Evan had fallen asleep under the covers. Lifting them up, she saw nothing but wrinkled white sheets underneath.

Kathleen felt a breeze on her arms and shivered, then heard the sound of raindrops against the window. She turned to look, and then focused on the chair underneath the window sill. It was a stool, actually, that had been pushed underneath, as if someone wanted to climb out. Gasping at the thought, she ran to the window and examined the dark mesh of the screen. It was open at the bottom, like someone had raised it and lowered it, but not all the way.

Kathleen felt the room begin to swim and her stomach lurch. "Evan, Evan, answer me," she called. But she knew it was in vain. Evan was gone.

She gripped the top of the dresser for balance and tried to gather her thoughts. Her purse was on its side, the wallet open. She reached for it, hands trembling. Unfolding the wallet, Kathleen looked inside.

It was empty. There had been several twenty and ten dollar bills inside, how much exactly, she didn't know. Evan had to have taken it, there was no other explanation.

Flipping on the light, Kathleen searched the rest of the

room for clues or a note. Surely he would have left something. She looked under the bed, inside the closets and around the suitcases. She found nothing.

Kathleen sank down on the edge of the bed, her head in her hands. Her thoughts were frantic and erratic. Where would he have gone? And why? The answer to the second question was clear. *Grace.*

Kathleen wiped at her eyes. They were stinging and dry. Her mouth was like sandpaper. Kathleen wiped at her forehead. It was time to think clearly. Kathleen took a deep breath, trying to clear her head. What would Henry do? She had all but lost her stepdaughter, but she wasn't going to lose her grandson. One way or another, she would find him.

She heard the front door slam and Grace's voice call out. Kathleen walked to the doorway of the bedroom and stood in the frame.

Grace was bent over, placing a gallon of milk and some cheese into the refrigerator. She stopped when she saw Kathleen's expression.

"What?" She straightened up, a confused look on her face, trying to anticipate what her stepmother was going to say. "What is it?"

"It's Evan." Kathleen managed to say his name in a whisper, starting to cry. "He's gone."

Chapter 53

GRACE TRIED TO comprehend the words her stepmother had just spoken. "He's gone?"

Kathleen nodded, one hand pressed to her chest.

"Are you sure? He's got to be hiding. He likes to do that at home." Grace said. She was making excuses and knew it, trying to stay calm.

"I checked the bedroom, the closet, under the bed and the covers."

Grace started pacing, trying to ignore the panic catching in her throat, her heart beating twice as fast as normal. She started calling Evan's name.

Kathleen interrupted. "I found the window in the bedroom open part way. A stepstool was pushed underneath it."

Grace stopped and stared at her stepmother, unblinkingly. "What did you say?" Grace wasn't sure she wanted to hear it.

"I think he may have crawled out the window."

"He wouldn't leave," Grace exclaimed. "He couldn't." As she said the words, she began opening closets and peeking under tables in a frenzied pace. Striding to the sliding glass door, she pulled hard for it to open and stood on the porch, calling Evan's name.

"He's got to be here. He's just upset." Grace was talking to herself, more than anyone else, trying to make herself feel better.

Out of the corner of her eye, she saw Ryan through the window of his house. "Maybe Evan's next door," she said to Kathleen.

Grace waved her hands furiously at Ryan to come out on his porch.

Ryan finally looked up, his eyebrows knitted together; trying to figure out what Grace could want that was so urgent. "Need some help?" He offered.

"Do you have Evan?" she called out. "Is he over there with you?"

Ryan looked at Grace blankly and then cast a look back inside his open door. "No," he said slowly. "I haven't seen him in a while. Why?" He started to look concerned, which wasn't making Grace feel any better.

Ryan seemed to read the seriousness of the situation without Grace saying a word. Kathleen stepped out on the porch, arms crossed tightly in front of her chest.

"I checked the garage," she said. "One of the bicycles is missing."

Grace gasped.

"I'm coming over," Ryan yelled. "Give me a sec."

Less than two minutes later, there was a rap on Kathleen's front door and Grace heard his voice calling out. "He's really gone?" Ryan exclaimed. He had jogged across the lot and was breathing hard.

Grace nodded, trying to stay calm. Her skin prickled with worry. Horrible thoughts raced in circles in her head.

"We've looked everywhere."

Ryan nodded. "Kathleen, we're going to look for Evan.

Can you stay here by the phone and wait? Maybe call some friends and ask them to be on the lookout? Someone needs to stay here in case he comes back."

"Of course."

Grace grabbed for her car keys.

Ryan put his hand on hers. "I'm driving. You can spend your time looking and thinking about where he might have gone. You can spot him more easily than I can."

Before they left, Grace stopped and hugged Kathleen. Her stepmother was pale and stricken with grief, wringing her hands. She dabbed at her eyes with a tissue.

"It's not your fault," Grace said, her own eyes filling with tears.

Ryan reached over and squeezed Kathleen's shoulder. "We'll find him, okay?"

Chapter 54

G RACE LOOKED AT Ryan's hands as he drove. They were solid and capable. How may people had he cared for? How many lives had he saved?

He was sweet and good. Such a wonderful, kind person. He didn't have any obligation to find Evan or to help her fix her problems. It must be true. He cared about her a lot.

They were nearing his office. Grace looked over at Ryan quizzically. "Your office?"

He pulled into the driveway and parked. "You never know."

"Okay," she said, following him up the ramp and to the door.

"He liked it here. Maybe he thought this was a safe place to go."

But the office was empty and dark. There was no sign of life anywhere. The doors to the rooms were open, white paper on each exam table, ready for patients. The halls were dark and their footsteps echoed as the walked from one room to another, checking to make sure Evan wasn't behind one of the doors.

"I keep it locked, but Evan's smart enough, he could have found a way in." Ryan paused at the door to his office. "I don't have a security system. Just never got around to it, I guess."

"He's not here," Grace said out loud. She knew she was stating the obvious and was starting to feel hopeless. "Where could he be? I just can't believe he'd take off like this. It's so unlike him."

Ryan walked toward the door. Grace followed him, not knowing where to go next. Ryan drove away from the office, heading toward the far end of the lake. She didn't ask where they were going. She didn't know what to do, so she let him drive.

The sun was sinking in the west, causing streaks of purple and pink to cut across the deep blue of the sky. Grace watched as the scene before him changed and unfolded as the yellow ball got lower and lower, finally out of sight behind the hills in the distance.

She decided that it was possible Evan went up to the place where Henry's memorial service was held. Perhaps he wanted to say goodbye, or talk to him, in the peace of the building, away from all of the adults.

"What about Garrett Chapel? It's a stretch, but I think we should take a look?"

Ryan nodded. "Good idea. Let me turn here. We'll be there in a few minutes."

Grace's fingers twisted and squeezed together in her lap. Her lips parted, and she kept her eyes half-closed, praying for Evan's safety or a miracle.

As they rolled along, turning and shifting with the curves of the road going up the hill, Ryan decided to break the silence. "Evan's a great kid."

She looked over at him, eyes sore from crying, but dry. "Yes, I was just thinking the same thing." She sniffed back a tear and rubbed at her nose. She drew in a ragged, tired breath.

"We'll find him," Ryan said, his voice confident. His hand slid across the seat, fingers finding Grace's palm.

She trembled at the touch, so wanting to believe Ryan's words. Grace knew that neither one of them were going to give up until they found her son. If it took them a week, and Evan was on top of the Empire State Building in New York City, they would track him down.

They reached the top of the hill. The shadows were getting longer over the road and the sky was turning gray. They stopped at the edge of the chapel parting lot. Both opened the doors of the car simultaneously. The air had a slight chill.

Grace shivered, looking at the empty parking lot. "He's not here," she cried out, walking away from the car toward the chapel. Her voice was carried off in the evening breeze. "He's not here. There's no bicycle."

"You don't know that," said Ryan following after her. "He could have put it anywhere."

Grace broke into a run. She reached the doors of the chapel, breathing hard. Her hands pressed up against the wood, then pulled at the giant doorknobs. They wouldn't budge. Grace tugged angrily, without success.

Ryan came up behind her, gently moving her away. He knocked hard with his knuckles. The sound echoed in the trees surrounding the chapel.

The sound of metal on metal startled them both. Grace and Ryan stepped back from the doors of the chapel as they swung open.

All at once, Grace burst into tears when Reverend Spencer's face appeared in the opening. At the sight of the minister's kind expression, she covered her own face with her hands, sobbing.

Ryan's arm slid around her shaking shoulders. He squeezed her gently.

"We're looking for Evan."

Grace heard Reverend Spencer's muffled reaction.

"Evan?"

"And if he's not here," Ryan added, "then, we need a miracle."

Chapter 55

KATHLEEN HUNG UP the phone. The police officer said there was no sign of Evan anywhere around town. They would be patrolling all night, on the lookout for a little boy on a bicycle.

The fire chief had assured her he would call if Evan turned up, taking her home phone number just in case.

Tripp, her attorney, offered to drive around the lake, stopping at restaurants or ice cream shops. She thanked him and said, yes, that would be fine. He promised to swing by at the Mennonite farm on the top of the hill first. Perhaps he went to visit Adam's family?

Her hands dropped in her lap. She stared out the window, unable to see what usually gave her so much pleasure.

The lake, filled with boaters, the trees swaying in the night air, and the cool breeze coming through the window did nothing to comfort her. She was numb with fear, too frightened to think of what could have happened to Evan.

Kathleen sat next to the window, Henry's ashes by her side. She lit a candle, the flame illuminating the carving in the sides of the box. The wood glowed reddish brown. She felt it necessary to bring her husband along. Henry would give her strength.

"Where is he? Where did he go?" Kathleen spoke softly to Henry, knowing he wouldn't answer.

The candle flickered and cast her shadow on the wall, long and lean. The sun was dropping in the distance, coloring the sky.

The phone rang. Kathleen said a silent prayer it was Grace, telling her she had Evan in the car, they were coming home and everything would be all right.

The voice on the phone was Reverend Spencer's. "Grace and Ryan Gordon were just here. They wanted me to check in with you. They haven't found Evan yet."

Kathleen's heart sank. She clutched the phone tighter and tried to breathe. Kathleen swallowed, trying to catch her breath.

"Kathleen? Are you there?" Reverend Spencer's voice was urgent. "What can I do? Shall I come to the house? Please say something."

"I'm here," Kathleen managed to say in a small voice.

"I know you must be panicking. Of course, you've called the police?"

"Yes, everyone," Kathleen said. "They're all looking, everyone is looking." She stared out into the growing darkness. "We're looking for him, too. But, it's getting to be nighttime. And he could be all alone, lost…" Her voice broke. "And it's my fault."

"Nonsense," Reverend Spencer said firmly. "You can't blame yourself for this. What could you have done to cause him to run away?"

Kathleen thought for a moment, and then answered. "Everything."

Chapter 56

R YAN'S PHONE BEGAN to hum as he and Grace drove back toward town. Lights across the lake were flickering on, like houses winking at each other across the pool of deep water. Grace had always loved this time of the day. But tonight, the growing darkness seemed to put her further away from finding Evan.

Her hand squeezed at the damp tissues she held in her lap. They bumped along the road in silence, swerving to avoid potholes and sticks.

Ryan snapped the phone from its holder, looked at the caller ID and held it up to his ear. "Ryan Gordon," he answered. His voice was tense.

Grace tried to listen to parts of the conversation. She heard the other person talking in a muffled voice. A patient, she was sure. Ryan's beeper had been going off incessantly.

"Really?" Ryan's voice brightened. He grinned at Grace.

"What?" She mouthed, pressing a hand on his leg. "Tell me!" A thrill of excitement coursed through her.

Ryan handed the phone to her wordlessly and put both

hands back on the wheel, still smiling. He pressed the accelerator with such force that Grace was slammed back into her seat.

She almost dropped the phone, but managed to catch it before it fell to the floor mats.

"Hello?" Her voice shook with anticipation.

"Miss Mason, we have some very good news."

RYAN WATCHED AT the needle of his speedometer hit eighty on the road leading downtown. He turned the corner to the college on two wheels, squealing the tires. Grace hung on for dear life, smiling from ear to ear. They grinned at each other deliriously.

Ryan pulled up to the library, parking in dead center in front of the steps. The library was lit up, every light on. The front doors were propped open.

Grace jumped out before Ryan could get it into park. Bounding up the steps, she ran through the doors and looked around, the light blinding her momentarily. Evan and Dr. Mark Jensen were waiting at a table in the corner of the room.

"Mom!" Evan called out to her.

"Oh sweetie!"

Evan ran to Grace and threw his arms around her waist. Grace started crying all over again, tears hitting the top of Evan's head. She put her hands on his shoulders and held him out at arm's length, not letting go.

"Let me look at you. Are you all right?" She ran her eyes along his arms and legs, searching for signs of a struggle or fight.

"I'm fine."

Grace squeezed him again, this time tighter.

Ryan jogged through the doors and over to where Grace and Evan were standing in their embrace. He squeezed Evan's shoulder playfully.

"Hey, sport. Am I ever glad to see you! You gave us all a big scare. Your mom and grandma were really frightened something bad had happened to you."

Evan hid his head in Grace's shirt.

Mark Jensen walked up and shook Ryan's hand. "Nice to see you, Doc."

"Thanks. You found him?" Ryan raised an eyebrow and looked in Evan's direction and then back at Mark.

"The campus security department did." Mark chuckled.

"Really?" Grace looked up from Evan.

"Seems this guy here had come into the library, hid himself in the stacks near the back wall and fell asleep."

"Yeah." Evan volunteered. "I hid Dr. Gordon's bike behind the library. I came inside and lay down. I was real tired after riding all the way here."

Mark nodded. "Apparently, when he woke up, all the lights were off and everyone had left the building. Locked up for the night."

"It was dark and spooky!" Evan's eyes were wide. "And so I tried to leave."

Grace hugged her son close and stroked his hair. She leaned over and kissed the top of his head.

"That's when the alarm sounded," Mark explained. He looked at Evan, amused. "The security guards get a call from the building in case someone tries to break in. In this case, someone was trying to break *out*. When no one here answered the phone call, they sent an officer to check it out. And, of course, they called me and my staff right away."

"He gave me snacks. I was hungry," Evan said.

"He was a hungry little boy all right," Mark agreed. "Two bags of chips, a snickers bar and a can of Sprite."

Grace kneeled down next to Evan and looked him in the eyes. "Please don't ever do this again. You scared me and a lot of other people who care about you."

Evan nodded, his eyes starting to water. He rubbed at

them with the back of his fists.

"It's all right, honey. You're safe now." Grace stood up and turned to Mark. "Thank you so much."

"No problem. Just glad he's all right." Mark shoved his hands into his pockets. "If it's all right, I've got to get home. I'm going to shut off the lights and lock up. Again." He smiled at Evan.

Grace took Evan's hand and began to lead him toward the doors.

"Oh, come back any time." Mark called out. "During school hours, of course."

"Thanks. I will." Evan answered. He squeezed Grace's hand.

"Just one question, sport," Ryan walked beside them. "Why the library? I never would have thought about looking here."

Evan smiled and looked up at the sign. "I knew someone would find me eventually," he pointed to the letters, "because the building has my name on it."

Chapter 57

KATHLEEN STOOD AT the doorway, searching for the lights of a car. It was a warm night, the air heavy with moisture and sweet with the scent of pine. She gave another glance at the phone, then stepped outside, her chest tight from sitting inside for so long.

Grace and Ryan had called fifteen minutes earlier to tell her that Evan was safe and sound, but she couldn't relax—couldn't imagine breathing regularly—until she saw her grandson with her own two eyes.

Headlights passed, but didn't stop. Semi-trucks hurried by, carrying their loads to another city, and teenagers gunned their engines, loud music blaring from their speakers. A few other pickup trucks drove by, pulling fishing boats. Kathleen listened again for the sound of approaching cars, but heard only the chirps of crickets and the call of a lone owl.

The walkway was lit with tiny solar lamps, casting a round glow on the plants edging the bricks. Kathleen hobbled a few more steps, careful to use her cane, and watched a worker ant scuttle across the stone.

Finally, the familiar sound of Ryan's truck made her heart jump. When she heard the crunch of tires on gravel, Kathleen squinted up toward the road. Headlights flashed through the trees, splintering the light into little pieces. The pickup rolled to a stop and Ryan cut the engine.

Kathleen's chest pounded. Truck doors opened and she heard footsteps, the sound of tennis shoes hitting pavement. She heard Grace and then Ryan say hello, and after that, a child's voice—Evan's small, sweet voice—cried out.

"Grandma," he called to Kathleen. "Here I am!"

Then, he was in her arms, wrapped up tight. He hugged her back, pressing his head into her chest. Kathleen stroked his soft hair and counted her blessings.

He had disappeared on her watch. If something had happened—the worst—the unthinkable, it would have been her fault. And Grace, with every right, would have never forgiven her.

But everything was fine.

Evan was all right.

He was home and he was safe.

Tears coursed down her face so quickly that Evan's face was blurry when she released him and held him out at arm's length.

"Look at you. You're here," Kathleen was able to gasp. She hugged Evan again. "I'm so happy.

Evan yelped a little. "Too tight, Grandma, you're squeezing me too hard!"

Ryan and Grace laughed as Kathleen released him.

"Phew!" Evan exclaimed, stretching his arms above his head. "I can take deep breath now."

"Oh, honey," Kathleen explained, "I was afraid to let go."

Chapter 58

RYAN WAS RESTLESS. He watched the lake from his window. There was so much he wanted to say to Grace.

He could see faintly through the trees that Kathleen's kitchen light was still on. He fought the urge to run next door and confess his feelings.

Ryan paced the house. He kicked off his loafers and stretched out on the couch next to a stack of mail he needed to go through. "Now's as good a time as any," he said aloud.

There were bills, advertisements for a new cell phone and more credit cards, an invitation to a business opening in town. Most he tossed aside.

Then, a newsletter containing a color photograph of the college library caught his eye. An article followed about Henry, his contributions to the university and a scholarship program he had created. Ryan scanned the article and set it aside. Everything reminded him of Grace and her family.

His wife stared at him from her photograph on the table.

"Tell her," his wife's expression seemed to say.

He stood up and stared out the window. The moon, big and bright, hung over the lake like a white spotlight, making a path across the water to his dock. Stars glinted in the distance. Ryan stepped out onto the porch and leaned against the wooden railing. The air had cooled considerably. He thought about swimming. The idea was appealing; the water would be cool and was likely the only thing that would clear his head.

He checked again to see if the light was still on at Kathleen's. A subtle glow spilled out the window into the yard connecting his house and hers.

Out of the corner of his eye, though the window, he saw a shape move toward Kathleen's dock.

The moon offered some light, casting a yellow glow over the water. He glanced over at Kathleen's house. It was dark now and well past midnight according to the clock on his wall.

The figure moved again. She was sitting. Ryan could tell then, his eyes adjusting to the darkness. The shape of her body, the curve of her back told him what he hoped was true. He had trouble trusting his eyes. No, they weren't lying. It was Grace.

He couldn't let her go without telling her.

Ryan didn't bother with shoes. The grass was soft and rustled under his feet. He couldn't remember if the door had made a noise when he shut it behind him. Did she know he was there? Should he call out and tell her he was there? He stopped, not wanting to frighten her.

She remained motionless.

His legs propelled him forward. He was closer, a few yards away.

Before he could speak, his foot caught, throwing him off balance. He grabbed for the air, found nothing and fell, feet over hands, a few feet from the water's edge.

"Need help?" Grace called.

"I'm okay," Ryan answered from the ground. He jumped up, brushing the dirt off his legs. "My pride's hurt worse than my body." Although his leg was killing him, he didn't say so.

The clouds moved away from the moon, illuminating the beach.

Kathleen's rake lay at his feet. Grace followed his eyes and laughed.

"My stepmother's unquenchable need to clean everything, including the beach, gets people into trouble."

"So much for a graceful entrance."

"Don't worry about it." She waved him over. "No rakes over here. Coast is clear all the way to the end of the dock."

Ryan didn't move. He watched her hair shine in the light at she moved her head. Her chin titled down, her eyes curious. He searched for something to say. His legs started moving again. He couldn't help himself. The first board of the dock creaked under his weight.

"Is your stepmother asleep?"

Grace nodded. "Finally, yes. Evan too."

"Packed?"

Grace laughed, looking up at him as he walked toward her. "Not even close, which is so unlike me. Usually I'm ready to go, bags waiting by the door." She caught her breath and looked down at her hands, turning her wrist. Her watch was missing. "I'd estimate I have a whole twelve hours. Plenty of time."

Ryan stood over her, unable to decide if he should sit or leave. Grace made room. The docked moved under her shifting. He decided to sit.

They sat close; the width of the dock decided that. He could smell her hair, soapy clean. Her skin seemed to glow. His arm brushed hers as he settled himself and hung his feet into the water.

"I don't want you to leave." There, he had said it.

Grace cocked her head. The slightest curve of a smile tickled at her right cheek. "That seems to be the consensus."

"No. You don't understand. I don't want you to leave. You."

Grace was quiet, looking at the water.

"You don't know me," she said. "Not well enough to say that."

"I do know you a little bit. I know you through Henry and Kathleen. Your father talked about you all of the time." Ryan swallowed. "And—And I want to know you better." Damn, he was tripping over his words. He felt his face flush in frustration.

Grace tipped her head to one side and studied him. "But I wasn't very nice, at times, even when you insisted on helping me." Her cheeks reddened. "I've made some bad decisions, haven't given Kathleen enough credit, and then, there was that awful date." She rolled her eyes and put a hand to her forehead.

Ryan pressed a finger to her lips and held it there for a moment. He wanted Grace to stop talking about the past. He wanted to kiss her for an hour, wrap his arms around her, and make her forget about anything other than a future together.

"I understand why you were so upset. Things are better, though. You're happier, I can tell. Evan loves it here," he added. "And Kathleen cares about both of you."

Ryan took his finger away, and let his hand fall to his side. He wanted to add, 'And I do, too," but didn't want to scare her off any more than he already had done. Instead, he smiled at Grace, and watched her shoulders relax.

"You sound like my father. The eternal optimist." Her voice quavered slightly. She tilted her head back, letting her hair fall down her back, and looked at the moon. "I miss him so much."

"We all do."

"Every day I wake up and have to remind myself he's not here. There are times I can't believe that he won't come walking down here and sit with us on the dock." Grace drew in her breath, stretching her hand out for emphasis.

"I know," Ryan admitted. He'd thought about it a dozen

times, looking for Henry's face, the sound of his steps, his voice calling out between the two houses.

"I thought my stepmother would be lost without him. Flailing around, moping, unable to move. On the couch, ready to curl up and die without him. Needing everything. Needing me. I figured she'd be begging me to stay."

Ryan was silent. The water lapped at their feet.

"She's fine," Grace continued with a slight shrug. "After all, she's painted her house pink. Who in the world does that? Not someone who's ready to throw in the towel and give up on life."

"She does need you," Ryan said. "She's afraid to say it. And maybe she's afraid of admitting that she needs you and Evan." He knew, deep down, that Grace knew it too. "Kathleen's giving you space. Plenty of it. I think that it's all she can do."

Grace nodded.

"As far as the house, who cares? If she paints it orange next week, that's her prerogative. She's trying to find herself, like a teenager away from home for the first time. Can't you see that?"

Grace tilted her head up and down, slowly. "You're right."

"I think so," Ryan agreed. "If she doesn't keep moving or changing or finding something to do, she'll have to think about being alone. And that's harder than it looks."

"You're by yourself."

"Exactly. It's harder than it looks," Ryan repeated and gave her a meaningful stare. If he could transfer his thoughts to her, he would. He was having such trouble admitting that he didn't want to live without her.

When Ryan fell silent, Grace finally met his gaze.

"You could stay," Ryan told her.

"I have a job and a house. Then, there's Evan's school to think about…" Grace's voice trailed off. She tucked her legs up, hugging them to her chest. With a sigh, she rested her head on her knees and looked out at the lake.

"Can't you see that you have people who love you, right here?" Ryan said finally. "Right now? Don't you realize that?"

Grace turned her head toward him. Her eyes were glittery with tears. "How do I know that it's real? Can I ever trust that? How can I be sure that everyone won't...leave me?" she stopped and caught her breath. "E-Everyone that I loved with all of my heart—everyone except Evan—is gone."

Ryan inched closer and let Grace cry. He didn't say anything more, just slid an arm around her waist, pulled her close, and allowed her tears to fall. He hoped that somehow, expelling the grief would be a release, emptying her body and soul of some of the sorrow. Maybe then she could fill the deep, vast spaces in her heart with love.

She would have to open herself up. Take chances. And he knew from experience that it was petrifying.

There were no guarantees about tomorrow or the next day. He couldn't predict the future or make certain nothing bad would ever happen to her or Evan again.

But he would do his damndest—every moment for the rest of his life—to make Grace happy.

Ryan watched the water folding over on itself, pushing toward the shore and then away. The movement was like Grace and Kathleen, two identical waves, never quite finding each other in an entire ocean of water. They were made of the same stuff—salty-sweet and stubborn—funny and smart. The two women could be stronger together. Better together. They could lean on each other for support, but neither wanted to make the first move.

Neither one wanted to be the first to say she was sorry.

Chapter 59

KATHLEEN WAS UP before dawn; right before the sun decided to blaze its glory over the hills and kiss everything it touched with light. Now, from the sky to the water, everything was shades of gray, matching the stones and pebbles beneath the water she was watching.

Henry's ashes, in the mahogany box, sat next to her on the dock.

A family of ducks cruised by, the mother edging her three fluffy babies along with her beak, every once in a while quacking an order for good measure. Just in front of the dock, they stopped, waiting for her to notice them or give a handout.

"No bread today," Kathleen said out loud, as if the ducks could understand her. "Sorry." This was time for a private conversation.

Mother duck quacked a reply and seemed to look at her curiously. Without another sound, they continued on their journey, leaving a faint ripple behind them on the surface of the water.

"Oh, Henry, She's confused, I can tell," Kathleen said out

loud. "What do I do?"

Up until this very moment, she had been proud of the way she hadn't tried to convince Grace to stay another day or another week. She'd avoided, for the most part, any major confrontation. She didn't want to fight or argue.

Kathleen would have been happy to talk, but she wasn't going to be the one to ask. After all, Grace had been the one to stay away all these years.

If she had asked, Kathleen would be honest. She would tell her that, yes, absolutely she felt wholly responsible for the accident that killed Grace's mother. There wasn't a day that went by that she didn't regret it. Didn't think about it. Didn't see the twisted metal, the terrified teenager, and the heartbroken father and husband when he returned home from his business trip.

She didn't mean to inject herself into the Mason's life after the funeral, but the guilt propelled her forward. It gave her purpose, gave her something to do, and think about other than her own miserable existence with her awful husband.

Kathleen cooked casseroles for both of them, brought over cookies and candy for Grace. Often, she would be there three nights a week, never lingering a long while. She basked in the glow of Henry's praise. He would thank her profusely, and they would talk about the weather or her small garden. Grace was in her own dream world; quiet, focused on her schoolwork. She never made a sound, just drifted in and out of the kitchen, then disappearing back into her bedroom for hours.

It had turned into something more with Henry by chance. Out of loneliness, a little desperation, perhaps. And out of familiarity. It was easy, comfortable; never a moment of awkward conversation. They were friends and had been for years.

Should she have pulled away when Henry kissed her for the first time? They kept it a secret for so long. And she'd tried not to love him.

Kathleen inhaled. As if in a dream, the sun lifted itself behind her, casting a golden glow on the water in front of her. A fish jumped and dove, making a splash, sending rippled circles toward the pebbled beach.

Life would continue, with or without her. The sun would come up, babies would be born, and people would die.

Kathleen pulled the box of Henry's remains—all that she had left of him—closer to her. Just then. the wind caught her sleeve, tugging at strands of hair. She inhaled the sweet smell, of lake and air and trees.

Henry was telling her to let go. It would be okay.

She could take care of herself. She might get bumped and bruised along the way; she had proved that this week. She'd still make mistakes. But she was cheating herself if she didn't live, and live fully.

Resting the box on her knees, Kathleen traced her finger along the smooth wood, caressing what was left of Henry.

What was she thinking though? She was too caught up in saving pieces of him, keeping his clothes, his books. They were tangible, things she could touch and feel. She had better than that. She had fabulous, wonderful memories.

Birds called to each other in the trees, the branches waved good morning and a small boat came into sight, a lone fisherman casting his line, hoping for a bite.

With a fluid motion, Kathleen stood and released a handful of him. The ashes glinted in the sunshine, drifting in the air, finding their way to the surface of the water, where they floated, and then gave themselves to the lake.

Chapter 60

GRACE PACKED THE last of the clothes, carefully setting the photograph her father sent her on top of the dresser. She wanted to give it back.

After zipping up her suitcase, she looked out the door into the kitchen for a sign of her stepmother.

Evan was inspecting the last of his cereal, holding pieces under the milk, and then letting them pop back up.

"Ten minutes," she called out to him.

"Okay," he answered.

It wasn't the most enthusiastic response she had ever heard him give, but at least he was resigned that they were leaving. And it was happening today.

"Where's Grandma?" Grace asked.

"Down by the water," he replied, slurping the last of his cereal from the bowl.

Grace prayed she didn't get another idea about going out in the Sailfish by herself again. She held her breath and looked out the window. The dock was empty.

"Um, are you sure? She's not down there." Grace said.

Before he could reply, the screen door swung open, creaking on its hinges, and Grace jumped at the noise. Whirling around, she saw her stepmother in the doorway, her hair blown, face flushed, and the mahogany box in her hand.

Their eyes met and held for a long moment.

"I guess that it's a day for all sorts of goodbyes," Kathleen finally said and managed a small smile.

Chapter 61

RYAN LOOKED AT the clock for what seemed the millionth time that day. His hands were jumpy and he couldn't seem to write a sentence without stopping and thinking about Grace and Evan.

He typed notes into the laptop, pecking, pausing, and completely unable to focus. He glanced at the wall again, watching the hands on the clock move steadily.

Eleven-fifteen. They were leaving in less than three hours.

"What's with you?" his nurse finally asked.

"Nothing," he said, but they both knew he was lying.

He'd been short with his patients this morning, unable to make the normal conversation he enjoyed so much. He always knew grandchildren's names, remembered anniversaries and just about every other detail people gave him. This morning, he was blank. His head began to ache. The phone rang incessantly. A baby wailed in the waiting room.

"Dr. Gordon," his nurse began. He looked up. "You don't look so great."

He didn't feel so good either. Ryan shut down the laptop, closed the cover, and slid the machine across the counter. He needed a break.

"I'm going to get some air," he said, to anyone who would listen. Ryan gazed down the row of patient rooms, filled with people waiting to see him. He might as well be on a walk to death row.

Outside his office, in the back parking lot, he leaned against the brick of the building. A pep talk was what he needed; it always worked in medical school. But he couldn't think of a word to say to himself.

He stood up again and began to walk, then kicked at the stones in his parking lot. One shard of a pebble skimmed the toe of his shoe, launching into the air. It landed squarely on his truck's window, cracking the driver's side glass into a perfect spider's web.

"What else is going to go wrong?" Ryan heaved a sigh and stretched his arms above his head. His watch face glinted in the sun. Fifteen minutes had passed. It was time to go back inside.

As Ryan headed for the back door, a gray van pulled into his parking lot. The vehicle was long and large, with a bright floral bouquet painted on the side above the company's phone number and website.

The driver rolled down the window.

"Doc Gordon? Got a delivery here."

"Can I take it in for you?" Ryan asked, walking over to the van.

The man raised an eyebrow. "What are you doing outside? Aren't you supposed to be in there seeing patients?" He jerked his thumb toward the office.

Ryan grinned. "Yes, sir. Just playing a little hooky. Needed some air."

"Yeah, okay." The man sounded doubtful, but jumped out of the truck, walked around to the rear bumper, and opened the twin back doors.

Inside stood rows of blossoms and floral arrangements, all secured firmly for the day's journey. Ryan could barely see the driver's seat over the lilies, carnations, and yards of colorful ribbon.

The man thrust a vase full of yellow roses in Ryan's direction. There were at least a dozen, maybe more.

"Wow!" Ryan exclaimed. "Let me guess. Birthday? Anniversary?" His staff was always celebrating something. He looked around the bouquet of flowers to the man.

"I dunno. You tell me."

Ryan squinted and leaned closer, not understanding.

"Open the card and read it, I guess," the driver told him.

"I can't do that," Ryan exclaimed, starting to chuckle.

The delivery man wrinkled up his forehead and pointed at the small white card attached to the vase.

"Why not? They're for you, doc."

Chapter 62

KATHLEEN POPPED THE truck and watched as Grace dragged her suitcase to the curb. "Sure you don't want me to come in?"

"Thank you, but it's okay. We can manage." She eyed Kathleen's air cast, thinking the last thing that her stepmother needed was to hobble around the Rochester Airport.

The terminal was alive with passengers. Cars parked all around Kathleen's. Horns beeped. There was more than one squeal of tires.

Evan unfolded himself from the backseat, his red backpack on his shoulders.

Kathleen reached for him, wrapping her arms around him. She put her face close to his, holding her hands under his chin when she stepped back.

"You come anytime your mom says you can, okay?

Evan nodded. "When I get bigger, I can come by myself."

Grace stopped. "Without me?"

"Maybe." His voice sounded hopeful. "I didn't know if

you'd want to come back."

Kathleen looked from daughter to grandson. "You're both welcome anytime."

"Thanks for everything. We had a wonderful time," Grace added with a sincere smile.

Kathleen hugged Grace back and then Evan again.

They turned.

"It's home if you want it to be," Kathleen whispered. The words slipped out before she had a chance to catch them. Grace didn't turn around. She probably hadn't heard. And that was better. Yes, she told herself. It was better that way.

She watched for a long time, until they disappeared through the sliding glass doors.

Chapter 63

RYAN WATCHED THE speedometer hit eighty as he sped by tall cornfields and rolling hills. A few cows, bits of hay in their mouth, turned their heads to look at his car drive past. They were used to tractors and slow-moving vehicles. Oh well. If the police caught him, a ticket was worth it. He had the money to pay for it.

The note from Grace said three words. He rolled them over and replayed them in his head, making sure he understood them. *I'll miss you.*

As he turned onto the highway, police lights were flashing blue and white. A car, heading the other direction, was in the median, hit head on by a tractor trailer. Ryan shook his head. Senseless. Someone might have been asleep at the wheel.

He looked at the clock again. There was barely enough time to get to the airport. He might be able to catch her, but now, with the accident, he had to make a decision. He surveyed the scene. The ambulance hadn't made it yet, although he thought he heard sirens in the distance.

Ryan pulled the car over to the side of the road. He

wished he'd brought a bag with emergency medical supplies in it. He didn't even have a band-aid. Waiting for a pickup to go by, he jumped out and across the road to where two state troopers stood.

"Can I help, I'm a doctor?" Ryan's heart was pumping. He could see by the look of the two vehicles, it had been a violent crash.

The taller man looked up. "Thanks. Appreciate it. We've called the ambulance."

Ryan looked from one man to the other.

"One is already gone. The other one is hanging on by a thread. Don't think she's gonna make it either."

"What happened?" For some reason, the question gnawed at him.

The tall man pushed up his sunglasses with his index finger. "Drunk, we think. The driver of the rig. Smells like a damn brewery inside the cab. Beer bottles everywhere." The trooper shook his head. "He's from out of state. Mississippi, I think."

Ryan took a step back. Mississippi. A weird coincidence.

"What about the other car? Was he in the right lane?" Ryan felt like he was annoying the troopers, but they patiently answered his questions.

The ambulance siren sounded, this time, closer. It came over the crest of the hill as the trooper answer.

"She. It was a woman. Just bad luck. Wrong place at the wrong time."

As the trooper said the words, Ryan hung his head. Out of the corner of his eye, he saw chips of silver paint on the tractor trailer.

"What kind of car was the woman driving?" Ryan walked a few steps closer to the accident scene. He could smell burned rubber and smoking oil.

The answer was in the ditch. An older Mercedes, silver. The license plate, bent in three places, spelled out HM KM.

Chapter 64

KATHLEEN HOVERED IN the place between dead and alive for what seemed like a decade. She saw herself in the car, seconds after the tractor trailer veered into her path.

Her body was broken, the last breath of her life snuffed out in an instant. Her head was bloodied, her arm tangled in the bent steering wheel. The driver of the truck wasn't in much better shape. She watched as he too lifted himself up from his body, pulling away. He stepped out easily from the truck, looked around and disappeared into the grassy edge of the highway.

Beside Ryan and the state troopers, within inches from their bodies, she heard them talking about her, but their voices sounded like they were being carried by the wind.

She was transparent, dust off the road flew through her, and pebbles tossed from a passing car clinked against the asphalt behind her. Kathleen could see through her hand when she reached out for Ryan's arm. Her fingers moved through him, pulling like she was in deep water and then out and easily through the air. She couldn't touch him or let him know she was there.

His face was broken, his lips set and drawn, his eyes frozen. She wanted to let him know it would be all right. She was fine with her life ending like this. She had taken care of what she needed to.

Kathleen watched as he dialed his cell phone and asked for the number of the airport. Ryan cradled the phone next to his cheek and stepped away from the officers. She could hear every word clearly. He asked for the flight numbers, whether the plane had left and what could be done to reach Grace in an emergency.

The ambulance screamed up and two paramedics jumped out, medical bags in hand. As they ran to the scene of the accident, Kathleen could see them slow as the troopers waved them down. Kathleen's car had started smoking heavily, black clouds curling up into the sky with the pungent odor of gasoline and oil mixing with the sweet smells of summer.

Before anyone, Kathleen saw the flame, tiny and orange at first, licking the edge of the hood of her Mercedes. She shouted out of habit, but heard no voice. Kathleen pushed against the pavement to run, but her legs wouldn't carry her.

The car's explosion shook everything except Kathleen. Debris flew in all directions. Pieces of curled metal shot from the vehicle, now charred beyond recognition. The impact flattened the policemen and paramedics against the ground.

Ryan was yards away; eyes closed, on his back, one arm thrown above his head, fingers outstretched. Ryan's cell phone had tumbled even further. He lay motionless on the side of the road.

Above the commotion, Kathleen thought she heard Grace's voice answer the cell phone.

Then, everything went dark.

Chapter 65

Braving the maze of ticket counters, security check-points, and bathroom breaks, Grace and Evan made it to their gate. A-10, it proclaimed in large letters.

A voice boomed from the speaker overhead, interrupting. "Flight 485 to Atlanta has been delayed. Passengers please stay in the gate area for further announcements."

"Looks like we're going to get home a little later than we expected, Evan." Grace settled as best she could into the plastic back of her chair.

Evan pulled out his Nintendo 3DS, clicked it on, and started playing. It held his attention for less than three minutes. "Can I go watch the airplanes take off?" His eyes were soft and wide.

"Sure, honey, just stay where I can see you."

Evan lined up with two other children, both with their noses pressed to the glass.

Out of habit, Grace checked her cell phone. No messages.

The voice sounded again. "Passengers scheduled to depart on Flight 485. A repair crew has been called. Please stay in the gate area for more information."

Evan said something to the boy next to him, half a head shorter. He turned and waved at Grace, who waved back.

A sky cab flew by with a tiny, frail woman clutching her chest. Without thinking, Grace turned to call out to Ryan. He was a doctor. He would help.

She stopped herself before the words came out and leaned back against the firm seat. Grace was used to having him there. She missed him already.

"Attention please," the voice commanded. "Attention, please, in the terminal." the voice repeated. "Passengers Grace Mason and Evan Mason. Please see the agent at the counter for a message."

Grace wrinkled her nose. What could that be about? Surely, they weren't being bumped from their flight.

She motioned for Evan to come away from the window. He galloped over like a pony. Gathering her bag, she walked, holding Evan's hand, to the woman waiting.

Wordlessly, she handed over the phone.

Carefully, Grace tucked the receiver between her ear and shoulder. "Hello?"

There was no answer.

"Hello?" she repeated, then shook her head.

Grace paused and looked at the receiver. The line had gone dead. "There's no one here." She handed the phone back over the counter.

The woman murmured an apology. "I'm sorry, ma'am. The person on the line said it was urgent."

"Urgent." Grace's throat caught. She swallowed hard. "But not an emergency. Are you sure it was for me?"

"Is your name Grace Mason?" The ticket agent started to look annoyed.

When Grace nodded, a cold shiver crept down her spine. In the back of her mind, more questions began to surface. It couldn't be a coincidence. The person knew her name and knew she was here.

Grace stepped closer to the counter and leaned in. "Man or woman? The person who was calling."

The agent thought for a moment. "It was a man. Someone young, but not a teenager, though."

"Was he calm or frightened?" Grace was grasping at straws.

The airline employee shrugged and gestured toward the crowd. "I'm sorry. I don't think he was upset or anything. It's hard to tell, though, it's so noisy in here, especially around flight time."

"Thank you. Maybe he'll call back." Grace had trouble believing her own words.

Immediately, she dialed Kathleen's home number with her own cell phone. The short, pleasant voice mail greeting instructed her to leave a message.

"Kathleen, it's Grace. I'm sure you're driving, but we just received a strange call here at the airport. Could you give me a call back?"

Grace turned and walked back to Evan. She checked her cell phone. No messages. Was it Ryan? She had thought it was a nice touch to send the flowers. Unexpected, but yet friendly and still interested. They could see each other at Christmas or Thanksgiving or some other holiday. Deep inside, she knew it was too long to be away from him.

Pulling her cell phone up in front of her face, she shook it like it was broken. Cradling it in her palm, she stared at the screen, daring it to light up with Ryan's number.

When it didn't, she scrolled through her numbers. The ten-digit code stared back at her. Grace hit send, then stopped the call after the fourth ring. He wasn't going to pick up. He was busy. He was at work.

If it was an emergency, involved Kathleen, and somehow he knew about it, surely his staff would call back.

A fellow traveler brushed by her with his suitcase, head-phones on, oblivious to the noise surrounding him. Her arm tingled at the touch and she rubbed it. Men with briefcases and women with strollers rushed by her, both ways, as if the corridor was a highway during rush hour. She imagined the security guard directing traffic, waving his arm and pointing to who was next to make a left hand turn.

Grace blinked several times, trying to convince herself everything was all right. She forced her legs to move closer to Evan. He was still sitting in the same place, knees crossed, head bent over his Nintendo 3DS. She stared out the window at the hundreds of planes moving, taking off, and climbing toward the sky.

The overhead paging system blared. "Attention passengers on Flight 485 traveling to Atlanta, Georgia, we will be boarding shortly. Please have your boarding passes out and available for the ticket agent when your row is called."

"Is that us?" Evan looked up at her, not blinking, his shoulders hunched against the gray plastic of the seats.

"Yes, finally," Grace answered, but made no move to gather her bags.

Evan stood and stretched his arms over his head. "So, we're going?"

The counter agent opened the door leading to the jet way. Grace looked at the phone hanging near the counter. It didn't ring again for her. No one was paging her. The call must have been a fluke. Mason sounds like...well, some other names, she guessed.

"We'd like to welcome our Gold Star passengers first and anyone seated in First Class. If you are traveling with small children, you are welcome to board at any time."

Grace folded herself into the bench and gathered her bags at her feet. Her lips were parched and her vision dimmed for an instant as she stared at the rows of departures and arrivals on the wide television screens. She checked her cell phone again.

"What is it, Mom?" Evan tugged at her sleeve. He wasn't used to the glazed over person sitting next to him.

"Now boarding Zones A and B," the voice overhead called out. A small line began to form at the counter and people shuffled forward with their bags.

Stay, her inner voice cried out to her. Just for a little while, what would it hurt? But home is in Mississippi, she argued back to herself. That's where you need to be. You have a life there, a house, a job.

"C'mon, Mom," Evan was tugging harder now, this time on her pant leg. Grace patted him on the head and smoothed a cowlick. She smiled at the awkward curl.

"This is the final boarding call for Flight 485 to Atlanta. All ticketed passengers should proceed to the jet way."

Grace looked down at the boarding passes and checked their seats. They inched closer to the doorway leading to the jet. Hand outstretched, the ticket agent reached for the papers. Nodding at Grace and grinning at Evan, she waved them on and took the next person's papers. "Have a nice flight."

After the tunnel leading to the open door of the plane, Evan and Grace found their seats, wedging bags in the small crevices around them. Evan looked out the window at the men outside. He pressed his nose to the window, leaving a small grease mark. His breath fogged up the glass.

Grace closed her eyes. It had been nine days. She had made it. This was where she needed to be. Going back to her life. Grace started crying.

Chapter 66

DAZED BUT THANKFUL to still be alive, Ryan pushed himself onto his elbows, hanging his head between his shoulders. His neck hurt, his eyes were burning and the smell of smoke and rubber was putrid and dirty, filling his lungs.

Blue and white lights flashed to the side of him. The blacktop was warm and oily under his fingertips. Half of him was on grass. It tickled the hairs on his arm. His whole body ached. He attempted to move his legs and get into a sitting position. Ryan tried hard to remember where he was and what he was doing.

With a push, Ryan managed to roll over on his back in what seemed like an hour. He stared up at the sky, blue and clear. He tasted blood in his mouth, salty and warm. A lone bird swooped overhead, darting over the smoke drifting from the center of the highway.

Rolling his head to one side, he saw flashers, red and blue, a road block in place. Traffic was backed up for miles. Ryan shut his eyes. The noise became louder, rushing at him like in a movie theater. People were shouting and talking, horns beeped, and a tow truck rumbled nearby.

"Over here," he heard someone call.

Footsteps came closer and stopped inches from his face. Ryan looked at several pairs of worn work boots, dust covered. Knees came closer and a hand was on his forehead.

"Blast must have sent him flying." One pair of work boots said. "Hey, man," the voice said to Ryan. "You okay?"

Ryan started to laugh at the absurdity of the question, but ended up coughing and hacking to catch his breath. He nodded and tried to sit up. A hand forced him back down. A thick cotton blanket was draped over his arms and legs.

"Don't move. Lie still," another man said. His voice was gruff, but calm. "Got another ambulance coming to take you to the hospital. They should be here in five minutes or less. We'll get you away from the wreck." The man turned away from Ryan and spoke to someone next to him.

"They've gotta take that lady. Darndest thing. Found a pulse on her when we dragged her from the car. One of the paramedics thought she was a goner. Good thing someone else checked."

Ryan's heart jumped. *Wreck. Kathleen. Mercedes. Was she alive? Get to Grace.* Visions of the accident scene flashed in his head. He saw the crumpled bumper of the car and the tractor trailer lying cock-eyed across the road, skid marks making black streaks across the pavement.

Ryan shook his head from side to side. Where was his cell phone? He felt as if his brain was swollen and might explode. Lifting a finger, he opened his mouth to speak.

Grace. Kathleen. He couldn't make the words come out in more than a whisper.

Ryan's head started to clear. Emergency vehicle sirens screamed in the distance. The police and firemen turned their attention to the noise. Their backs to Ryan, he eased himself up into a sitting position and felt for his keys. In his pocket. Good. He turned to look for his cell phone. It was a few feet away, shattered into several pieces.

Ryan stood and took a deep breath, his ribs protesting at the pressure. The officers were busy supervising the transfer of Kathleen into a waiting helicopter. Ryan caught a glimpse of her face, covered with a clear oxygen mask and tubing.

She was so pale her skin looked almost translucent. Her eyes were closed and she looked peaceful, unmindful of the commotion around her. Men in blue jumpsuits gently placed the stretcher inside, jumped on board after her and sat down. Ryan read the words on the side of the helicopter. Strong Memorial Hospital. He had friends there. She'd be well-cared for.

Ryan looked around for his pickup. It was still sitting by the side of the road, up and away from the action. He slid behind the bumper of one of the fire trucks and made his way to the vehicle. Pressing the key fob, the headlights on his truck flashed twice. Ryan opened the door and slid behind the wheel.

Kathleen was taken care of, for now. She was hanging on, he was sure of it. He needed to find Grace though. Before it was too late.

Chapter 67

GRACE SHIFTED IN her seat. The flight attendants walked through, checking and rechecking seatbelts. She was uncomfortable and the man behind her kept lowering his tray table, then shoving his back in place.

She closed her eyes. They would be back in Georgia in a few hours, then Mississippi soon after that. She could sort out her feelings there. It was weeks before the school year started. She could even fit in another visit before the end of the summer. She wouldn't say anything to Evan just yet. Anything could happen between now and then.

The captain came over the intercom. "Good afternoon. This is the captain speaking. I'd like to welcome you on board." He paused and cleared his throat.

Never a good sign, Grace thought. Wasn't it time to be taxiing out? She glanced at her watch. They were already late.

"We've been informed there's some weather in Atlanta. Fog and light rain currently. I've asked the guys on the ground to top off our fuel tanks because of that, so it's going to be a few more minutes here before we can taxi out to the runway. I'll be checking back with you in just a little while with a revised schedule for getting into Hartsfield. Thanks for your patience."

Several passengers groaned. The man behind her pushed the seat back again. Grace tried to ignore him and patted Evan's leg. It was hot inside the cabin. Grace reached up and adjusted the air vent.

"You think Grandma's going to be okay by herself?" Evan's voice was muffled. His knees were drawn up to his chest. His eyes welled up with tears, brimming to the edges.

Grace bent her head down to his, trying to block out the lights and sounds around them. She wanted him to feel safe, his face told her so. She chose her words carefully.

"Yes. Grandma is going to be fine. She said so. Didn't you hear her?" Grace added. "And Ryan's going to keep an eye on her. Doesn't that make you feel better?"

Evan nodded. A lone tear trickled down his cheek in an uneven line. He blinked and looked away, unsure if he should be sharing his thoughts.

After wiping his tears away and kissing his cheek, Grace took his hand and squeezed it.

"But Grandpa died and we weren't there," Evan said in a soft voice.

"I know. I know." Grace tried to comfort him, patting his hand, then rubbing his shoulder, but Evan slumped against the seat, pressing his head against the wall of the airplane.

Grace looked around the plane, hoping some idea would pop into her head and make him forget about issues with his grandmother. She sighed, watching a man in front of her reading the newspaper. He looked vaguely familiar, though she couldn't see his face. Where had she seen him before?

The man stood up, adjusting his briefcase, and slipped off his sport coat. He towered over her, nearly touching the ceiling of the plane. When he turned to open the overhead bin, Grace caught his profile. It was in a photograph in the cottage. It was a group photo, everyone holding drinks and celebrating.

He must be a friend of Henry and Kathleen's.

Their eyes met.

"Hello." Grace managed to squeak out. It probably was a mistake. The man was about to sit down, but stopped at the sound of her voice.

"Don't we know each other?" he asked, scratching his chin.

Grace shook her head quickly. "I don't think we've met."

"Tripp Williams," he replied. He grinned and stuck out a huge hand. Grace liked the look of his face and the way he held himself, confident and assured.

"And you are…?"

"Grace. Grace Mason." She shook his hand over the top of the seat.

A flicker of recognition crossed his face. "Aw, you're Henry's girl. That's right," he exclaimed in delight. "Kathleen Mason's stepdaughter?"

"Right."

"And this must be your boy." He pointed at Evan, who was still facing the window.

Grace nodded and leaned forward, lowering her voice. "He's not really happy. He doesn't want to leave."

"Do you?"

Grace thought for a moment. "I guess I'm torn." She looked down at her hands, then back up at Tripp. She paused, thinking how odd it was to share her feelings with a stranger. "I don't really want to leave either."

"No place like it. I could never leave for very long." He moved aside for one of the flight attendants to walk through. "And you live in Atlanta? Big job?"

Grace laughed. "Not really. I'm a teacher's aide. We live in Ocean Springs, Mississippi."

"That's right; Henry mentioned that. Your father was always very proud of you."

The sentiment warmed Grace inside and she reached for

Evan's hand again. "Thank you for saying that. Do you have children?"

Tripp chuckled. "I'm on my way now to Fort Lauderdale. My oldest lives there. Going to spend a week away and play with the kids. Spoil them rotten. I'll love every minute of it." His big face was wistful. He rubbed a thick hand over his head.

Grace wondered where his wife was. Tripp seemed to read her mind.

"My wife died ten years ago. Cancer. Made me wake up and realize that life's too short." He laughed. "I sound like a country song. What's that one? Live like you were dying?"

Grace knew the one he was talking about. It hit home with lots of people.

"I love that part...what is it?" He started to sing in a voice resonating with emotion. "And I loved deeper and I spoke sweeter. And I gave forgiveness I'd been denying..."

Grace blinked in amazement. Evan stared, his mouth open. What was with everyone singing lately?

She thought about the words. *I gave forgiveness I'd been denying.* That could have been written for me, she thought.

The entire cabin got quiet. Someone from the back shouted, "Encore! Encore!"

"Sound a little like Tim McGraw, don't I?" He whispered behind his hand after taking a little bow.

An annoyed flight attendant tapped him on the shoulder, standing on her tip toes. "Excuse me. Your *American Idol* performance is going to have to wait. We're done fueling and air traffic control should be giving us clearance for departure."

"Nice talking to you." Tripp winked and settled down in his seat.

Grace stared ahead into the cockpit. The pilots were busy checking buttons and switches. Another flight attendant walked by, counting heads for the third time.

I gave forgiveness I'd been denying.

Grace's pulse quickened. She stood up, pulling at Evan's sleeve. "Get up," she said. She fumbled for her cell phone and turned it back on.

He wrinkled his brow at her and didn't move from the seat. "It's too late to go to the bathroom, Mom."

"Stop," she yelled, hit the call light, and motioned at the flight attendants.

"Is she going to sing too?" she heard someone say.

Grace grabbed her bags off the floor and motioned for Evan to follow her. "Mom, what are you doing?" He insisted, heaving a sigh. She didn't care what anyone thought at that point. She rushed toward the woman about to close the door.

"Please," she said, trying to catch her breath. "We need to get off."

Her cell phone began ringing. She ignored it, looking directly at the flight attendant.

"Ma'am, I know you've been waiting a long time, but we really are leaving now. We're about to close the door. Please take your seat." She gestured to the row where Grace and Evan had been sitting.

Grace shook her head.

She had to see Kathleen. She had to apologize. And she hadn't shared her real feelings with Ryan. They had a few more weeks before school started. They could get to know each other better. She didn't have to leave right now.

Grace took Evan's hand in hers. "We are getting off this airplane if we have to jump out."

The flight attendant moved aside, rolling her eyes. She made a crazy sign, twirling her finger around her ear at the other flight attendant in the back.

Grace's cell phone started ringing again.

It was Ryan.

She waved at Tripp, and he smiled back. Grace shouted above the noise of the ringing and sound of the engine. "Life's too short, right?"

Chapter 68

RYAN TRIED GRACE'S cell phone for the fourth time. It had gone to voicemail three times. He had left several messages. Maybe her phone was dead. Maybe she was already in the air. He checked his watch. There was no telling. He just had to keep on trying.

Ryan had borrowed the cell phone from a passenger at the Rochester Aiport. Someone took pity on him racing around to try and find a pay phone. He figured he looked desperate or crazy. Maybe both.

The phone clicked and stopped ringing. Please don't go to voicemail. He heard Grace's voice. It sounded like she was standing a few feet away.

"Hello?"

"Grace it's me." The thought didn't occur to him that she didn't know who "me" was until he said it.

"Ryan!"

"Listen," he interrupted. "Where are you?"

"Getting off the airplane."

Ryan felt like punching the nearest wall. "You need to be

here. Here, meaning New York."

She cut him off. "I'm right here."

He turned around. He had to blink to make sure what he was seeing was real. Grace was standing in front of him, Evan at her side. They looked disheveled, but happy. Evan jumped into his arms.

"What? How? I thought you said you were getting off the plane. That you had landed." He remembered he had borrowed the cell phone. "Thanks so much," he said, handing it back.

Grace put her hand on her head and shrugged her shoulders. "We never left. I made them let us off the airplane. It was so funny. There was this guy...you probably know him... he started singing this song and the next thing you know...I knew I had to be here. I couldn't leave just yet." She took a deep breath, about ready to continue. Her mouth opened. She hesitated and looked at him. "What is it? I know it sounds silly..."

Ryan reached for Grace and pulled her close. His hands found the small of her back, the smooth stretch of skin between her shirt and her jeans. "Don't talk, just kiss me."

His mouth pressed into hers. At first, her touch was hesitant and shy, holding back. He hugged her closer, pressing his body tight against his. She responded, kissing him back, deeper, longer. He could stand here forever, he thought, lost in the way she felt.

A few people whooped and clapped.

With all of his strength, Ryan remembered that they were still in the airport. Still holding Grace around the waist, he stepped away, and took Evan's hand.

"I hope you don't mind, buddy," he motioned toward Grace. "I really like your mom."

Evan smiled. "I can tell."

Grace, pink-cheeked, giggled at both of them. "So this was the reason for the urgent phone call? That's so sweet."

"It wasn't exactly the reason," he replied.

She stopped then, realizing that Ryan's clothes were

ripped and dirty. His face was scraped and raw in a few places. "Wait a minute. You're hurt! What happened?"

He summoned the courage to tell her about Kathleen. Ryan took her hand and pulled her toward the door, still holding onto Evan.

"Your stepmother. She's been hurt pretty badly. She needs you."

Chapter 69

KATHLEEN'S EYES OPENED into slits, just enough to see dozens of tubes and wires sticking out of from all parts of her body. She was numb from head to toe and a machine next to her beeped every few seconds. She tried to turn her head but couldn't. Her arms felt weighted down. An IV dripped every few seconds. She watched a fuzzy line beat across a nearby screen.

A nurse in white appeared in front of her. She bent down to check the tubes and wires, and then pressed buttons on the machine to her side. She hummed as she went, looking concerned but not panicked at the results being printed off.

Kathleen tried to call out to her. Her mouth opened slightly, and then went slack with exhaustion. It was as if every move of her body was like moving a mountain of dirt. Her muscles cried out under the strain.

She tried to think about where she had been and how she had gotten here. What day was today? Who brought her here? She couldn't remember much about anything. It exhausted her to think about more than right now.

The nurse paused to straighten the sheets at the end of the bed. Laying them gently against her legs, she patted the layers into place. Reaching her arm, she plumped Kathleen's pillow. She smelled faintly of baby powder and soap, clean and fresh.

Kathleen longed to ask her to open the window. A deep breath of the outside air was what would make her feel best. The nurse paused and lifted Kathleen's wrist, taking her pulse. She counted silently to herself, looking at the silver watch on her wrist.

"Okay," she murmured. "That's good. Your pulse is getting back to normal. Things are looking up. You'll be getting your strength back in no time."

Opening her eyes wider, Kathleen watched her check the IV bag. The nurse turned to adjust a clip and was startled to see Kathleen awake.

"Well, hello," she said. Bending down, she patted Kathleen's arm. "Glad to see you've taken a break from napping. You've been through a lot in the last few hours. We'll take good care of you."

The woman's eyes were steady, a deep blue with flecks of gold. Her face was round, but happy, sprinkled with freckles across her nose.

Her next words stopped Kathleen cold.

"We just have to find out who you are." She paused. "If you remember, you could tell me your name. Your car was pretty badly burned. There was a small explosion. All of the paperwork, all of your identifying information, your purse and wallet, was destroyed."

Kathleen strained to form the words and answer. It was no use. She shut her eyes, breathing heavily.

An oxygen mask was slipped over her nose and mouth. "There, there," the nurse said. "I didn't mean to frighten you. Plenty of people are like this after a head injury. You're just lucky to be alive. We have plenty of time to talk about it later.

I'm sure your children and husband will be looking for you."

Kathleen pressed her head against the pillow, thinking hard. She couldn't remember her own name. Did she have children? Was she married? The questions started swimming around in her brain, white capping like waves in a storm.

Chapter 70

RYAN DROVE AS fast as he could without being danger-ous. He knew Grace was frightened at the news about her stepmother, but didn't want to alarm Evan by giving them too many details.

He had seen enough accident victims. This crash was serious. The other driver hadn't made it. That was certain. He had passed the coroner's van going in the direction of the wreck while he headed for the airport.

He tried to make small talk with Grace. "So, what about your luggage? What happens to it?"

Grace's eyes were glued to the road ahead of her. Trees flashed by the windows. She tried to joke. "I guess they'll have an all-expenses paid trip to Atlanta."

They exchanged glances.

"That's the last thing I'm going to worry about. We can buy a few things until we can have the luggage delivered or I go back to get it." She paused. "I'll have to go back and pack the rest of it up sometime." Grace looked out the window and then at her watch.

Ryan tried to be casual, but not too pushy. "So you changed your mind?"

Grace nodded, glancing in the back seat toward Evan, who had drifted off to sleep. "It's time I realized what was really important." She rubbed at her temples. "There's nothing keeping me in Mississippi, other than my pride." She gave a forced laugh. "And that's about gone."

Ryan smiled. He hoped Kathleen would pull through the accident to find out. There were no guarantees.

Grace seemed to read his thoughts and tilted her head in his direction, lowering her voice so that Evan couldn't hear. "Ryan, what are the chances? How bad was it?"

Ryan swallowed, weighing what he could tell her. Most of it would be guessing. He wasn't the one taking care of her, taking her vital signs and assessing the damage her body sustained. He didn't know if he could even give an objective analysis now. He was too close, cared too much about the outcome. His professional judgment could be clouded. It happened all the time with husbands and wives, fathers and children. He couldn't take the risk.

"I'm not sure," he said, which was the most honest and logical answer. "Let's just see what the attending physician says. It's a good hospital. One of the best in the area for trauma." He was careful to speak in a way that wouldn't alarm her too much. "Grace, it's out of our control right now. We have to trust they're doing the right thing."

Ryan wished he had a relationship, other than casual phone referrals with someone at the hospital. This would be the time to call in a favor, however large.

Grace buried her face in her hands. "I just don't know what I'll do if I lose her, too." Her voice cracked with the finality of an eggshell bouncing off a hard surface, shattering into a hundred tiny white pieces.

Ryan scratched his head as the car screamed up under the tower of the sign that said Emergency in big red letters.

Evan woke up when the car stopped, looking around, his eyes half-shut, his face lined with indentations made from pressing his face against the door and window of the car. His hair stuck up in clumps.

"Where are we?" Evan peered out the window, furrowing his brow at the fading sun and bright, starched white lights behind the huge sliding glass doors.

"At the hospital," Ryan heard Grace say, though he guessed Evan would figure it out after he came out of his sleep state. "We have to check on Grandma. She's here."

Grace seemed to hesitate, torn between wanting to rush in and find out the news versus staying in the security of the car, where not knowing could be better.

Ryan nudged her with his words. "We'll go park. Go ahead in and let them know you're there. We'll find you."

The door clicked shut behind her, leaving Ryan and Evan alone in the car. They both watched Grace whisk through the glass.

He'd have a better time of it keeping track of Evan. Grace would have enough on her mind trying to digest what was happening. Or what had already happened.

Chapter 71

THE ROUND-FACED NURSE with the freckles had adjusted Kathleen's bed. She was propped up and comfortable, despite the array of noise and conversation that floated around her.

A doctor had been in to examine her. It was someone different than from the emergency room where she had arrived. He was young, maybe thirty, with small round glasses. He peered over his clipboard and asked her the same series of questions everyone else had.

What is your name? Where do you live? Do you know if you have a husband? The wedding ring on her left hand caught the light and glinted. She nodded, looking down at it. Children? Do you remember anything about the accident?

All Kathleen could do was shake her head. Her voice was coming back and she managed to whisper no to the last question.

The young doctor smoothed his lab coat and made a few notes on her chart. He explained she'd be staying a few days for observation and tests. He was frowning, and Kathleen could tell he didn't like what was in her chart.

The nurse and he conferred at the other end of the room near the doorway. Another nurse and a woman with long, dark hair appeared in the doorway. She looked familiar, but Kathleen couldn't quite put a name with her face.

The doctor put his hand on the woman's arm and gently turned her toward the hallway. They spoke in hushed tones. Every few minutes, the woman turned and looked at Kathleen. At one point she gasped and put a hand firmly over her mouth.

Whatever could be wrong and why are they talking about me? The very sight of them started to aggravate her. The call button was a fingertip away. Kathleen edged her hand down the white bed sheet, closer to the round red circle. Exhaling and drawing another breath with all her might, Kathleen pressed it and let her hand fall to the side.

At the sound of the alarm, the trio in the doorway jumped, turned and all stared at Kathleen. She'd make a face if she could. The nurse was the first to move.

"Getting better, eh?" She asked, bending close to the bed. "What do you need, love?" While waiting for an answer, she checked the IV line. The liquid dripped at a steady rate.

The girl walked toward Kathleen. She was lovely, from the wide shape of her eyes to the gentle curve of her chin. Her brown hair was shiny and hung down her back with auburn highlights.

As she came closer, her mouth parted slightly, as if she wanted to speak, but didn't know what to say. The girl tilted her head, looking at the intricate web of machines and wires surrounding the bed. She bit her lip. The nurse gave her a gentle push toward Kathleen.

"It's all right," she said, nodding her approval.

Kathleen blinked, trying to place her. Her eyes shut, trying to remember. Nothing. Not a flicker. Was she another nurse? No, the dress was all wrong. An administrator person?

An attorney? An insurance adjuster? Hopefully not, although it was possible, with being involved in an accident. Kathleen finally hoped it wasn't someone from Hospice. She was bruised and scarred, but not ready to go just yet.

The nurse smiled broadly and took the woman's elbow, leading her even closer to the hospital bed. The look on her face was a mixture of hope and relief.

"Ma'am, it's your stepdaughter." She nodded at Grace and turned, leaving the room in a whisper of rubber soles on gray laminate.

Chapter 72

GRACE LEANED AGAINST the cold tile, her shoulder and head touching the endless wall of squares. The hospital smelled like all do, of strong disinfectant. The scent permeated her very being. Phones rang and doctors were paged in code overhead. Nurses scurried like mice in and out of rooms, stethoscopes around their necks, pills in hand.

Her stepmother didn't know her. Kathleen had looked at Grace blankly, slowly pointed a shaking hand toward the door, and then turned her head toward the wall and refused to look at anyone.

Grace, trying not to burst into tears, had been told to wait outside her stepmother's room until the physician caring for Kathleen was called back to the area. "He'll explain," she had been assured. But Grace had so many questions, waiting to be answered. "Try to be patient," the nurse said. "You need to speak with the doctor."

A janitor in a dark green jumpsuit ambled by pushing his squeaky cart, waving to a nurse down the hall. They smiled and greeted each other silently, exchanging waves.

As he rounded the far corner of the hallway, Grace caught a glimpse of Ryan and Evan. She rubbed at her eyes, wiping away a stray tear and sniffed loudly. She couldn't breathe and her eyes were stinging. She willed the corners of her mouth into a small smile.

Ryan hugged her and Evan wrapped an arm around her waist. She melted into the embrace and for a moment was able to release her fears.

"Amnesia," she said in a halting tone when Ryan released her.

He nodded, making eye contact with Evan and tousling his hair.

"What's am-nee-sa?" Evan's eyes were wide. "Is her knee broken?"

"Just a sec, honey." Grace put a finger to her lips. "No her knee isn't broken, thank goodness."

Ryan leaned in toward Grace. "But she's all right otherwise?"

"I think so. A few bumps, bruises, burn marks. But otherwise, tired. She's okay."

"That's good news."

Grace tried to smile. "Yeah."

"How bad is it?" He meant the memory loss, she knew. He was concerned, she could tell.

"When can we see her?" Evan interrupted. "Where is she?"

Grace held up her hand. "Not now, buddy." She pointed to the room across from where they were standing. "She's in there. But it might not be a good time. She needs to rest."

Evan's glanced toward the door. His face fell. "But I wanted to see her," he protested, making a scuff mark on the shiny floor with the edge of his tennis shoe. It left a black mark in the shape of a Nike swoosh on the ground.

"I know," Grace patted his head. She looked over Evan's head at Ryan and raised an eyebrow. She didn't know how much to share with Evan, when she knew so little herself.

Ryan shook his head. "Why don't you let me do some checking? There's a snack machine at the end of the hallway. I saw it when we came in. Hungry?" He peered at Evan, who nodded.

Grace hesitated. She looked from Kathleen's doorway to Ryan's face.

"Trust me. I'll find out what's going on."

Grace sighed and tried to be thankful that Ryan could get involved, no doubt faster than she could.

"C'mon, let's get something to eat." Grace took Evan's hand in hers and led him down the hall.

Grace took a few more steps and looked back at Ryan. He had already disappeared.

Chapter 73

B<small>Y THE TIME</small> Ryan returned, candy bar wrappers, the plastic from cracker packs and several cans of soda had filled the table next to the waiting room sofa.

Grace was trying to absorb herself in a woman's magazine. As he walked toward them, Ryan could see her eyes closing, and then flying back open. She was clearly exhausted. Evan was sprawled across the edge of a loveseat in the corner, one leg resting on the floor. He had found a racing magazine and was anxiously flipping pages.

"Hey there," he said. Grace jumped, spilling her magazine on to the floor. Evan waved, and then turned his attention back to the pages.

Ryan motioned for Grace to follow him. She picked up the magazine and set it on the table. Her eyes were tired. They faced each other near a window, just out of hearing range of Evan, but close enough to keep an eye on what he was doing.

"Well?" Grace twisted her fingers together, squeezing and releasing. Her shoulders were hunched and she was doing the best she could to keep it together for Evan's sake.

Ryan covered her hands with his. "They think she's going to be fine."

Grace let out a breath. She swallowed, closing her eyes. "Tell me the rest."

"She's suffered quite a few abrasions from the air bags, and she's had the burns on her arm looked at by a specialist. They should heal nicely. Nothing's broken."

Grace relaxed a little more, listening, this time with her eyes open.

"And..." she prompted.

"And, the amnesia is what's tricky. No one's sure when and if her memory will return." Ryan paused, letting his words sink in. Grace gripped at the window sill, motionless.

"They've scheduled an MRI and some other tests, just to get another look at what's going on. They should know something more in the morning, maybe even this evening."

Grace looked out the window at the skyline. The sun was sinking, sending streaks of red and purple against the gold and blue. It was a brilliant sunset. "We should be there. At the lake. She would feel better, I just know it."

Ryan smiled. "We all would. It's a good idea, but not reasonable right now. She has to stay and get these tests, let them observe her overnight, monitor everything and then maybe we can talk about it tomorrow. Maybe tomorrow she'll recognize you."

They sat in silence, inches between them. Ryan had conferred with the hospital's best minds. There were a lot of unanswered questions. Time was the only thing that might really help.

According to the nurses, Kathleen was still agitated and upset, complaining she didn't know where she was and what she was doing there. Ryan would share that later, if it came up. For now, Grace had enough to worry about.

"Can I take you home? I mean to Kathleen's?"

Grace ran a finger across the edge of the window. She was

deep in thought. "I guess that's best. She's stable. We can come back in the morning."

Chapter 74

KATHLEEN WAS TIRED of ice chips. She was tired of having an IV stuck in her arm. She was tired of someone taking her blood pressure every five seconds. Sliding her hand to the cord and call button, she pressed down with her index finger as long as she could.

"Yes?" The voice on the intercom was harried. "Can I help you?"

"You certainly can," Kathleen snapped back. Her throat hurt like someone had rubbed sandpaper inside it, but that wasn't going to stop her from talking and trying to get out of this place.

How long could they keep a person here with no reason? She pressed the call bell again. No nurse in the doorway yet. Where were they? She poised her finger to press again when a voice called out from the hallway.

"Please don't."

Kathleen's finger glided to rest on the bed. "I wasn't going to," she said, looking away from the woman's gaze. The nurse was staring at her, not flinching.

"We've just changed shifts, so I am Martha, your nurse until the morning. I've been told you were in an accident?"

"That's what they said." Kathleen pressed down on the sheets, smoothing the edges flat. Even that motion was a chore.

"From the looks of you, you're lucky to be alive," the nurse checked a monitor and gave Kathleen a sidelong glance.

"I wish everyone would stop overreacting!" Kathleen's voice rose to a shrill pitch. "I don't remember any accident."

Martha was quiet, surveying the way Kathleen was acting. She stepped away from the monitor into Kathleen's line of vision. Hands on her hips, she jutted out her chin. "Okay then, what was it that you needed?"

"Needed?"

Martha pointed in the direction of the red button resting on the bed. "Your call button. You've rung it several times."

Kathleen looked at the call button. Had she pressed it? Yes, she supposed she could have. But what is it that she had needed. The clock on the wall ticked off the seconds. She stared at the second hand, sweeping across the numbers.

"It's time for me to go home," she announced.

A smile played on Martha's lips. "Who's going to take you?"

It was Kathleen's turn to be silent. She pursed her lips. Now that was a problem. Where was her car? Surely she had parked it outside.

"You told your stepdaughter to leave."

Kathleen bent her head to make sure she heard Martha correctly.

"You told her to leave," Martha repeated. "Right when I started the shift. I was at the nurses' station when they got on the elevator. Three of 'em. A little boy, your stepdaughter, and her husband. I think he said his name was Dr. Gordon, from down near Keuka Lake?"

The people didn't mean a thing. But images of the waterfront sprung into Kathleen's brain. She could almost taste the fresh air and hear the lapping of the blue-green waves against her dock. Then, it was gone.

"Yes. Of course," Kathleen said. She was tired of everyone thinking she was crazy. These nurses just wanted her to get better, didn't they? This one looked so hopeful.

Martha looked pleased. "There now, you are getting your memory back! Wonderful! Good news! I've got to put a note in your chart."

In a flash, Martha was gone.

Kathleen started to reach up to rub her forehead. Her wedding ring caught her eye. Where was her husband? Had he been here?

A flash—a snippet of memory—echoed through her mind. A crinkled smile, graying hair and kind eyes were there and then gone.

The sky outside was almost black, with the streetlights arcing yellow lights down into circles on the streets below. Kathleen's eyes were heavy. Before she fell asleep, she formed a plan.

Saying "yes" to the stranger's questions just might get her out of the hospital. Then, she could figure out what was going on and get her life back, once and for all.

She fell asleep, thinking about the strange girl, the young boy, and the doctor.

Chapter 75

It took Grace a glass and a half of chardonnay before she could relax. She swirled the liquid in the wide-mouthed glass, watching the wine cling to the sides. She was curled up in the chair near the front porch. She had propped open the sliding glass doors and a delicious breeze wafted through.

The house had an eerie quiet to it. On the floor next to her, Evan opened his backpack and started spreading toys in a semi-circle around his crossed knees. The occasional clatter of matchbox cars made Grace feel a little bit better.

"Want me to run to the store? Hungry?"

"Afraid we've maxed out on the hospital candy supply. I'll be paying for it tomorrow," Grace joked, patting her stomach.

"Nah, a little sugar never hurt anyone." Ryan tried to lighten the mood.

They smiled at each other. Ryan walked toward the door and Grace followed. She stopped him, putting her hand on his shoulder. He took her hand and squeezed it in his.

"Thank you. You've been wonderfully kind." She meant it. Grace hoped he knew that.

Ryan's cell phone started buzzing. He looked down. "Sorry, duty calls," he apologized.

Grace held open the door. Its hinges groaned in protest.

"One more thing." He stepped closer, almost toe to toe with Grace.

She started to ask what it was, until Ryan leaned in and kissed her on the lips. It was different this time. She didn't feel awkward or pull away. He left without a word through the darkness to his house, just yards away.

Grace was still dazed when she turned to shut and lock the door behind her. She blinked, hoping Evan had missed the whole thing.

He was staring at her curiously.

"We're just friends," she said, not believing it herself. How could she explain it to Evan when she couldn't make sense of it herself? She would think things through, examine the many feelings that were pinging around in her heart and make sense of them.

Evan narrowed his eyes. "Mom."

"Sorry...I shouldn't have..." she let her voice trail off. She didn't know whether to apologize or bury herself in the ground outside. She wished he hadn't seen it.

"I like him." Evan answered. "It's just..." His voice choked up.

Grace slipped down beside him and put an arm around his back.

"It's just...with Papa and now Grandma...will you and Ryan die too?" His face scrunched up like a crinkled paper bag.

Grace sucked in her breath and held Evan closer. "Oh." She searched for the right thing to say.

"I don't want you to die," Evan wailed, this time louder.

"There, now," Grace stroked his head. "Both of us are going to be around for a long time."

Evan sniffed, rubbed his nose, wiping the tears away with

the edge of his shirt sleeve. "What about Grandma?"

"She's going to be fine," Grace said. "She's pretty banged up right now, but she's getting a lot of help from the doctors and nurses. Ryan says it's a really good hospital."

Grace squeezed Evan. He leaned into her, putting his head on her shoulder.

"We'll know more tomorrow. Ryan says we will."

Grace hoped it was true.

Chapter 76

KATHLEEN AWOKE TO a face hovering inches away from hers. Opening her eyes as wide as she could, she screamed out loud, startling the person invading her personal space.

A night's rest had made a world of difference. She had managed to drown out the beeps and clicks of the monitors by sandwiching her head between the two pillows. She pushed them close to her ears, drowning out most of the ambient noise. Then, she was able to drift and finally fall into a deep rest. She had even managed to go right back to sleep after one of the nurses had cracked open the door around midnight to check on her.

This kind of wake up call would never do, however. Kathleen was sure the scare was about to kill her.

The woman in question had turned pale, her freckles standing out on her skin like brown dots on white paper, and now gave Kathleen plenty of space.

"Good morning," the woman said timidly. "I see you have your voice back."

"Yes, I suppose I do," Kathleen said gruffly. "What do you want?"

"Just checking on you to see if you need anything before I leave."

Kathleen looked at her blankly.

"I'm Martha," the woman put a hand on her chest and smiled. "Remember me from last night?" She didn't look away.

"Sure I do," Kathleen said, making her voice stronger and confident. "Martha," she repeated. The woman's face relaxed. It was obviously what she wanted to hear, regardless of whether it was true. Kathleen was sure she was writing everything she said down in her chart.

"Glad to hear it," Martha replied, bustling around the room, looking for something to help with. "I was afraid you didn't remember. If you didn't make any more progress, they might order more tests."

Kathleen shut her eyes, trying to remember what tests she did have. There was a hazy thought of lying in a big tube, but it disappeared faster than she could hold onto it. It was no use. She shook her head.

"Oh, I didn't mean to worry you. All of yesterday's tests came back perfectly normal. I think they're waiting on one more. If that's okay, they'll probably let you go in a few days. It'll be up to the doctor of course. He'll be in shortly to do rounds."

As she walked out the door to the hallway, a woman carrying a tray came in. She set the breakfast down on the table near her elbow. A nutty smell wafted up from the cup.

"Mmm. Coffee. I need another cup to wake up," the woman smiled and left.

Coffee? Did she like coffee? What about this muffin and bacon? Kathleen's stomach rumbled at the thought of eating. She unwrapped a fork and knife and stabbed at the fluffy scrambled eggs. Before she could swallow, the door opened again.

"Kathleen, I wanted to come last night, but it was too

late." The man was short and bald, with a "clergy" tag on his shirt.

He took quick steps over to her bedside with a furrowed brow.

"Ryan and Grace called to fill me in," he began, sinking down into the chair across from the bed. "They thought you wouldn't mind if I came over."

Kathleen swallowed and nodded. "It's so nice to see you," she answered.

"Are they going to let you go home today?" His eyes seemed to sparkle at the thought. "You have such a lovely view from your house by the water. So peaceful and calm. Just the thing to make you feel better."

Kathleen wanted to agree, but couldn't remember where her house was or what it looked like. She started to tell him about the tests and the doctor making a decision to go home, but stopped.

An idea popped into her head.

"Actually," she sat up straighter and adjusted her hospital gown, "they're letting me go home today... this morning."

His eyes widened. "That is good news!" he exclaimed.

"Do the kids know?" she shook her head. That question she could answer honestly. Her mind raced.

The clergyman stood up. "Well, I guess I'll be seeing you soon, then, if you're all cured."

"Wait," Kathleen stopped him. "Could you do me a favor?"

"Of course. Anything."

"Give me a ride home?" The words spilled out of her mouth. "The...kids...they're busy this morning." After she said the words, she immediately wished she could erase them like chalk from a blackboard.

He frowned.

"They could come later, after dinner, of course," she corrected herself. "But, as you say, I'd heal a lot faster at home.

And I'd like to go this morning."

Kathleen looked out the window and out of the corner of her eye, saw his reaction relax.

"Can you help me? Give me a ride home? You know where it is, don't you?"

"Did you think I'd forgotten?"

Kathleen laughed. "Just teasing."

"I have several people I need to visit this morning. It could be an hour, maybe less. Will that be okay?"

"I really appreciate it. It will give me time to get everything finished here." She held up the arm that held the IV. "Have to get disconnected."

The clergy man smiled and stood up to leave.

"Oh, and Reverend? I'll be ready to go whenever you're finished."

Chapter 77

THE PASTOR'S BIBLE was sitting on the seat when he opened the car door. His name was embossed in gold letters on the black leather.

Kathleen had pondered what she would do if she was forced to identify him. A coughing fit or a fainting spell could come in handy, but the truth would be easier. She simply couldn't remember, no matter how long she thought about it or stared at his profile. She waited for something to spark her memory—a hand gesture, the shape of his eyes, the sound of his voice—nothing worked.

And, in her desperation to get back and find anything she knew, he was the most unlikely candidate to be a serial killer. Memory loss or not, she still had instinct.

Reverend Spencer had been easy to persuade. She didn't like to manipulate, but could do it occasionally if she really needed to get her way. The minister was an easy target, gullible and caring to a fault. Kathleen wondered if that could happen if you shut yourself away from the world, only coming out to make hospital calls and preach sermons.

Kathleen, still in her hospital gown, a blanket draped over her shoulders, laid out her plan of escape while looking at the fire escape chart on the wall. They took the stairs from the third floor to the ground.

Reverend Spencer had protested at first, asking about using a wheelchair to leave the hospital, but had no choice to follow her after she descended the first flight of stairs and started down the second.

By the time they got to the bottom, Reverend Spencer was red-faced, winded, and holding his chest. For a moment, Kathleen thought they'd have to rush back inside to the emergency room, calling for help, where someone would realize she was actually supposed to be in a room upstairs. She might have a tough time explaining that he was abducting her. After a few minutes, his color returned to normal and he began breathing deeply again.

His car was parked steps from the entrance—a lucky break for a quick escape, Kathleen thought. Before Father Spencer drove carefully out of the parking lot, he waited for every car to pass, looked both ways several times and finally turned on to the main highway. He gripped the wheel as if bracing for a crash. His back was ramrod straight and he didn't take his eyes of the road.

In the car, Kathleen watched the speedometer creep up in increments of two miles an hour until they topped off at a speed of exactly thirty-one miles per hour. A speed limit sign passed by Kathleen's window, with sixty-five spelled out in twelve inch letters.

Did he not see it or was he just ignoring what was normal and reasonable? Perhaps there was a rule for clergy about only going half the normal speed limit. It would be rude to ask why and point out this minor detail. Other cars passed, some drivers with angry looks on their faces, shaking their fists. Some were just bewildered at this turtle of a car in the middle of a rabbit race.

She shivered and pulled the blanket around her more tightly. The sun was shining, beaming inescapably through the window onto her shoulders, but somehow she didn't feel it. Where was she going? What did her house look like? Would she finally remember anyone's name? Kathleen forced herself to stop worrying.

She was glad to be out of the confines of the brick building. She should be thankful they weren't caught and dragged back up to the third floor by security. She watched in the rear view mirror as the hospital disappeared behind other buildings.

Kathleen wanted to reach for the radio and turn it on. Music would lighten her mood, some kind of noise other than the sound of the engine purring and her own breathing. She caught herself watching Reverend Spencer as he drove.

"I know I'm a terrible driver," he said without looking at her. His voice had a hint of a smile in it. "I should have told you before you got into the car."

So he did know. And he was okay with it. It was good to be comfortable with who you were. Reverend Spencer had that peace about him, like he was okay with the world. Kathleen wondered if it was the religion or a gene he was born with that somehow happened to be deleted from her system between age twelve and now.

"Kathleen, did you really have an okay to leave the hospital?" Reverend Spencer asked. The words made her heart want to split open in a gaping wound that needed a dozen stitches. She had to catch her breath before she could answer.

"Well, no," Kathleen bit her lip at being found out. "Why did you let me?"

Reverend Spencer smiled, keeping the odometer at thirty-one. "I figured you were going to do it anyway. It might as well be someone you knew and trusted to help you get home."

To help you get home. The words sounded safe and at the same time, magical, to Kathleen's ears.

"Yes." It was all she could say.

"You've been through a lot these past weeks. With Henry gone and Grace leaving, why, you'll be alone most of the time. I'll be there to help if you need it," he said.

"Of course," Kathleen answered, wondering who Henry and Grace were and where they had gone.

Reverend Spencer made a careful turn off the highway, following the exit ramp. There was a stoplight at the end, on green. Kathleen could see him hesitate, then press the accelerator.

She was on her way.

Chapter 78

THE THIRD FLOOR of the hospital was in an uproar by the time Grace and Ryan reached Kathleen's empty room. Departments and broom closets were searched, security guards were dispatched to scour the parking lots, lunch rooms, and lounge areas.

"Who's been to visit Mrs. Mason last night and this morning?" Ryan demanded. "Let me talk to the nursing supervisor." He was trying, not too successfully, to keep his cool. He knew the hospital was understaffed, the nurses were overworked with too many patients, but there was no reason for a grown woman to go missing.

Grace was on the phone with the police at the nurses' station, describing her stepmother in height, weight, and build.

Ryan heard her explaining. "Wearing?" Grace paused. "She would have been wearing a hospital gown. All of her other clothes were thrown away after the accident." Grace listened as the person asked more questions. "That's right. Her family physician is right here. He could better explain that."

He raised an eyebrow as Grace pointed to the phone. She

held it out to him.

Ryan cradled the phone to his ear. "Hello? Yes, that's right. She suffered some injuries, one of which caused some memory loss. Short-term and long-term." He paused. "Danger to others? No, I don't believe so. We're just afraid she's wandering around somewhere. Yes. Thank you."

Ryan handed the phone back, looking grim. "They're sending out a patrol car, but there's no telling which direction she went. There's not much to go on."

"Should we stay here? Go look for her?"

Ryan scratched his head. "Let me think." He called to one of the nurses. "Can you tell me who all was on the floor this morning? Anyone at all."

The nurse crossed her arms and closed her eyes. "Hmm. The cleaning people were here early, the cafeteria lady came to deliver breakfast, and one of the electricians stopped to fix a broken light bulb. That's about it. It's been pretty quiet until this."

She saw the look on Ryan's face. "Sorry."

Another nurse stepped up, "I think one of the ministers was here. He'd traveled a long way to see your stepmother. Gavin Chapel, maybe?"

"Garrett Chapel?"

The nurse brightened. "Yes, that sounds right."

Ryan could feel Grace catch on to this glimmer of hope.

"I'm certain he was in to see her," he said. "Maybe he saw something or knows what's going on."

The second nurse nodded and scurried toward a phone. Within a minute, Reverend Spencer was being paged overhead. She returned breathless, "He'll be able to hear that anywhere in the hospital, even down in the morgue."

Grace's hand flew up to her mouth. Ryan put a hand on the other arm, hanging limply at her side. "Don't even think about it." But he knew she was.

Chapter 79

L OOK AT THAT!" Evan exclaimed, pointing out the window. His eyes were wide, glancing from Grace to the area in front of his grandmother's house. "What's going on? Is Grandma here?"

A small crowd had gathered, including policemen, Reverend Spencer, several neighbors, and Mark Jensen from the University. They were all talking at once.

Grace stepped out carefully and was almost unnoticed, except for Evan slamming the door to Ryan's truck. The dozen or so faces in the crowd swiveled to face Grace. The expressions ranged from surprise to shock. Grace walked toward them, Evan pulling on her arm to drag her closer.

A rally of questions erupted like a volcano. Grace could barely discern what people were saying.

"Thank goodness you're here. We're so worried about Kathleen," one woman said. Grace recognized her from a few doors down

"What's going on?" another neighbor asked. "I heard about the accident."

"Have you talked to Kathleen? Reverend Spencer said that he's concerned for her safety."

Despite the days events, and anxiety of her stepmother's disappearance, Grace wanted to chuckle. Her stepmother had developed quite the reputation over the past week. Who knew what the rest of the neighbors were thinking, but not saying.

"I thought you'd be back in Mississippi by now," Mark Jensen stepped up first and shook her hand warmly. "Nice to have you back. Maybe you can shed some light on this whole situation?"

"Let me try," Reverend Spencer interrupted. "Grace, your stepmother talked me into driving her home from the hospital. She was determined that she was leaving, was not going to wait for the doctor, and I figured that she'd be safer with me than in a taxi, or God forbid, hitching a ride back to Penn Yan." Reverend Spencer wrung his hands in dismay. "As soon as we arrived, I told Kathleen to go on ahead and get settled in the house. I needed to make one phone call and rearrange a few appointments so that I could stay with her until someone else came home."

Ryan nodded. "Of course."

"When I got to the front door, it was still closed up tight," Reverend Spencer continued. "And Kathleen was no where to be found."

"I'm sure there's an explanation for all of this," Grace said. She bent down to Evan's ear. "Run ahead and check the house for grandma," she urged her son, who flew out of her grasp and headed for the door. By the time she reached the front steps, he confirmed Kathleen wasn't inside.

"Nope, not here," Evan said, out of breath. His face was flushed. "I checked all of the rooms."

Grace pushed the door open further and stepped in next to Evan. She was thankful the crowd didn't follow her. They stood outside in hushed silence, each wondering what to do next.

"Wait a minute. I have a feeling I know what Grandma's up to," she whispered to Evan, putting her arm around his shoulders.

"You do?"

Grace gazed out the window, far off into the distance. A familiar blue and white sail with a black Sailfish near the top floated into view. A slender woman in a bright orange life vest was navigating, sitting straight and tall.

"Grandma!" Evan exclaimed.

Chapter 80

WITHIN FIFTY FEET of shore, Kathleen slowed the sailboat. Letting out the line, the vessel came to a stop, bobbing gently in the wake of other boats in the distance.

She was grateful to Reverend Spencer and she would make profuse apologies as soon as she navigated back to the dock. She couldn't wait, though, to explain or ask permission. As soon as she walked into the door of the cottage, the moment she laid eyes on the mahogany container, everything came back. Henry, Grace, Evan. She remembered everything. Her husband's heart attack, the funeral, even the tree falling on the house.

It was time to say goodbye, once and for all.

Unaware that she had an audience on the shore, Kathleen lifted the box with Henry's remains, setting it beside her hip. In one fluid motion, she opened the top and scooped out a handful of ashes.

The silver specks caught in the air stream, creating a ghost-like apparition in the shape of a person waving goodbye. A hand seemed to stretch out and meet Kathleen's before dissolving and drifting to the water's surface, the specks making hundreds of tiny round ripples.

After watching Henry's remains float and disappear, Kathleen pulled in the sail and adjusted the rudder. As she came closer to shore, she tossed the ashes again and again. This time, Kathleen didn't stop. She continued sprinkling Henry's remains until the container was empty.

When the last of the ashes were gone, Kathleen steered the Sailfish toward the cottage. It was then that she noticed all of the neighbors and friends gathered outside her house. She lifted an arm and waved, signaling that she was fine.

Ryan waved back and spoke to Reverend Spencer, Mark Jensen. She couldn't hear the conversation, but she knew he was reassuring them.

No one had to worry. Kathleen was all right. She was safe.

One by one, her friends and neighbors left the yard. When they were all gone, Grace and Evan walked to meet Kathleen at the shoreline.

Dripping water from the waist down, Kathleen unbuckled her life vest. She turned in time to see Evan break free of Grace's hand and run toward her full speed.

Kathleen bent down and held her arms open. The force of Evan's hug nearly knocked her to the ground. He buried his head in Kathleen's shoulder. Tears formed at the corner of her eyes.

"We're back and we're not leaving," Evan said, breaking free of her grasp. He did a little dance and then jumped in the air. "We're staying!" he shouted. He ran to the edge of the dock, teetering on the last board. Without hesitating, he jumped in, clothes and all.

Grace held back a laugh and took Kathleen in a wet embrace. "We're going to stay a while longer."

They linked arms and walked to the water's edge, waiting for Evan to swim to shore. He lay on his back, spouting water from his mouth like a whale.

"I thought you'd be in Mississippi by now," Kathleen finally said, squeezing Grace's arm.

"It's a long story," Grace admitted. "Something...or someone...just wouldn't let us leave."

Kathleen nodded her eyes on Evan. His skin shone in the sunlight, the splashes from his hands and feet sending droplets airborne. "Henry was just telling me."

Grace tilted her head to look into her stepmother's eyes. "My father was telling you?"

"Yes."

"I thought you let him go...before we left." Grace searched her stepmother's eyes. Kathleen looked away, then back at Grace, facing her.

"I tried. I tried to force myself. I started to, then just couldn't do it. You were leaving," she admitted, "I wanted you to think everything was okay and that you could go and not worry about me. So, I pretended to let him go so you could leave."

Grace was silent, listening.

"It was his plan," Kathleen continued. "Henry was telling me just now," Kathleen smiled through her tears. "When I let him go for real. Then I understood."

Grace raised an eyebrow. "His plan?"

"Don't you see? He died to bring us back together. It was his only wish."

Chapter 81

RYAN LOOKED FROM Kathleen to Grace, and then over at Evan. The sheer joy on everyone's face was unmistakable. He raised his glass, standing to preside over the table.

"I propose a toast," he began.

Grace and Kathleen giggled, raising their glasses. Evan joined in, not to be left out, his glass of milk nearly reaching the others as Ryan continued.

"First, to Kathleen. To starting over, being strong, and getting your way, no matter what." He paused. "Second, to Grace. For getting off the plane and taking a chance on spending the rest of the summer here, surrounded by the people who love you."

Ryan winked at Evan, who winked back.

"And to Evan. To keeping up with your Mom and Grandma. Many more adventures are waiting. You're the best, big guy!"

Everyone clapped and Ryan sat down.

He watched as Grace rose from her seat and lifted her glass once again. "I'm so glad that we're all here together," she said. "I feel so blessed and lucky to be surrounded by family and friends."

Kathleen smiled at the words, and Ryan watched as the women began to clink their glasses together.

"Wait, wait, I'm not through. I forgot something," he interrupted, motioning for Grace and her stepmother to wait for a moment.

Ryan sprang back to his feet and smoothed his shirt.

"Speech, speech," Evan called out, clinking his fork on his glass.

Grace reached over and tousled his hair.

With a grin, Ryan held up his glass one last time.

"Finally, I toast Henry tonight, who, of course, can't be with us, but is the reason we're all together now." He paused and looked at everyone around the table. "I know that he loved a good party, he loved this place, and he loved each and every one of you."

Grace gazed up at him, smiling, though her eyes glittered with tears.

"So, here's to Henry," Ryan said. "And in his honor, here's to love...and second chances."

With that, he bent down, and kissed Grace.

Chapter 82

KATHLEEN TUCKED THE covers up to Evan's chin. He smelled soapy-clean and could barely keep his eyes open as she brushed away a hair caught in his lashes.

"I'm so tired," he murmured, opening one eye into a slit. "Got to go to sleep." His head fell to the side. Kathleen watched the rise and fall of his chest.

"It's been such a day. So much excitement," she whispered, leaning over to click off the light next to the bed. The bed springs groaned when Kathleen rose to stand. Evan stirred beneath the blankets, then settled back to sleep. Kathleen stood next to the door, listening to the sound of his breathing.

She shut the door behind her and blinked into the brightness of the kitchen. The house was empty, the chairs pushed neatly back under the table. Candles were snuffed out and the dishes, silverware and glasses were washed and stacked neatly on thick towels next to the sink.

An empty bottle of champagne sat on the edge of the counter. She smiled at it, thinking of Ryan's toast.

For a moment she couldn't move, thinking of all that had

happened in her life over the last two weeks. It was overwhelming and immeasurable. She glanced around at the familiarity
of her home. The clock on the wall, the magazines stacked next
to the sofa, her curtains drawn away from the window so she
could see the beauty of the lake, day or night.

Her hand poised over the light switch, Kathleen paused.
She could see the water so much better with the lights off. The
moon was out and the stars would be winking at each other
in the night sky. With one finger, she darkened the room. Yes,
that was much better.

Kathleen moved toward the sliding glass doors. She savored the anticipation of the peace that awaited her. For a moment, she felt a tinge of sadness. Henry wouldn't be out there,
stretched on a chair, feet up on the wooden railings, ready for
conversation.

Then, she swallowed the feeling, tucking it back inside
her. She pushed open the door, letting the air caress her face.
Her skin was bathed in the glow of the moonlight. Overhead,
constellations sparkled like fine jewels sprinkled across a sheet
of black velvet.

Henry's stardust.

Kathleen stepped out further and leaned against the railing. Voices floated up from the dock.

Grace and Ryan were there, sitting so close they could
have been one person. Her head was on his shoulder; her arm
was around his waist.

Kathleen didn't try to listen, but heard the words anyway.

"When I came, I had every reason to leave. Now I have
every reason to stay."

Epilogue

GRACE STOOD ON the steps of the Mason Library, the breeze tugging at the edges of her silk dress. She had come miles and miles to where she was today, to Mississippi and back, to realize that home was right here.

Her father, in his infinite wisdom and grace, knew it would take more than an invitation to a society dedication to change her life. It had taken the photo of the little girl, his death, and a long journey to make her realize that she had to start living again.

Her stepmother had, after all.

Kathleen settled into a nice routine working at the local greenhouse, giving advice to about hanging baskets, container gardens, and potted plants. The Mercedes had been replaced by a newer, more reliable model, and was used often to ferry Evan back and forth to school events.

Once in a while, Kathleen would give in to a lunch invitation from an old friend of Henry's, but most of the time, was content with sitting by the lake with a good book and a glass of wine. Despite popular opinion, Kathleen resolutely denied any interest in Tripp Williams, though he seemed to be a regular at the cottage, and never missed the Mason family supper on Sunday afternoons after church.

In a rush of bravery, Grace gave up the security of her teaching job, applied to graduate school, and sold her house in Mississippi.

Evan was happily settled in a new school, making friends with a group of boys who shared his love of swimming and water sports. He still went to work with Ryan on Friday afternoons and now insisted that medical school was in his destiny.

Grace didn't argue. Who was she to predict the future?

Perhaps most surprising of all—Ryan did the unthinkable. The week after Grace and Evan escaped from the airplane and decided to stay, he cut back on his hours at the office, hired more staff, and alternated call with his nurse practitioner.

Now, days for Grace and Ryan were something to be treasured and savored. Life had taken on a deliciously predictable quality. For Grace—it was college—even though she was the oldest student in many of her graduate school classes. For Ryan—it was more downtime, spent with the people he cared about most.

Grace shielded her eyes with her hand to look up at the letters carved into the brick and mortar of the library. *Mason*. She was proud of her father, of his legacy, and their name.

Music from a string quartet filled the air. She wasn't alone. Her stepmother, looking lovely, handed her a bouquet dripping with pink and yellow roses.

Evan took her arm like a grown up, ready to lead her down the aisle.

The great wooden doors of the library swung open to reveal a transformed room. A fairytale of flowers, tulle and soft candle light greeted her, along with the delighted faces of nearly one hundred guests.

She stepped into the light and squeezed Evan's hand in

the crook of her arm. Her stepmother took her place in the front row, gently patting the seat next to her where her father would have been sitting.

And there, at the end of the red carpet, was Ryan, waiting for her.

Acknowledgements

First and foremost, to my wonderful sons, Patrick and John David, I love you! Mom and Dad, thank you for support, sharing your passion for big dreams, and turning off the television every summer of my childhood...there's no better way to spark the imagination!

My wonderful early readers include Maxine Kidder, Laura Pepper Wu, Elizabeth Wright, Doug McCourt, Lizz Gentry Woodrich, Ron Wright, Lorelei Buzzetta, and Tobi Helton.

I am indebted to Damonza, who created the fabulous cover for Stardust Summer. Hugs to the talented formatting gals at Duolit, Toni and Shannon, y'all rock!

Jeweled princess crowns to each my fellow authors... Tracie Banister, Jen Tucker, Juliette Sobanet, Samantha March, Lynnette Spratley, Kimberly Kincaid, Barbara Barth, Tonya Kappes, Pj Schott, Kat Kennedy, and Cindy Roesel. Yes, Dina Silver, you can be queen!

To Yvonne Edeker—the best neighbor in the entire world—thank you for sharing your front porch. Thank you, also, to Lisa Hirsch, Cecelia Heyer, Ginger Jesser, Heidi Pritchett, Colette Chmiel, Jana Simpson, Ted and Linda Hicks, Jessica Sinn, Ashley Wiederhold, Valerie Case, Laura Howard, Rebecca Berto, Kat Kennedy, Charles McInnis, Mandy Reupsch, Linda Moore and Ellen Odom for your support and friendship.

To the folks at my favorite bookstore, Page & Palette in Fairhope, Alabama, much appreciation for supporting my novels. Hugs to the gang at Carpe Diem for always keeping my coffee mug full!

My readers...I am wowed by your support and kind words! I've had such a fantastic time meeting everyone at book signings, book clubs, and writing groups. And yes, I would LOVE to come talk at your event, too! Please email me at laurenclarkbooks@gmail.com. You can also find me on Facebook, Twitter, my blog, and website, laurenclarkbooks.com.

If you enjoyed this novel, please consider writing a review on Amazon, BN.com, or GoodReads. For an author, there's no higher compliment!

About the Author

Lauren Clark writes contemporary novels sprinkled with sunshine, suspense, and secrets. A former TV news anchor, Lauren adores flavored coffee, local book stores, and anywhere she can stick her toes in the sand. Her big loves are her family, paying it forward, and true-blue friends.

Lauren is a member of the Gulf Coast Writers Association, the Mobile Writers Guild, and a monthly contributor to Parents & Kids Magazine's Mississippi Gulf Coast Edition. Check out her website at www.laurenclarkbooks.com.

STARDUST SUMMER
READER'S GUIDE

1. Grace Mason seems content living a quiet, sheltered life in Ocean Springs, Mississippi. How does the physical distance from her father, Henry, help shield her from a painful past?

2. As readers, we never actually "meet" Henry Mason. From Grace's memories and others' descriptions, what was Henry like as a husband, father, colleague, and friend?

3. How do you view Evan's relationship with his grandfather, Henry, at the outset of the story? Is it unfair that Grace keeps them apart?

4. Kathleen appears open and loving toward Grace, despite the emotional void that exists between them. Do you see Kathleen's actions as genuine or simply obligatory as the stepmother in a blended family?

5. Ryan Gordon is a well-loved and respected physician in Penn Yan, New York. What lessons did he learn from focusing on his career rather than his wife and marriage?

6. Evan is an innocent observer of the chilly interaction and often sharp exchanges between Grace and Kathleen. What does he interpret from this situation?

7. Everyone handles grief and loss in different ways. Does Kathleen appear to be taking inappropriate risks after Henry's death? Are her actions justified?

8. How much does setting play a role in Stardust Summer? What does the concept or idea of "stardust" symbolize in the story?

9. At several points during the novel, Kathleen is unable to let go of Henry's ashes. What do you think she's feeling when she finally releases his remains?

10. Throughout the story, Grace continually rejects Ryan's friendship, and, later, his romantic advances. Why? What is she afraid of?

11. Is Kathleen's decision to paint her house pink a wise choice? What does it signify about her life without Henry?

12. After a great loss, forgiveness can seem almost impossible to offer. Why does it often take a crisis to bring a family back together again? Can you think of a similar example in your own life?

13. Does Grace eventually forgive herself for not mending her relationship with Henry before his death? Why or why not?

14. Are you pleased with the ending of the novel? Where do you see Grace and Ryan in five or ten years?

More from Lauren Clark

Pie Girls

Coming in 2013

Visit www.laurenclarkbooks.com

Read on for an excerpt from

Dancing Naked in Dixie

by Lauren Clark

CAMELLIA PRESS

Available from Camellia Press

Chapter 1

"THE NEW EDITOR needs you, Julia." A stern summons from Dolores Stanley leaps over the cubicles and follows me like a panther stalking its prey.

"Just give me a minute," I beg with a wide smile as I sail by the front office and a row of hunch-shouldered executive assistants. Steaming Starbucks in hand, my new powder-white jacket stuffed in the crook of my arm, I give a quick wave over my shoulder.

I am, after all, late, a bit jet-lagged, and on deadline. A very tight deadline.

A glance at my watch confirms two hours and counting to finish the article. I walk faster. My heart twists a teensy bit.

I don't mean to get behind. Really, it just sort of happens.

However, that's all going to change, starting today. I'm going to organize my life, work, home, all of it. I'll be able to check email on the road, never miss an appointment, and keep up with all of my deadlines.

Just as soon as I can find the instruction manual to my

new iPhone. And my earpiece.

Anyway, it's going to be great!

So great, that I'm not the least bit panicked when I round the corner and see my desk; which, by the way, is wallpapered in post-it notes, flanked by teetering stacks of mail, and littered with random packages. Even my voicemail light is flashing furiously.

Before I can take another step, the phone starts ringing.

In my rush to pick it up, I trip and nearly fall over a pile of books and magazines someone carelessly left behind. A thick travel guide lands on my foot and excruciating pain shoots through my toes. My coffee flies out of my hand and splats on the carpeting. I watch in horror as my latte seeps into the rug fibers.

"Darn it all!" I exclaim, snatching up the leaking cup and setting it on my desk. Other choice expressions shuttle through my brain as I catch the edge of the chair with one hand to steady myself. I frown at the offending mess on the floor. *Who in the world?*

Until it dawns on me. Oh, right. I left it all there in my hurry to make my flight to Rome. My fault. I close my eyes, sigh deeply, and the strap of my bag tumbles off my shoulder. Everything—keys, mascara, lip gloss, spare change—falls onto the desk with a huge clatter. Letters and paper flutter to the floor like confetti in the Macy's Day Parade. Just as Dolores sounds off again, her voice raspy and caffeine-deprived.

"*Now*, Julia."

My spine stiffens.

"Be right there," I call out in my most dutiful employee voice. Right after I find my notes and calm down.

As I start to search through my briefcase, a head full of thick silver curls appears over the nubby blue paneling.

"Hey, before you rush off," Marietta whispers, "how was Italy? Was it gorgeous, wonderful?"

"Marvelous," I smile broadly at my closest friend and

conjure up a picture postcard of Rome, Florence, and sun-drenched Tuscany. Five cities, seven days. The pure bliss of nothing but forward motion. "From the sound of it, I should have stayed another day."

Marietta studies my face.

It's the understatement of the year. I hate to admit it, but the prospect of inhabiting an office cubicle for a week intimidates me more than missing the last connection from Gatwick and sleeping on the airport floor. Claustrophobia takes over. I actually get hives from sitting still too long. Most days, I live out of suitcases. And couldn't be happier!

I'm a travel writer at *Getaways* magazine. Paid for the glorious task of gathering fascinating snippets of culture and piecing them into quirky little stories. Jet-setting to the Riviera, exploring the Great Barrier Reef, basking on Bermuda beaches. It's as glamorous and exhilarating as I imagined.

Okay, it is a tad lonely, from time to time, and quite exhausting.

Which is precisely why I have to get organized. Today.

I sink into my chair and try to concentrate. What to tackle first? Think, think.

"Julia Sullivan!"

Third reminder from Dolores. Uh-oh.

Marietta rolls her eyes. "Guess you better walk the plank," she teases. "New guy's waiting. Haven't met him yet, but I've heard he's the 'take no prisoners' sort. Hope you come back alive."

All of a sudden, my head feels light and hollow.

I've been dying to find out about the magazine's new editor.

Every last gory detail.

Until now.

"I'm still in another time zone," I offer up to Marietta with a weak smile. My insides churn as I ease out of my chair.

Marietta tosses me a wry look. "Nice try. Get going already, sport."

I tilt my head toward the hallway and pretend to pout. When I glance back, Marietta's already disappeared. Smart girl.

"Fine, fine." I tug a piece of rebellious auburn hair into place, smooth my suit, and begin to march. My neck prickles.

I'm not going to worry. Not much anyway.

My pulse thuds.

Not going to worry about change. Or a re-organization. Or pink slips.

Focus, Julia.

The last three editors adored me.

At least half of the North American Travel Journalist Association awards hanging in the lobby are mine.

The best projects land in my lap. Almost always.

Well, there was the one time I was passed over for St. Barts, but I'm sure what's-her-name just had PMS that day. And I did get Morocco in February.

This last trip to Italy? Hands-down, one of the choice assignments.

I round the corner and come within an inch of Dolores Stanley's bulbous nose. As I step back, her thin red lips fold into a minus sign. Chanel No. 5 wraps around me like a toxic veil.

Dolores is the magazine's oldest and crankiest employee. Everyone's afraid of her. To be perfectly honest, Dolores doesn't like *anyone*, except Marietta—and the guy in accounting who signs her paycheck. And that's only twice a month.

Most of the office avoids her as if she's been quarantined with a deadly virus. "Good morning, Dolores," I say with forced cheer.

As expected, she ignores me completely. Instead, Dolores heaves her purple polyester-clad bottom up off the chair, and lumbers toward the editor's office. Breathing hard, she pushes open the huge mahogany door, frowns, and tosses in my name like a careless football punt.

I follow the momentum, shoulders back, hoping Dolores doesn't notice my shaking hands.

Stop it, Julia. No worries, right?

Dolores pauses and murmurs something that sounds like 'good luck.' *Wait. Dolores wished me luck?* That freaks me out completely. I want to run. Or fall to the floor, hand pressed to my forehead, prompting someone to call the paramedics.

Too late. The door clicks shut behind me. The office already smells different. Masculine, earthy, like leather and sand. I crane my neck to see the new person's face, but the high-back chair blocks my view; an occasional tap-tap on a keyboard the only sound in the room.

I fill my lungs, exhale, and wait.

Light streams onto the desk, now piled high with newspapers, memos, and several back issues of *Getaways*. A navy Brooks Brothers jacket hangs in the corner.

I gaze out the window at the majestic skyscrapers lining Broadway, a blur of activity hidden behind a silver skin of glass and metal. A taxi ride away, three international airports bustle with life. Jets ready to whisk me away at a moment's notice. My pulse starts to race just thinking about it.

"Not in a big hurry to meet the boss?"

The gruff voice startles me. My knees lock up.

"Sir?" I play innocent and hope he'll blame Dolores.

The chair spins around. Two large feet plop on the desk and cross at the ankles. My eyes travel up well-dressed legs, a starched shirt, and a red silk tie. They settle on a pair of dark eyes that almost match mine.

For a moment, nothing works. My brain, my mouth, I can't breathe. It absolutely, positively may be the worst shock-of-my-life come true.

"David?" I stutter like a fool and gather my composure from where it has fallen around my feet.

The broad, easy grin is the same. But the hair is now

a little more salt than pepper. The face, more weather-beaten than I remember.

"I told them you'd be surprised." David's face flashes from smug to slightly apologetic.

I say nothing.

"They talked me out of retirement," David folds his arms across his chest and leans back. "Said they *had* to have me."

"I'll bet," I offer with a cool nod.

His face reveals nothing. "Not going to be a problem, is it?"

Of course, it is! I dig my fingernails into my palm, shake my head, and manage to force up the corners of my mouth.

"Good." David slides his feet off the desk and thumbs through a pile of magazines.

I stand motionless, watching his hands work. The familiar flash of gold is gone. I glower at his bare finger, incensed to the point of nearly missing all that he is saying. I watch David's mouth move; he's gesturing.

"…and so, we're going to be going in a new direction." He narrows his gaze. "Julia?"

I wrench my eyes up. "A new direction," I repeat in a stupid, sing-song voice.

David frowns. With a smooth flick of his wrist, he tosses a copy of *Getaways* across the desk. He motions for me to take it.

"The latest issue," he says.

Gingerly, I reach for it. And choke. *That's funny.* I purse my lips. *Funny strange.* The cover story was supposed to be mine. My feet start to tingle. I want to run.

Instead, I force myself to begin paging through for the article and stunning photos I'd submitted—shots of the sapphire-blue water, honey-gold beaches, and the lush green landscape.

With forced nonchalance, I search through the pages. *Flip. Flip. Flip.* In a minute, I'm halfway through the magazine.

No article. No Belize. No nothing. My fingers don't want to work anymore. I feel sick.

"Julia, what is it? You seem a little pale," David prods. He leans back in his chair and stares at me with an unreadable expression.

I continue looking. *Where* is my article? Buried in the middle? Hidden in the back? More pages. I peek up at David, who meets my dismay with a steady gaze.

What kind of game is he playing?

I yank my chin up. "No, nothing's wrong," I say lightly, "not a thing."

Inside, I'm screaming like a lunatic. *There must be a mistake.* My bottom lip trembles the slightest bit. I blink. Surely, I'm not going to…lose my…

"It was junk. Pure and simple," David interrupts, the furrows on his forehead now more pronounced. He jumps up and folds his arms across his chest. "Bland, vanilla. The article screamed boring. It was crap."

Crap? Don't mince any words, David. He might as well toss a bucket of ice water on my head. I shiver, watching him.

"Let me ask you this." David stops walking back and forth and puts his fists on the desk. "How much time did you actually spend writing and researching the article? Just give me a rough estimate. In hours or days?" David's finished making his point. He sits down and begins glancing through a red folder.

My mind races. Last month? Right. Trip to Belize.

Focus. Try to focus.

I fidget and tap out an uneven rhythm with my shoe. Excuses jumble in my head, swirling like my brain is on spin cycle.

David clears his throat. He opens a manila envelope, thumbs through the contents, then gazes at me with the force of a steam-driven locomotive. "Are you taking care of yourself? Taking your… prescriptions?"

The words cut like a winter wind off the Baltic Sea.

I grope for words. My thoughts fall through my fingers.

My attention deficit isn't exactly a secret. Most everyone knows it's been a problem in the past. But, things are under control… it's all been fine.

Until now.

I start to seethe. David continues to gaze intently and wait for my reply.

What are you, a psychiatrist? I want to spout. *Not to mention all of the HR rules you're breaking by asking me that.*

"I'm off the medication. Doctor's orders. Have been for several years," I answer, managing to give him a haughty *the-rest-is-none-of-your-business* stare.

David backs off with a swivel of his chair. "Sorry. Just concerned," he says, holding one cuff-linked hand in the air. "So, *exactly* how much *time* did you *spend* on the *article*?" David enunciates each word, stabbing them through my skin like daggers.

"Five hours," I blurt out, immediately wishing I could swallow the words and say twelve. "Maybe seven."

David makes a noise. Then, I realize he's laughing. At me. At my enormous fib.

My face is scarlet, glowing hot.

Head bent, David flips through a set of papers. He pauses at a small stack. I recognize the coffee stain on one edge and the crinkled corner. My article.

"Let me quote verbatim to you, Ms. Sullivan," he says, his tone mocking. "Belize offers the best of both worlds, lovely beaches and a bustling city full of good restaurants. Visitors can find fascinating artwork and treasure hunt for souvenirs downtown."

He stops.

Surely, my article was better. He must have the draft. Oh, there wasn't a draft. Oops. Because I hadn't allowed myself much time. Come to think of it, I banged most of it out on the taxi ride from the airport. I accidentally threw away most of my notes in a shopping bag, which wasn't really my fault. I was late for my plane. And then…

"So, I killed it." David ceremoniously holds the papers over the trash can and lets go.

I watch the white papers float, then settle to their final resting place. Maybe I should jump in after them? My legs start to ache. Why did I wear these stupid Prada boots that pinch my left heel?

"But, all is not lost," David says dramatically. "I'll give you a chance to redeem yourself." He drums his fingers on the desk. "If you can up the caliber of your writing. Spend some time. Put your heart into it."

I don't say a word. Or make a sound. Because if I do, I'm sure to sputter out something I'll regret. Or, God forbid, cry. *Redeem myself? Put my heart into it?*

Deep breath. Okay, I can afford to work a teensy bit harder. Give a tad more effort here and there. But, the criticism. Ouch! And coming from David, it's one hundred times worse. The award-winning super-journalist who circled the globe, blah, blah, blah.

David cracks his knuckles. "Look, I know it's been tough since your mother's illness and all." His tone softens slightly. "Her passing away has been difficult for everyone."

I manage not to leap over the desk and shake him by the shoulders. *Difficult? How would he know?* My blood pressure doubles. *Stay calm. Just a few more minutes.* Doesn't he have some other important meeting? An executive lunch?

David drones on like he's giving a sermon. I try to tune him out, but can't help hearing the next part.

"Julia, it's affected your writing. Immensely. And look at you. You've lost weight. You're exhausted. I want you to know I understand your pain—"

"You *don't* understand," I cut in before I can stop myself.

My mother died two years ago. She was sick before that. I still miss her every day. *Damn him. Get out of my personal life. And stay out.*

We stare each other down, stubborn, gritty gunfighters in the Wild West.

"Fine," David says evenly and breaks my gaze. "So, as you've heard, the magazine is going in a new direction. The focus group research says…" He glances down at some scribbled notes. "It says our American readers want to see more 'out of the way' places to visit. Road trips. A Route 66 feel, if you will."

Focus groups. I forgot all about that obsession.

David pauses to make sure I'm listening. For once, he has my undivided attention.

"According to the numbers, they're saturated with Paris, London, the Swiss Alps. They want off the beaten path. Local flavor. So, we're going to give it a shot. We'll call it something like 'Back Roads to Big Dreams.'"

What a horrible idea. I swallow hard. Our readers don't want that! Who did he interview in these focus groups? The Beverly Hillbillies?

David continues, immensely pleased with the concept. "The emphasis is going to be on places that offer something special—perhaps historically or culturally. But the town or city must also be looking toward the future. Planning how to thrive, socially and economically. It's going to be part of a new series, if it turns out well." David puts emphasis on 'if' and shoots me a look. "What do you think?"

Is he joking? He doesn't want my opinion. Does he honestly think I like the idea?

David pauses. Apparently, he expects a response. An intelligent, supportive one.

"Sounds… interesting," I manage to squeak out and shift uncomfortably. I predict that I'll be spending a full day spinning half-truths. I'll likely be offered a lifetime membership in

Deceivers Anonymous if I don't die first.

David snatches up his glasses. *Glasses?* When did he start wearing glasses?

"I know you're our token globe-trotter, but I'd hoped you'd be more enthusiastic." He taps his Mont Blanc on his desk calendar and then points to the enormous wall atlas. "I'm thinking Alabama."

Something massive and thick catches in my throat. My head swivels to the lower portion of the map. I begin to cough uncontrollably.

Ever so calmly, David waits for me to quit.

When I catch my breath, my mind races with excuses. The words stumble out of my mouth, tripping over themselves. "But, I have plans. Tickets to the Met, a fundraiser, a gallery opening, and book club on Monday." I don't mention the Filene's trip I'd planned. Or the romantic date I've been promising Andrew, my neglected boyfriend.

David waves a hand to dismiss it all. "Marietta can handle the magazine-related responsibilities."

From the top drawer of his desk, he produces an airline ticket and a folder with my name on it. He sets them on the edge of his desk. Something I can't decipher plays on his lips.

I keep my voice even. "What about Bali?" I had planned to leave for the South Pacific a week from Friday. "It's on my calendar. It's been on there…"

David shakes his head. "Not anymore."

The words wound me like a thousand bee stings.

"Alabama," David repeats.

I swallow, indignant. He's plucked me off a plum assignment without a thought to my schedule. My new boss is sending me to who-knows-where, and he looks perfectly content. I narrow my eyes and fold my arms.

"Seriously David, you're sending me on an assignment to…Alabama? *Alabama*?" I sputter, searching my brain for an appropriate retort. "I'd rather—I don't know—*dance naked* for my next assignment than go to Alabama!"

The announcement comes out much louder than I intend and reverberates through the room. Dolores probably has her ear pressed to the door, but the phrase bounces off my boss like a cotton ball.

David smothers a chuckle. "Suit yourself."

"It's a done deal, isn't it?" I finally manage, my voice low and uneven. The answer is obvious. The airline ticket and folder are within my grasp. I don't move a centimeter toward them. For all I know, the inside of one of them is coated with Anthrax. For a brief moment, I picture myself, drawing one last ragged breath, on the floor of David's brand-spanking-new office carpeting.

"It's your choice." David swipes at his glasses and settles them on his nose. "Deadline's a week from today. That's next Wednesday. Five o'clock. Take it or leave it."

I stifle an outward cringe at his tone, and the way he's spelling it out for me. Syllable by syllable, like I'm a toddler caught with my hand in the cookie jar.

Take it or leave it.

Not the assignment. My job.

It's your choice.

David's fingers hit the keyboard. Click-clack. "Oh, and leave your notes on Italy with Dolores. I'll write the article myself."

That's it. The meeting's over. I'm fuming. Furious. I want to rip up the papers an inch from his face and let a hailstorm of white scraps fall to the carpet.

Take it or leave it.

I start to turn on my heel and walk out like we'd never had the conversation. David will come around, won't he?

Then, I stop. It's a joke. An awful, terrible joke. Do I have other job prospects? Do I want to change careers? What about my apartment? What about the bills?

Fine. Okay. Have it your way, David.

I catch myself before I stick my tongue out. He probably has surveillance cameras set up on a 24-hour loop.

David knows I'm beaten.

So, I bend, ever so slightly. In one quick motion, I reach out to tuck the folder and ticket under my arm. In slow motion, the papers slip through my fingers like water between rocks in a stream.

Damn! The clatter of David's awkward typing stops.

So much for a smooth exit.

On the ground lies a square white envelope and matching note card. I swoop down to gather my mess.

Though I'm trying not to notice, I can't help but stare at the delicate pen and ink lines on the front of the card. There's no lettering, just thin strokes of black that form the outline of a majestic mansion and its towering columns. Before I can stop myself, I flip open the note card, expecting a flowery verse or invitation. Some event I'll be expected to attend for the magazine? A party?

There are only a few sentences inside, barely legible, scrawled in loopy, old-fashioned writing. *David, Please help*, I can make out. Underneath, a scribbled signature. An *M*, maybe?

Hmph. There's no end to what people will do to get a story. Gifts, money, flowers, I've seen it all. Traded for a snippet of publicity.

I refold the note and hand it across the desk. It must not be particularly important, because David takes the card and sets it aside without glancing at it.

Necessary papers tucked securely in the crook of my arm, I straighten up, flick an imaginary piece of lint off my skirt with my free hand, and begin to walk out. My feet brush the carpet in small, level steps.

I reach for the doorknob, inches from the hallway.

"Have fun! Don't forget to check in," David calls after me. "Oh, and send a postcard."

I scowl. His voice is ringing in my ears.

That's low. Lower than low. He knows I collect postcards. Make that *used to*. In my past life. I want to stomp out—have a proper four-year-old temper tantrum. Be in control, I tell myself. Keep your chin up. Walk.

David can go to Hell!

I make the most horrible, gruesome face I can think of. Surveillance cameras be damned.

Visit Visit Amazon, BN.com, Smashwords or www.LaurenClarkBooks.com to purchase your copy of *Dancing Naked in Dixie*.

CPSIA information can be obtained at www.ICGtesting.com
Printed in the USA
LVOW01s1649170713

343354LV00018B/696/P

9 780984 725090